# DON'T MESS WITH THIS WITCH

E. B. LOROW

IMAGINATION UNLIMITED

Don't Mess With This Witch

E. B. Lorow

This book is a work of fiction. Names, characters, places, and incidents are either products of the author's imagination or are used fictitiously. Any resemblance to actual events, locales, or persons is entirely coincidental.

Cover by C. K. Gregory



Published by Imagination Unlimited

Edited by Peg McChesney



Contact info, http://lizlorow.com/contact

Newsletter sign-up, https://landing.mailerlite.com/webforms/ landing/k4k4w4

## *DEDICATION*

*To my parents who never told me what to do, but supported me and respected my right to make stupid decisions while I figured out life on my own.*

# ACKNOWLEDGMENTS

I'd like to thank my agent Nicole Resciniti for all her help and guidance.
She has the overwhelming responsibility of leading the Seymour Agency as well as being my champion and negotiator for fifteen hot rom-coms, published under another pen name.

Also my critique partner New York Times bestseller Tamara Mataya, an incredible editor and sensitivity reader, deserves thanks for helping this lucky author make her debut in the young adult world.

To readers who write reviews, share social media posts, and offer word-of-mouth advertising, thank you! Your support and encouragement mean the world!

# CHAPTER 1

"Hey, Fish Face! Over here!"

*Lake Pirate* waved madly. I sighed, but made my way over to him and *Just Jen*. They were sitting in our usual spot in the cafeteria, so I didn't see his need to announce my hated nickname so loudly. Yes, I hate it, but I can't let anyone know that. The more you object to something in here, the more the other kids will use it to make your skin crawl. *Jerks.*

"What's this emergency assembly all about?" I stepped over the long bolted down bench and took a seat at the attached table. Goddess forbid we have anything that can be easily lifted and used as a weapon.

"Nobody knows," Just Jen said. "I guess we'll all find out together."

She's called Just Jen because people often mispronounce her real name, Jenika. Seriously, what's so hard about putting the accent on the second syllable instead of the first? So she sighs and tells them, 'It's just Jen.'

My name is *Genevieve*. But I have to put up with Fish Face, because I slapped my old history teacher in the face with a fish. I call it 'accidental conjuring.' They called it assault. That's why I'm here.

Eventually everyone had filed in, settled down, and that's when the administrator Mrs. Whitehall finally spoke.

"I'm afraid I have some alarming news. As you know there's no way to leave Haven without serving your time and demonstrating you have control over your powers...and most importantly that your attitudes have changed for the better. Unfortunately, there's been a breach. Student Logan Holderness seems to have gone missing."

There was dead silence while she waited for that to sink in. A moment later we all broke out in cheers.

It's not that we're ass-hats... Well, we are, but not for that reason. It was the sign of hope we'd been waiting for. Most, if not all of us, wanted *out* of this place. We were told from our first day, it couldn't be done.

"Quiet... Order!" she cried, until the din died down.

"Now, if any of you know anything about this— anything at all—we need you to come forward. Rest assured there will be no reprisal for sharing what you know. We understand the fear of reprisal from your fellow students for 'ratting out' someone, so we will give you time to speak with any of your teachers, discretely."

*Ratting someone out? What is this? The nineteen thirties?*

I had no classes with Logan, and I don't think I'd actually exchanged two words with him. He was a senior, a cool, good looking guy—make that a *great* looking guy—in a surfer dude way. Blond, tousled hair and blue eyes.

I would have liked to have known him better. One thing for sure, Logan didn't look like he belonged here. Some of our fellow inmates definitely looked the part with neck tats and black leather jackets.

"In order to facilitate your ability to communicate privately," our administrator Mrs. Black Hole continued, "we're lifting the ban on telepathic communication, *temporarily*." Okay, her name is Mrs. Whitehall but Black Hole seems better suited to her. You go to her with any concern and it winds up in a big black hole. She's nothing if not unfeeling.

*"You dirty rat..."*

Wait. Was that Lake Pirate in my head? It didn't sound like him, unless he was lowering his voice on purpose.

I wanted to jump for joy. I missed being able to communicate without fear of being overheard.

*Hey, Just Jen. Can you hear me?*

*"I read you loud and clear, Fish Face."*

Sigh. Even in private conversation, I can't shake the name. Whatever…

"*So, what do you think of our prison break? Did you know it could be done?*" she asked.

*Nope. No clue. Did you?*

"*No. But if Lawless Logan got out, that means…*"

*Maybe we can too?*

"*Exactly!*" She was facing me and grinning like a loon. Her bright white teeth in her tawny face were hard to miss. I think she might be mixed race, but I never asked. To me, she's Just Jen.

*Get ahold of yourself. You don't want them wondering what we're saying to each other.*

"*Oh, yeah. Like catching a note being passed.*" She quickly faced the makeshift podium. "*Can they eavesdrop?*"

*I don't know. It's best to keep facing forward and not cause suspicion.*

Mrs. Whitehall was scanning the room, silently, probably tapping in on all our telepathic conversations, hoping to pick up a stray clue.

After a few long moments of silence, Mrs. Whitehall cleared her throat. "I have another announcement. We have a new student joining us today. Francine Costa, from Connecticut. We don't usually mention this, but I hope you'll give her some space and let her settle in. Let's not add to her stress."

"What kind of stress? And what's so special about

her? She never said what she did or why she'd already stressed out, did she?" Lake Pirate asked aloud.

"It's probably something she has to share herself, if she wants to. Privacy and all that crap," Just Jen said.

"What privacy?" he asked. "That's one of the worst things in this place. They know everything about us."

"Yeah, but we don't know everything about each other, thank The Goddess. Only what we want to tell."

"Yeah. I guess so." He shrugged.

"So are we going to be dismissed or what?" I asked no one in particular.

Mrs. Whitehall scanned the crowd one more time, then sighed. "You're dismissed. Resume your schedule at the beginning of your next class. Meanwhile, return to your rooms."

Judging from the depth of that sigh, she must not have heard what she was hoping for. That means no one knew anything…also that I managed to keep my limited knowledge under wraps. *Whew.*

At that moment a tall willowy blonde entered the room. She wore designer jeans that fit like they were made for her and a haughty expression that said, *I'm too good for the likes of you.*

"Um, I'm sorry she's late, Mrs. Whitehall," Guard Simmons said. "Her admission interview took longer than usual."

Francine shot him a glare.

Simmons is one of the non-magical guards they have here. Most magicals would consider a guard's job beneath them, so they have to hire non-magicals and give them certain advantages. He keeps his keys on a ring which hangs from a chain around his waist. Other staff members have them but keep them concealed. I guess the rest of the magical staff aren't too worried about us overpowering him. He carries a Taser and as an ex-football player he has fast reflexes and muscles. Not one of us teens could best him one-on-one without our powers. And they'll never give us that much power back until we're out of here.

When we were finally allowed to leave the assembly, I found myself walking beside him down the stark white hallway, trying not to let my sneakers slip on the newly mopped linoleum floor. "Hey, Simmons."

He stared at me. "Yeah?"

I'll never get past how harsh his scarred face looks up close. "What took so long with the new girl's interrogation? I mean *interview* and *evaluation?*"

He stopped, crossed his arms and frowned. "Wouldn't you like to know?"

"Well, yeah. I would. That's why I asked."

"That's privileged information." He resumed walking and was gloating just a bit, so I didn't feel too badly about taking him down a peg.

"You know, you're not one of the privileged ones here. You're not a witch."

He smirked. "How do you know?"

"We were told."

"By who?"

I could've corrected him and said the word he was looking for was *whom,* but the taunt wasn't worth it. Yeah, I kinda liked to poke his ego, but nobody here was really hung up on grammar—unless it made a spell go haywire.

There are certain times when a comma makes all the difference. For instance, 'Let's eat, Bobby,' is appropriate at the dinner table. However 'Let's eat Bobby' is appropriate on a raft in the ocean. It's the same with a written spell—and all newbie witches have to write their spells first, then get a high priest or priestess to check for incorrect spelling and punctuation that could make it mean something completely different. The Goddess can take things incredibly literally.

Anyway, I wanted to get some dirt—I mean, *information* about the new girl and Sim wasn't always able to keep his mouth shut. I did like that about him.

I strolled along beside him and casually asked, "So what's up with her? She looks stuck up."

He rolled his eyes. "Yeah, she comes from money. I don't know how her dad made his millions at such an early age, but he was filthy rich before she was born. All those millions could have been inherited. New money people are worse than old money people since they toss it around just to prove they've got it. And some filthy rich people, new or old, think they can buy their way out of anything."

"Can she? Buy her way out of anything, I mean."

"Ha. She's here, isn't she?" His snaggle-toothed grin was enough to put most people off. Some of his teeth looked like they were fighting each other for a place in his mouth and others were simply missing. I felt a little sorry for him, but he seemed content. This guy's intimidating characteristics were required here. I guess everyone needs to be needed.

So, all I've got so far on 'new girl' is that her name is Francine, she's rich and spoiled, and apparently *thought* she could get away with anything, but she didn't. I wonder if Daddy will come to her rescue at some point in the future. Or maybe he's teaching her a hard lesson. At any rate, it was more than we knew before.

Simmons glanced over at me. "So, do you know anything about that jailbreak?"

"Is that what we're calling it? A jailbreak?"

He shrugged his muscle-bound shoulders—at least I think he did. They seemed to reside up around his ears most of the time. "It seems appropriate," he said. "You boys and girls are stuck here, locked in your rooms at night, told what to do twenty four-seven…sounds like jail to me."

"Didn't you ever get in trouble when you were young?"

He smiled briefly, then schooled his features. "I was

on the football and hockey teams. Athletics kept me busy and out of trouble. You might try that when you get out of here."

"I'm getting out of here?"

He looked like he'd swallowed a bug. "Oh, I don't know. That's not what I meant."

I hung my head and tried to look pathetic. I probably didn't have to try too hard. "I thought… Well, I thought you may have heard something."

"Not really. But what you did seems minor compared to some of the others."

"Yeah, assault and battery with a fish." I shook my head.

He laughed out loud. Usually the staff tried to make us feel bad about whatever we did. I'm kind of glad he saw the humor in it.

"Hey, wait. You distracted me. I was supposed to be finding out what you know about the jail break."

*Damn.*

Suddenly he halted and jammed his hands on his hips. "I know you know something. Tell me!"

"Tell you what?"

"You know what."

He leaned over me and narrowed his eyes.

I rolled mine. "Simmons, if you're going to play 'Good cop/Bad cop' you need to have more than one cop."

He opened his mouth to speak, then looked

confused and shut it fast. I had reached my room so turning away from him, I waved and said, "See Ya."

"Not if I see you first."

At least he didn't answer, 'wouldn't wanna be ya.' That earned him a nasty shin bruise from one of the older kids a few months ago—and the kid added six months to his sentence, but he still says it was worth it.

Anyway, I'm surprised Simmons didn't try to ask me more about the incident. I'm glad I managed to deflect his question until he lost his train of thought long enough to reach the relative safety of my room. That wasn't hard to do.

Other staff were like a dog with a bone. You couldn't get them to let go of a question until you vomited up some sort of answer. And to the magicals—in other words most of the staff—a lie was something they could detect pretty easily.

Yeah, it's a good thing I was able to shield my thoughts in the cafeteria. Because *I do* know something. I knew Lawless Logan got into the off-limits library, *somehow.* I'd watched him go in, and of my own volition I'd played lookout.

When he returned he winked at me. I don't know why he'd trusted me, except that most of us kids really wouldn't *'rat on each other'*. We were all in this together, some more permanently than others. I don't exactly know what he did, but the rumor is that he'd never get out. Too bad. He's too cute to be locked up. A real waste of boyfriend material.

I couldn't wait to get out of here. I didn't quite know where I would go when I was released, but maybe my aunt would take me in. My parents had given up on me and said they hoped this place would straighten me out. And yet they hadn't visited me to see if it was working or not.

My aunt had. I actually got the feeling that she liked me. She'd laughed at my nickname Fish Face when I told her what happened, but she gave me a sympathetic look a moment later. Seriously, who would slap their teacher in the face with a fish on purpose? I was handing in my history homework and noticed her lips and bulging eyes resembled a fish. Somehow my paper turned into a wiggling sea bass, which I couldn't hold onto.

My aunt was also the one who brought me things. We couldn't have much, but she would bring me a postcard of a sunset over the ocean, and with a touch of her fingers the sound of waves crashing and salty air smell would tickle my senses. Or she'd conjure a couple of exotic flowers—nothing with thorns though. They'd confiscate those weapons before I could put them in a paper cup.

I liked nature and my aunt knew that. Except the old gnarled orange trees and scrub pines outside, we had no natural beauty here. So she tried to bring me something pretty, and I loved her for it. Maybe she'd let me go to her place in the Superstition Mountains of Arizona, a long way from here. When I get out, I don't think I can get far enough from this place.

I only have another few minutes of peace and quiet before I have to get to my next class. And, *oh goody*, it's Coping Mechanisms 101. That's where they give us upsetting situations and we talk about how to cope like a 'normal person' would. Why we'd do that when we have magical powers and can freeze time or disappear from any situation is beyond me. I guess it's so we don't freak out the public.

Yeah, the teachers are always concerned about us keeping our powers a secret. They seem to think non-magicals would feel threatened and turn on us. Somehow I can't see them burning us at the stake again, but I guess you never know…

I have to admit that making the occasional jerk-face wonder if he's losing his mind has been kind of fun. Once I ran down an alley, hid behind a dumpster, and then just vanished. If people are running after you, they expect to see you behind that dumpster, right? Instead, I popped up to the top of the nearest building and peeked over just to enjoy their confused reactions. I know. I know. That's not very nice. So off I go to learn how to behave like a nice, normal girl. Snort.

## CHAPTER 2

Lake Pirate rushed into my room. He wasn't allowed in a girl's room, but his philosophy seemed to be; *everything is all right as long as you don't get caught.*

"We have a nickname for the new girl," he said, excitedly.

I was in the middle of changing my shirt. I whirled away from him, picked up the shirt I was about to put on and covered my chest with it. "Ever hear of knocking, dude?"

"Sorry, I got carried away."

I peeked over my shoulder and he was still facing me.

"Turn around!" *Idiot.*

Lake Pirate pivoted, facing the door and crossed his arms. "Sorry. Sometimes I forget you're a girl."

*Wait, what?* "What do you mean by that?"

"Oh, it's not an insult. In fact it's a compliment!"

"I don't want to know what you're talking about, so I won't pursue it. Tell me about this nickname for the new girl."

"I will, as soon as you're ready. I want to see your reaction." He was still facing away from me. I put my hands on my hips and laughed "How long do you think it takes to put on a T-shirt?"

"So you're decent?"

"I'm always decent. And now I'm dressed too, so you can turn around."

"I never know how to deal with you girls. You confuse me. One minute you want to be treated like you're special, the next you want to be treated like everybody else. You can't blame me for not knowing what to do from one minute to the next."

I wanted to say, *Try using your common sense*, but I didn't think he had much. Instead I just rolled my eyes.

"Do you want to know what her new name is?"

"I said I did, didn't I?"

"Oh, yeah. Well, it's Alien."

I paused. "Alien? Why Alien?"

"When someone was talking to her about why she's here, she said it's because she alienates people."

I couldn't help laughing. "Okay, and how did she react to the name Alien?"

"We haven't really tried it out yet. Just Jen and I came up with it. I'm sure there will be others who like it. When should we spring it on her? I think the sooner the better. We don't want someone else to come up with a boring nickname."

"You mean like Just Jen? That's one of the worst nicknames I've ever heard."

"Yeah, I wasn't here when she came."

"I know. You came the same day I did."

"Right."

I shook my head. "Has anyone found out what this unusual stress is that Alien went through?"

"Not yet. We haven't found out much at all. You?"

"I got a little bit out of Simmons."

He bobbed like an excited puppy. "Tell me, what did he say?"

I shrugged. "Not much. She's from Connecticut. Some rich family with new money. Or old money. I don't know what difference the age of the money makes. Simmons says her daddy is throwing lots of money around. Maybe trying to… I don't know, get her out of here?"

"Could be," but then he laughed. "So whatever she did must be serious enough to keep her here despite his fancy lawyers."

"Sounds interesting. I can't wait to find out more."

"Do you think she'll actually tell us anything?"

"Probably not yet. To me, she looks like someone who'd rather turn her nose up and walk right past us than acknowledge our existence." I plopped down on my bed.

"I don't know. Maybe I can charm her into trusting me and telling me something."

I chuckled. "Yeah, you're so charming. No one can resist you."

He grinned. "That's what I think."

I have no doubt of that. Lake Pirate was nothing if not cocky.

He looked for a place to sit. There was only my bed so I scooted to one side, and he took the other.

"I'm kind of glad we have a chance to talk by ourselves," he said.

*Oh no.* This better not be what I think it is. He's not going to *ask me out*, is he? Like there's anywhere to go. That wouldn't stop some guys here. I held my breath and waited. *Please, please, please don't say the word girlfriend or boyfriend or anything other than friend-friend!*

"I was just wondering if, you know, if there was anything about that assembly this morning… Did you get any clues about how Lawless Logan got out of here?"

Oh, thank the Goddess. He just wanted to talk about regular stuff.

"Uh, I don't really know any more about it than you do. Hey, were you able to read my mind in the cafeteria when they lifted the ban?"

He thought about it for a few seconds, then shook his head. "No, I don't think so. Were you?"

"Yeah. I thought for a second you were communicating with me, but it didn't sound like something you would say and the voice was a little lower."

"No, I didn't say anything. At least not that I remember."

I projected a few words to him. Just asking what time it was. He didn't even look at his watch. Yeah, some of us wore watches since we weren't allowed to have cellphones.

Something was definitely off about Lake Pirate. Jim had no clue when his mind was being scanned or tele-pathically spoken to. I mean, we were all supposed to have the power only temporarily, but it didn't sound like he'd had it at all.

"So, Jim, I've been meaning to ask…what do you think happened on the boat? You said the beer and your buddies disappeared. Was it like they magically disappeared? Like one second they were there, and the next second they went *poof?* Or did they just throw the beer overboard and follow it by diving under the water?"

"I didn't actually see it. I was trying to hide the girls down below."

That sounded about right.

"Have you done anything else magical?"

"Well, sometimes I know when the phone is going to ring. Or when I'm going to get a text."

"Yeah? Is it when you're not expecting a call or text

at all? Or do you zero in on the other person's energy, so they think of you and call you?"

"Huh?"

"Never mind… How long did it take between the Coast Guard stopping you and when they boarded the boat?"

Lake Pirate considered the question for a few moments and then he squinted real hard. Apparently he was burning up some brain cells trying to remember the answer.

"It's okay. It's not really important. I just wondered what made the judge think something magical happened. Did the Coast Guard have a witness who testified against you?"

"Some guy was sitting with the boat owner's lawyer."

"Was it the boat owner?"

"Well, yeah. But there was someone else too. He wasn't wearing a Coast Guard uniform or anything, but he looked familiar."

"Familiar? Like you may have seen him in the Coast Guard boat that night?"

Lake Pirate shrugged.

"Did he say anything to the court?"

"To the court? Nah. He spoke to the judge, though."

I did my best not to smack my forehead…or his.

"But they spoke quietly. I couldn't hear, but I don't think I was supposed to."

"If you were able to read their minds, you would have at that moment, right?"

"Oh, definitely!"

"I wish I could have been there." I'll bet the poor kid was taking the fall for a magical so-called friend and didn't even know it.

"Were you ever in trouble before?"

He laughed. "Is the Pope Italian?"

"No."

"No? But he lives in Rome. Or Vatican City, next to Rome. I don't know exactly where it is, but it's in Italy, I'm pretty sure."

I took a deep breath and was about to get us back on track when he scooted closer. "Did you mean that? You really wished you were in the courtroom with me?"

"If I could have helped you, of course. What are friends for?"

He smiled. "We could be a little more than friends, you know..."

*Oh, yuck!* The conversation I dreaded before was happening! It's not that he has no redeeming qualities, but cute doesn't make up for brainless. At least it shouldn't.

"I'm sorry, Jim. I just can't... I don't want to jeopardize our friendship."

"How would being my girlfriend change our friendship? If anything it would make our friendship better."

"Look. The answer is no. I'd rather you be my forever friend than my future ex-boyfriend."

My door flew open.

"Who's in here? I hear talking."

*Oh, crap.* Bossy Rando. I think Mrs. Randall's real name is Bessy, but sometimes it's hard to remember the right names, especially when the wrong ones fit so well.

It was much too late to hide under the bed, but Jim tried to wedge himself under there anyway.

"James, stand up."

"Sorry, Mrs. Rando. We weren't doing anything. Just talking is all."

She bristled. "It's Mrs. *Randall.* You know you're not allowed in anyone else's room—especially not a female's room."

"If I know, how come you're telling me?"

Her face turned red, her nostrils flared, and her teeth clenched. *Oh, no.* She probably thinks he's being a smart-ass. By now she should know our sweet Lake Pirate is just a dumb-ass.

This bitch was the worst. In class, she set us up to fail, then looked smug when one of us did. Poor Jim didn't stand a chance.

"You're coming with me, Mr. Levy."

"Okay. Where are we going?"

"To the administrator's office."

"But she's a female. You said I couldn't be in a—"

A loud crack split the air and Jim landed on his ass. "Ouch."

"Are you coming?"

"Yeah. Give me a minute to get up, will you?"

He'd barely made it to his feet when she swept the air beneath him and he fell again.

I should say something. She just assaulted a kid, but if I opened my mouth, the bitch would do something else heinous, then probably add time to our sentences.

"Hurry up, Mr. Levy. We don't have all day."

This is just the kind of abuse of magical power she's known for. I held my finger to my lips, hoping he'd take the hint and just shut-up.

He limped out of the room after giving me a sad, puppy-dog look. Damn. If I had my full power… Well, I'd probably have my sentence extended by a year, if I did to her what I wanted to do.

I lay back on my bed and instinctively reached for my familiar—something I'd do at home whenever I was stressed. My arm curled around empty air. Sadness overpowered me, which soon turned to anger. I shouldn't be here. Neither should Jim.

I had just about had it with Bossy Rando. We all had. She, unfortunately, was one of the tenured teachers at this school. And get this…she's supposed to teach us how to use our powers responsibly. *Ethical Witchcraft* our course was called. Such a joke. I wish I could teach her a thing or two about that. *Wait a minute... Maybe I can!*

Soon I was marching down to the administrator's office before I had a chance to chicken out. I was nervous, but not because of what she could or would do to me. I just didn't want her to take it out on Jim. Frankly, I thought… Well, no. I didn't think. I just acted.

Striding into the office I noticed the door closed and instead of barging in, a little common sense reared its welcome head. Just in time, I realized finesse was required.

I smiled at the secretary and said, "Do you think I could possibly speak to the administrator as soon as she's free?"

"She's with someone right now. Can you make an appointment?"

"I'd like to speak with her right away. It's important."

"Fine. Do you have a class or can you wait?"

I checked the olde-timey analog clock on the wall behind her and decided that even though I had a class in five minutes, I'd take the demerit. My idea had to be acted on quickly.

"Yes, I'll wait. Thank you."

"Fine. Have a seat." She went back to her business, which seemed to have more to do with shuffling papers than anything interesting like playing Candy Crush on her computer. Or, maybe in here it was Angry Birds. I didn't know what appealed to prison secretaries. At least I was in the office, and now I had 'sort of' an appointment. Wait. Her secretary wouldn't have asked me to wait if she had something lined up right afterwards, right? I don't know her, but I don't think she's totally incompetent. So, okay, I'll call it an impromptu appointment with the administrator.

What class would I miss for this? As luck or irony would have it, it was Bossy Rando's class on the responsible use of magic. I snorted. The secretary glanced up at me and I just smiled. She shook her head and went back to her paper shuffling.

Soon the door to the administrator's office flew open and Bossy Rando stormed out. Nobody followed her, so I figured Jim must still be in there. I hope she didn't see me. I think she was too pissed to notice much around her. She would have had to look past her black aura.

Eventually Mrs. Whitehall opened the door wider and held it for Jim to slink out. He looked at me and opened his mouth. I gave him a quick headshake and he closed it. At last, he's getting my hints. Now if he'd just get the hint about us only being friends and nothing more…

Mrs. Whitehall strolled over to me. "Is there something I can do for you, Miss Howe?"

"Yes. I would like to speak with you, in private. It's important."

She returned to her office. "Please, come in." She closed the door behind me and I took one of the two seats opposite her desk.

When she had settled into her own chair, she leaned forward and steepled her fingers. "Something important? I'm intrigued."

"Yes, this morning you said we should speak up if we knew something and it would be kept confidential. Is that true?"

"I wouldn't have said it, if it wasn't."

"I know something about how Logan escaped."

She sat up straight and smiled. "At last. I knew you would come forward."

*She did? How did she...* Never mind. I had a lie to concoct, and no time for questions.

"I'm afraid that Mrs. Randall had something to do with it."

Mrs. Whitehall's brows shot up. "Is that so? And what exactly makes you think that?"

"Well, I saw her close the door to the library, but she didn't lock it. A few moments later Logan came along and slipped inside."

The administrator leaned back in her chair and folded her arms. "And do you feel it was prearranged? Or simply an opportunistic act on Logan's part?"

"I don't think it was opportunistic. He wasn't where

he could see her when she left, but moments later he strode straight to the library door and opened it, as if he knew it would be unlocked."

"And where were you when all of this was going on?"

*Oh, boy. That's the $64,000 question.* I hadn't exactly perfected this little speech. Now I had to come up with something brilliant in three seconds or less, so it didn't look like I was thinking up something.

"I was waiting for Just Jen—I mean Jenika. She and I were going to study together, but there was some kind of delay on her part. So I was waiting for her." *Note to self, get Just Jen to back-up my story.*

"And you happened to be near the library?"

"Oh, not exactly. I was across the hall at the corner, so I could see Jenika coming from either direction, but the way Mrs. Randall strode past me, as if she were on a mission, piqued my curiosity. That's why I remember it so clearly."

"And Logan? Where did he come from?"

"Him? I'm not sure. I was staring at my shoes until I saw someone at the library door."

*Fortunately the library was at a crossroads, if you could call it that when you're talking about corridors. It was basically on the corner of intersecting halls, so he could have come from any direction.*

Mrs. Whitehall dropped her gaze to my shoes and shook her head. Probably because I was wearing the filthy worn-out Nikes I found more comfortable than stylish. Nah. She doesn't give a crap about our clothing as long as it doesn't violate the dress code, and that only says we can't wear anything provocative. Most girls at my suburban high school would have to go shopping for clothes that cover up all their provocative parts.

"I'm distressed to hear this, but I will follow up. Thank you for coming to me," she said.

"You won't tell anyone it was me who told, will you?" I asked.

"No, I won't. We promised anonymity to anyone who came forward."

"Thank you." It was all I could do not to let out a deep breath as relief washed over me. If Bossy Rando knew I had implied she was less than perfect, she would probably suspend me in mid-air and leave me there, then write me up for missing my next class.

## CHAPTER 3

At the top of the following hour I happened to meet up with Lake Pirate as we reached the classroom and I let him open the door for me. He made a flourishing gesture as if to point out that he was a gentleman. I considered turning and saying thank you, but that was too much. We weren't on a date; just getting to class.

In spite of his lack of… I hate to say it, but brain power? Common sense? Manners? Okay. All of the above, I couldn't help liking him a little bit. He was cute as hell. His light brown hair, a little on the long side, always looked kind of wind tousled. He had light brown eyes and long dark lashes I would envy, if I cared about my appearance in this hellhole.

I took my seat and wondered what today's situation was going to be. Sometimes she had us act them out. I hated role-playing, although it was kind of fun when somebody lost their cool and had to be wrestled to the ground.

"Good morning class," Mrs. Finnegan said.

Not all the teachers here were witches. Most were though, and a lot of them had master's degrees. Some witches were perfectly content with their bachelor's degree and teaching certificate. Mrs. Finnegan was one of them.

I'm guessing she's in her late thirties judging from the few gray hairs making an appearance from her black widow's peak. Her skin is ivory and all she needs is a headband, red lips and puffy sleeves to become Snow White. I guess that would make us her dwarves. She seemed a little more relaxed than most. She wasn't bad for a teacher.

"Before you get too comfortable..."

Everyone in the class groaned. That meant this was a role-play day.

She continued as soon as everyone was quiet. "I think today I'll have Genevieve and James act out a scenario."

"Damn," he muttered.

"Language, Mr. Levy," she scolded.

He sighed before apologizing—if you could call it an apology. "Sorry. But I'm not good at acting."

"You don't have to be. Just do and say what you would using the skills you've already learned."

He nodded, but still looked glum. We made our way

to the front of the room.

"Okay, you and Genevieve are friends and neighbors. You know each other's families well. Genevieve, you call James' mother out on some fault of hers."

I was stumped. She doesn't usually let us ad lib. "Um, like what? Something like 'Your mom's breath could kill an elephant?'"

Everyone in the class laughed—including Mrs. Finnegan. She nodded. "Okay, let's go with that. James, your friend has just said your mother has bad breath. What would you do?"

He scratched his head. "I guess I would stop and think about it first. Right? In this scenario, is it true?"

"Say it isn't. Now what?" Mrs. Finnegan prompted.

"I would be tempted to say I could smell her mother's farts from my house…"

The classroom broke into hysterical laughter.

Mrs. Finnegan held up one hand. "Settle down, class." Eventually the noise died down to a few titters. "You said you would be tempted to say that, but you wouldn't. Right?"

"Right."

"So what *would* you say?"

He sighed deeply. "I guess I'm supposed to acknowledge her feelings before expressing my own opinion."

"Good. Try that."

"I'm sorry you think my mom's breath could kill an elephant." The class cracked up again. To his credit, he quickly added, "but I disagree. I think her breath is minty fresh."

"Very good."

Suddenly the class started to get antsy. A few stomachs growled and I even felt my own start to roil. A girl named Wendy raised her hand and said, "Mrs. Finnegan, I don't think I can stay in class. I feel kind of…" at which point she barfed all over her desk.

*Oh, Goddess no.* Whenever somebody barfs that makes me want to barf. Apparently I wasn't the only one who gets like that. Suddenly Just Jen barfed too, and then a few girls raised their hands, asking permission to go to the bathroom, while simultaneously getting up and running for the door.

Most didn't make it. They slid in the pile of barf the others left behind and crashed into each other, creating a pile up at the door. Mrs. Finnegan looked a little green around the gills too.

"Um, class I think we should dismiss early." No sooner had she said that, then she dashed for the door and the kids who were finally upright made way for her. She rounded the corner and ran for the teacher's lounge as the rest of us bolted toward one of the bathrooms for students.

Most of us were running for the same lavatory, the closest one. I almost made it too. I just got in the door and realized all the stalls were full. I had to settle for a sink. I lost my breakfast along with everyone else.

Other classes were joining us in the bathroom too. "What's going on?" One of the younger girls asked.

"I don't know, exactly. Suddenly all of us got sick at the same time."

"Yeah, even our teacher got sick and ran out of the room," she said.

"Oh Goddess," I mumbled. Now the upset in my stomach was moving a little lower. "I need a stall. Quick!"

One of the girls who had been lucky enough to make it to a toilet came out and said, "It's all yours. I can't guarantee its condition."

I wasn't worried about what shape it was in. I just didn't want to soil myself, especially not in front of half my fellow inmates. Again, I just made it to the toilet bowl in time. The projectile vomiting may have stopped but it was followed by the most disgusting diarrhea I had ever had.

"I think someone in the cafeteria is trying to poison us," Just Jen said through the door.

"I hope not, but it's weird as hell. Why did we all get sick at the same time?"

A younger voice said, "Maybe it's a spell that wasn't worded right."

I had to think about that for a minute. How do you miss-word a spell and give everyone projectile vomiting and uncontrollable diarrhea?

When I thought my body was finally empty, I

cleaned up the best I could with the toilet paper available. Then I had to tiptoe around everybody's disgusting mess. I got halfway to my room when Lake Pirate met me in the hall. "Are you okay, Genevieve?"

Just the fact that he called me by my real name meant he was genuinely concerned.

"No. Are you?"

He shrugged. "I seem to be fine. I just don't know what's going on with the rest of you."

"Is anybody else *un*affected?"

We saw Simmons rounding the corner. "What the heck is going on?" he yelled.

"Everyone is sick," I said.

"I think you might need to help the janitor with this one." Lake Pirate smirked.

Simmons jammed his hands on his hips. I allowed myself a brief eavesdrop and heard him thinking, "Just for that, shithead, you'll be helping too."

Then I shut that down quick. If he knew I could still read minds after this morning, he'd report it for sure. I might need to trot out that power later.

Some more girls came stumbling out of the restroom and seemed as confused as everyone else. "What the heck was that?"

"I don't know. Do you know, Simmons?"

An announcement came over the loudspeaker. "Students. This is your administrator Mrs. Whitehall. Please proceed to your rooms. Basins and towels will be provided. Meanwhile, clean yourselves up as best you can and we'll find out what's going on."

Another voice, which sounded like the facility's nurse added, "Just lie down for a while. Don't come to the Nurse's..." Her sentence was followed by some retching that died out as if she was moving farther away.

Neither one of those two sounded very healthy. It seemed as if something was definitely affecting all magicals. Although I wondered why Lake Pirate wasn't affected. He seemed to be the only student who wasn't. Could he have been a fuggle all along? If so, how had he ended up here?

I waved to Just Jen and hurried to my room as fast as I could while still feeling somewhat ill. Before I went in I took off my shoes and left them at the door. I took a quick look at the hem of my jeans. It seemed like most everything missed them—that in itself was kind of a miracle. If I had been wearing my longer boot-cut pair I don't think the hem would've been clean. Thank goodness for ankle length skinny jeans.

I shut the door and peeled off my T-shirt then found something clean to wear. But then my stomach started to roil again. I unbuttoned, unzipped, and gingerly laid down on my bed, feeling like I must be turning green. Witches with green faces...one of those hated stereotypes, and yet now I pictured all of us looking that way.

"How weird is this?" Somebody had opened my door a few inches and spoken to me.

"Lake Pirate, if that's you, shut my damn door. I'm not decent."

"I thought you said you were always decent."

I have no witty retorts when I'm not feeling well. I just settled for yelling, "Get out" and hoped that convinced him I wasn't feeling up to having company. Fortunately my door shut gently, and I was able to just lay there, hoping to die.

It still sounded like chaos was going on out in the hallways. There was the occasional slip and fall. I didn't even want to think about the cause of that, or the outcome.

I laid there for maybe 10 minutes before my door opened a few inches and a bowl slid in. It was one of the large kitchen mixing bowls made of stainless steel. It kind of rolled around and made a high-pitched, tinny sound until it stopped in place. I didn't want to get out of bed to reach it, so I let it sit there for a couple moments. When I finally did get up. I peeked out the window and saw Simmons delivering the bowls to each room—with the help of Jim aka Lake Pirate.

What the heck? Do these guys have iron stomachs or is this something that only affects witches? If that's the case, how come Lake Pirate was helping Simmons and wasn't sick too? Again, that puzzled me.

I simply took the bowl, sat on my bed and hugged

it. I didn't know if this was over yet or not.

Some kind of calming music came over the loud-speakers. Maybe they thought it would help us get our bodies under control if we just relaxed and listened to classical music. *Yeah, right.*

It didn't work. My stomach was still upset. My trai-torous body made a couple more attempts to hurl, but it was so empty all I could accomplish were some dry heaves.

Mrs. Whitehall's voice eventually interrupted the music. "Students, we have a little information on this virus. It's something that only witches seem afflicted with, so about ninety percent of this wing has been affected. Please stay in your rooms and we'll keep you updated as we learn what to do about it. None of you will be penalized for missing classes until you feel better.

*A virus.* I guess that makes more sense than a poorly worded spell or mass poisoning.

But who brought it in—and why?

A minute later my door opened a few inches and Lake Pirate stuck his arm around it. He was holding a washcloth and towel. "I thought you might want these," he said. I couldn't see his face, but the good news was he couldn't see mine either. I shuffled over to his arm and gratefully took the damp washcloth and dry towel. I was able to mop some of the sweat off my forehead and felt a little better.

"Thanks, Jim."

"No problem, Genevieve."

Yep, it was serious when we were using each other's real names.

"Hey, how come you aren't sick?" I asked.

There was a long silence. Eventually he cleared his throat. "I… I'm not sure I'm actually magical. When I went before the judge he seemed to sit up and take notice when the prosecutor said the beer disappeared and so did my buddies on the boat. He seemed to think I did something, like twitch my nose or something."

"So, you're telling me you aren't a witch?"

"Maybe not. If this virus only affects witches, guard Simmons, the janitor, and I are the only ones who aren't affected…and if they're fuggles, well, I guess that means…I might be, um…"

He couldn't say it. He couldn't say the word *fuggle*. I understood why. We'd never said it with respect. I decided to help him out. "You mean you might not be magical?"

"Yeah. I guess that's what I mean."

"Give me a minute, I'll get dressed and you can come in."

"But I'm not allowed to."

"Has that ever stopped you before?"

"Good point."

"Is there anyone else in the hall?"

"Just Sim, and he's rounding the corner with a pile

of towels now. I'll give you a couple minutes to put on some clothes and then I'll come in."

So weird. What could I say to him? Had he never performed magic before? Didn't he question it when he was sent here? Maybe one of his buddies was responsible for the disappearing act, leaving Jim to take the fall. That would be a terrible thing to do. For whatever reason, I was curious enough to let him in and talk about it.

Happily, the school nurse left it up to us as to whether we were feeling well enough to go to classes or take the rest of the day off. Lie around in my room all day? Yes, please.

I was just about to take a nap when Just Jen peeked around the door to my room and slipped inside, closing the door behind her. She excitedly crammed her butt beside me as I lay on my bed.

"Did you hear what happened?"

"That's a pretty vague question. Can you give me a timeline? A who or a what?"

"About two hours ago Bossy Rando got fired!"

I sat up abruptly. "No way."

"Yeah. She was escorted out by two guards and Mrs. Black Hole. Actually, I think I'll call her Whitehall right now, because she's my hero."

"She fired her?"

"Yeah, you missed it. They waited until just after the end of class, but we could tell something was up. Three guards went in with Mrs. Whitehall. Most of us hung around the hallway and pretended to be checking our homework for the next class. There was a lot of yelling." Jenika changed her voice to sound like an angry Bossy Rando. "'You can't do this! I have tenure! You wouldn't have a clue how to keep these hoodlums in line, if it weren't for me…' Stuff like that. Then we saw her marched out, holding a cardboard box with her Venus Fly Trap plant and her wand popping out of the top."

I didn't know exactly what to think. That was awfully fast. Maybe there had been complaints about her before, and this was just the last straw. I wouldn't be surprised.

All the kids hated her, and now she was gone. I wanted to sing *Ding dong the witch is dead,* but that might sound like any one of us had melted into a puddle of green goo or something. At least Bossy Rando was gone from Haven. I couldn't ask for more than that.

"So how did you get out of class?" Just Jen asked.

"Um…my tummy is still upset. I went to the nurse, and she gave me the rest of the day off."

"Lucky you. I wish I'd thought of that."

I shrugged.

"So, what now?" Just Jen asked. "Do we keep looking into how Lawless Logan got into the library? The rumor is Bossy Rando let him and that's why she's gone."

"Where did you hear that?"

"That's what some of the yelling was about. Bossy said, 'The last thing I'd ever do is let that depraved delinquent into our library.'"

Lawless Logan? Depraved? I didn't think that was an apt description. Cute, funny, smart, and maybe delinquent, yes. More than a few of us had been called juvenile delinquents. That's kind of the go-to insult.

"So what do you think happened?" she asked.

I shrugged. I didn't want to confirm or deny the rumor. The less the others knew, the better. If they even suspected something devious and didn't come forward with it, they could get in trouble. If they did come forward, *I* could get in trouble. So, to protect her and myself, I kept my big trap shut.

"I would love to get into that library," she said. "I hear that if you touch the walls in certain places, they can talk."

"You mean just like the saying; *'if walls could talk...'* is a real thing?"

"It is here. Of course, nothing surprises me here," she said.

"But if that's true, why didn't the administrator just

touch the walls and ask how Lawless Logan got in there?"

"I don't know. Either the talking walls is a fallacy, or maybe they chose not to answer her."

"So, that's how he got out of here?" I murmured, sounding clueless. "He found his way into the library and got some kind of spell from there to transport out?"

Just Jen folded her arms and appeared to be thinking. "First, he would've had to find a way to lift the suppression of our powers. That in itself makes the library very tempting."

"And very off-limits," I added.

"Damn, I wish we could get in there."

"You and me both."

I really did wonder how Logan got in there. I would love to find a way in too.

"The door is always locked, but maybe someone forgot to lock it up at one time?" she pondered.

"That makes sense. I can't think of anything else."

"I wonder why they suspected Bossy Rando, instead of Simmons. It seems like he would be the one more likely to forget to lock it or maybe Logan lifted his keys when he wasn't looking."

"You think? I mean, that sounds like something Lake Pirate would try."

"I don't know. I was just tossing out ideas. Don't pay any attention to me."

I didn't want to get Simmons into any trouble. I imagine something like that could have happened, but setting up Bossy Rando was a lot more fulfilling. It threw suspicion off Sim, who the kids kind of liked, and got rid of the horrible bitch-witch, who would have us all locked up for life.

"Yeah, well whatever happened, I hope that's the end of it," she said.

"Me too."

"But I'd still like to get into that library!"

I suppose I should feel guilty. I'd gotten an innocent person fired. Or had I? She might be innocent of that one thing, but she was guilty of so many others. I'm sure it was as I suspected, this was probably the last straw in a long list of complaints.

She flopped back on my bed and let out a deep breath. "I can't tell you how relieved I am. I mean, I've always kept a low profile, just trying to get through without added time, but I might actually rather stay here than go home now."

Shocked, I stood up. "You what?"

She wriggled as if trying to get comfortable. "My step-father. I've never told you much about him."

"True. Is he awful?"

"He hates me."

I wish I could say something comforting, but I had nothin'. Being an empath, Jenika would know how he felt.

"He never wanted a kid. He married my mom after only knowing her a few months, and I came with the deal. After my mom was killed, he was stuck with me."

"I'm sorry. Was he abusing you?"

"No, nothing like that. We avoided each other as much as possible. He was seriously thinking of putting me into the foster system."

"Are you kidding me? A nice kid like you?"

She sighed. "Yeah, I guess I was cramping his style."

"Isn't there another relative you could live with? What about your dad?"

"Dead. Killed in Afghanistan. And my grandfather died a few days before my mom did. I think I told you she was killed in a drive-by. What I didn't mention is that she was standing in front of the church right after her father's funeral."

"Holy shit! So you lost two people you loved."

"In the same week." Her voice cracked a bit. She sat up quickly. "Well, I have to get to the next class. I wish I could stay and chat longer, but I'll probably see you at dinner, right?"

"Count on it. I'm starving."

"I thought your tummy was upset."

I couldn't help but smirk. "I think I'm making a miraculous recovery."

Just Jen rolled her eyes. "So you were faking it. Nice one, Fish-Face. Remind me to take a page from your playbook once in a while."

**CHAPTER 4**

FINALLY IT WAS DINNERTIME. THANK THE GODDESS! I thought I might starve to death. As I entered the cafeteria and saw what dinner consisted of, I wasn't sure I wouldn't starve to death anyway. I paused at one of the tables.

"What's that?" I asked of no one in particular at the table.

An older red-haired boy said, "Slop."

His buddies laughed, then a punk-looking girl said, "It's called the BRAT diet, because of the first letter of each food. Bananas, Applesauce, Rice and Toast."

"That spells bart."

The kids around the table laughed again.

"Okay, okay. I meant Bananas, Rice, Applesauce and Toast. Sheesh. So literal." The Goth shook her head and rolled her eyes at the same time.

"Because we were all sick earlier, this is all we get until tomorrow," the first boy said.

"You're kidding! We're being punished for getting sick?"

"Not technically, but it feels that way, doesn't it?" a blond-haired kid said. His hair kind of looked like Lawless Logan's, but it definitely wasn't him—not even with a glamor. This kid was short, skinny and Asian with a blond dye job.

"Does anyone know what that virus was? Or how it got in here?"

Everyone at that table shook their heads. "It might have been a spell," the red-haired boy said.

"What kind of spell could do that? And why would anyone here want to do something like that?"

*Shoot. I'll bet it was Bossy Rando on her way out the door.* I couldn't say that to these kids. I didn't know if they'd heard the so-called rumor yet. I sure didn't want to be the one to explain it.

When I looked over to the table where I usually sat, I saw Lake Pirate and Just Jen, but also an unexpected guest...Alien! Funny, I hadn't thought she seemed like much of a joiner.

I made my way over there and nodded to her.

"Fish Face," Lake Pirate said. "This is Alien."

The girl only reacted by rolling her eyes. At least she didn't verbalize her negative thoughts. I don't know if she was in a place like this before and learned to ignore the little barbs, or if she really just didn't care. I was voting for 'didn't care.' She looked bored.

"Is anyone eating?" I asked.

"I might," Lake Pirate said. "The toast with some mashed banana on top might be good."

Jen and I groaned and held our stomachs at the same time.

"You will not make this meal even more disgusting than it is already," I said.

He grinned and went up to the cafeteria line.

"You know he's going to do it just to gross you out," Just Jen said.

"Let him. I'm hungry enough to eat some toast or rice no matter what he does. Aren't you going to get anything?"

"I might. I thought you and I could show Francine, aka Alien, the ropes."

"Don't bother," Francine said, staring at her finger-nails. "I'll be out of here before breakfast."

I didn't want to let on that I knew anything about her. "How so?"

She looked down her nose at me. "I have contacts."

I looked closer at her brownish hazel eyes in case she was being literal, but I don't think she was.

"What sort of contacts?" Jenika asked.

"The powerful kind," she said. "My father has been accused of all kinds of crimes, but he's never spent a minute in jail." She leveled a look so deadly I thought maybe we should duck.

"Ho-kayyy," I said. "Well, in case you're stuck here like the rest of us, would you like us to show you how to go through the caf line?"

She let out a derisive snort. "It's not like I've never seen a cafeteria before. True, I haven't had to eat at many, but I think I can navigate picking up a tray and telling the workers what I want."

"Um, yeah. That's where you might get in trouble. The people behind the splashguard aren't 'workers'. They're inmates, like us. They're in a work-study program."

Her perfect brows rose. "You mean they're so pathetic that working in a cafeteria is something they have to study?"

I smirked. Couldn't help it. She was going to get herself in hot water before long. Just Jen and I looked at each other, communicating without saying a word. We didn't *have to* tell her how to behave here. We'd offered. She wasn't interested. That was her choice.

The two of us joined the line, picking up our plastic 'spork' and a napkin. We got a decent helping of every-thing along with a bottle of water. There was no, "I'll have this, but hold that..." You got what you got and the leftovers went poof as soon as you set the tray on the cart by the exit.

We rejoined her and Lake Pirate a few moments

later. I couldn't quite figure out why she was hanging with us. She didn't seem to want to be friends. Maybe we were just the least threatening group here.

I glanced around the room and looked at some of the other inmates as if for the first time. There was a table of tough looking guys. They were tatted up and wore a lot of black leather. They had nicknames like Flame-thrower, Boomer, and Bike-chain. They didn't scare me, but I could see how they might seem intimidating to a young ingénue.

Most of us were partial to the color black and wore it frequently—some even on their lips and fingernails. To witches, black is the color of protection—not evil, like some people think. Our ancestors who practiced their pagan beliefs had to do so in secret to avoid being burned at the stake. Wearing black helped them to blend in with the night.

"Here." I handed Alien my spork. "You can have my rice. I never eat it unless it's fried."

She stared at the one utensil in her hand and blinked. "What. Is. This?"

Just Jen, Lake Pirate and I tried hard not to laugh. We lost it anyway. When we could speak again, I said, "It's a ridiculous combination of spoon and fork, called a spork."

She leaned away as if it might bite her, rotating the thing back and forth, examining it. "I guess they're afraid you might stab someone, if they give you decent plastic silverware? Have the regular utensils been used as weapons?"

Lake Pirate shrugged. "I figure they must've had a problem with that in the past to come up with this weird solution."

She shook her head and tossed the spork over her shoulder. It clattered against the wall and then the floor. "That's stupid. I don't know about you guys, but I've watched enough shows on TV to know that a shiv could be made out of anything."

Just Jen laughed.

Alien glared at her. "You don't agree?"

"Oh, I agree all right. But these fork tines are pretty useless. I couldn't even comb my hair with it."

"And if you broke off the handle, by the time you filed it enough to be sharp it wouldn't be long enough to do much damage," I added.

Changing the subject, Lake Pirate asked, "So, what did you do to get in here?"

It's what we had all been wondering. So we all waited and listened until she said something.

"It wasn't that big a thing. My moods control the weather."

"Oh, you mean you caused it to rain for 40 days and 40 nights, and they were afraid we were all gonna drown?" Like Pirate asked.

She reared back and looked at him as if he'd lost his

mind. "No, dummy. I only made it rain for a couple of days and only on one very specific person."

We all sat up a little straighter.

"You can make it rain on one person?" Just Jen clarified.

"And only by being in a bad mood?" Lake Pirate added.

"Yeah. I was just learning to get control over the power and thought testing it out a little would be smart. The weather is not an easy thing to manipulate. I was kinda proud of myself, actually. And besides the jerk had it coming. He was a bully and he made this shy girl cry. So I thought I'd let the sky cry all over him for a couple of days."

Just Jen's eyebrows shot up. "How did anybody explain that? The fuggles must've had to twist logical explanations like pretzels."

"Fuggles?"

"It's a contraction of two words. You can probably guess which ones."

Alien smirked. "Yeah, I guess his father made him stay in the shower so he didn't ruin their floors."

"So, he didn't drown. Is that all you did?" Lake Pirate asked.

Alien shrugged.

I suspected there was more than that. Yeah, it's not good to rain on someone, but that's hardly a danger unless she put him in a box with no drainage.

"Was that related to the trauma you went through?" Lake Pirate persisted.

"What's with the 3^rd degree?" she snapped.

"We're just curious," I said. "You got the name Alien because you said you alienate people. But it depends on *how* you alienated them that would explain how you got sent here." I quickly added, "I guess. I mean, I don't know for sure…" Might as well not alienate the Alien, if I could help it.

She looked like she was gonna laugh, then quickly put the same scowl back on her face. "I hear they call you Fish-Face, because you hit a teacher in the face with a fish."

"Word gets around quickly here."

"I guess so. That doesn't seem really dangerous."

"I didn't think so either. I guess the thing is, my powers are wonky. That makes it harder to control them. Sometimes I'm just thinking of something, and *oops* it happens."

"That's kind of a pain in the ass, isn't it?" she asked.

"Tell me about it. It's hard to control your thoughts and sometimes the craziest things go through my head."

Lake Pirate chuckled. "Mine too."

Just Jen shivered. "I'd hate to see some of the things that wander through my brain come to life."

"So it was more than just hitting a teacher in the face with a fish, right?"

"Yeah, there were other crazy things. The fuggles were having a really hard time coming up with *logical* explanations."

"Gotcha. I had the same issue, but I didn't care," Alien said. "Let them know witches are around. Let them know we're superior to them. I say it's time to put the fuggles in their place."

Wow I can see why they say she alienates people. That kind of thinking would probably alienate the whole fuggle world.

"So you don't think you'll be here long?" Just Jen asked.

Thank you for changing the subject, my friend. I had no comeback.

"Hell, no. I'm sure my father will get me out of here very soon." Alien let out a long sigh. "Okay, I'm ninety-nine percent sure."

I was wondering who was pulling strings for her. If she gets out of here, he definitely belongs to that one percent they always talk about.

She folded her arms. "So if it seemed like there was something big going on when I first got here…that assembly was about something atypical, right?"

"Yeah. One of the kids escaped. Nobody knows how," Jenika answered.

"And if we did, we wouldn't tell them," Lake Pirate added.

I kept quiet and let the others take the lead on that one.

She smirked. "I guess you guys have to get out one way or another. Not everyone has superb lawyers on speed dial."

"I take it your father does?" Lake Pirate asked.

"Of course. He's a billionaire. I'm sure he's talking to them as we speak."

And I was trying so hard not to hate her.

"Won't they have to have another trial, or something? They can't just go to the judge and make him say, 'Whoops, I made a mistake. I sent an innocent girl to Juvie'."

She snickered. "No, they'll probably get another judge to declare a mistrial. They'll find some inappropriate proceedings or something, and get me off on a technicality."

"Damn," Lake Pirate said. "I wish I had someone who could do that for me."

Alien snorted and I could see why people might want to knock that smug look off her face.

"So what did you do to get in here besides rain on a kid?" he asked.

"What makes you think there was anything else?"

"If that was the only thing and your lawyers are so powerful, you should have just walked away with a slap on the wrist."

"True. I also rained on someone's wedding, but she was a bitch and deserved it."

"I thought it was good luck when it rains on your wedding," Just Jen said.

Alien laughed. "Yeah, frizzy hair is a real good look for a bridezilla. Especially when they take those wedding photos."

"Again. Not enough to get in here," I said, probably taking my life in my hands…

She laughed. "Fine. You got me. You know the huge amount of tornadoes and floods they had in the Midwest recently?"

My jaw dropped. "That was you?"

"What good is the power to control weather if you only cause a little rain here and there? I wanted to practice wreaking havoc on a grand scale, and I figured nobody would miss the Midwest."

I think my jaw dropped, only this time it hit the floor. The three of us just stared at her, dumbstruck. She studied her fingernails like they were so much more important than innocent lives. If I weren't afraid of what would happen, I might try to conjure a fish to slap her with on purpose.

Okay, so she wasn't just a snotty bitch. She was a huge, raging, psycho-bitch and apparently felt like she should be judge and jury of everyone. That gave me the heebie-jeebies. I hoped she *wouldn't* get out of here until they reformed her. *And I hope like hell I never run into her again.*

A crackling sound came over the loud speaker. That usually meant an announcement was to follow.

"Ahem…" the secretary began, "Would Francine Costa come to the office, please?"

"I'm outta here, bitches…" Alien said, gleefully.

## CHAPTER 5

Well, Alien was still there the next day—and the next, and the day after that! It looked as if she'd be staying awhile. We still didn't trust her, but for some damn reason, she wound up sitting with us in the caf each day. Of course, she acted like we were lucky she'd graced us with her presence.

At last it was visiting day. I was curious if her daddy and his fancy lawyers would show up, but to be honest I was much more interested in my own visitor. My Aunt Hilary was coming.

I know what you're thinking. Aunt Hilary = Ant Hill. Nope. I don't give cute derogatory nicknames to those I love and cherish. Even if the obvious name is right in front of my fish face.

I was so excited about seeing Aunt Hilary, I sat on my hands, trying not to bounce in my chair. Those of us with prearranged visitations—and there was really no other kind—waited in the large visitors' lounge, which was the size of my parents' open-concept living area. Speaking of my parents, I hadn't seen them in months. They occasionally wrote, but their letters were more like lists. I got the feeling they were trying to explain why they were too busy to visit their only child.

Anyway, the visitors lounge held a couple of couches, but mostly tables and chairs. I think the teachers' lounge was pretty much a duplicate, from what I could see when I peeked inside.

At last I saw my beautiful bohemian Aunt Hilary. She had long hair with gray streaks sprouting from her widow's peak, but it was still mostly medium brown. She usually wore it braided down her back. Today it was loose and wavy. She looked like a goddess.

Today's outfit consisted of a below the knee white broom skirt and an embroidered peasant blouse. The first time she came to visit she was wearing a tailored suit. It was all I could do not to laugh. She finally admitted she had an appointment with the administrator afterwards, and she wanted to look her most business-like best. She never told me what that meeting was about and when I asked, she deftly changed the subject.

I flew out of my chair and threw my arms around her. We gave each other a long tight hug. Aunt Hilary gave the best hugs.

"Hi, honey. I've missed you. How have you been?"

"I'm okay. This place is getting to me, but it wouldn't be doing its job if it didn't, I guess."

She gave me a sympathetic smile and we walked to one of the couches someone had just vacated. Lucky us. They were harder to get than the tables and chairs.

She took both my hands in hers and we sort of faced each other as much as you can when you're sitting side-by-side.

"What's new with you?" I asked.

"A few things. First, you know, that mark I have on my lower back?"

"Yeah, the one you affectionately call your tramp stamp?" I also liked that she was down to earth and never prissy. She got right to the point and spoke her mind.

She laughed. "That's the one. I know it's a lot to ask, but I think it might be a map, and I was hoping you would take a quick look at it and give me your opinion."

My eyes widened. "You want to flip up your blouse and pull down your skirt, to show me your tramp stamp? Here?"

She laughed and said, "No silly. I took a picture of it."

Now I felt like an idiot. She was fairly free and breezy, but even she knew enough not to gear down in the middle of a correctional institution with guards standing around, even if they were trying to look inconspicuous.

"I couldn't bring in my phone, but I know they let you have postcards so I just made a little 4 x 6 photo… like the kind we used to have developed when we used film in real cameras."

I chuckled. "Yeah, I've heard of those."

She presented me with the photo and said, "You know this is not a tattoo, right?"

I studied the lines and realized right away that it was anything but a tattoo. The lines were slightly raised as if they had been scarred into her skin, not inked.

She nodded to it. "It showed up shortly after I was struck by lightning. I didn't notice it right away. The area was red and blistered, but if this is a map I'm pretty sure it was the result of the lightning strike."

I dropped the photo. "Are you shitting me?"

She shook her head. "No, I wish I were. This happened about four years ago. I'm curious about it, because as much as I thought the marks would fade over time, they haven't. Not at all."

I took another look at the picture and, it did look as fresh as if it were etched on her body that day. But etched with lightning? That's a scary thought. "Weren't you afraid you might die?"

"Oh, yes. I was knocked unconscious. And it's a good thing. When I came to, my body was vibrating. I didn't know what to think. It took me a while before I could actually move."

"Well, no wonder. You were electrocuted. You don't just jump up from an electrocution and go about your merry way."

One side of her mouth curled up. She had this half smile thing, which wasn't exactly a smirk, but it was more of an, 'I know something you don't know' kind of smile.

"It's true" she said. "My eyes opened and I just laid in the dirt, quivering for a while. There was no one around. When I was finally able to get up I felt lucky to be alive."

"Did you ever go to the hospital?"

She snorted. "Hospitals aren't for me."

"Hospitals aren't for most witches."

"Exactly. Unless someone has to cut me open, I'll do what I can with my herbs and tinctures. I did make a poultice and treated the area for several days. The blisters went away, but the marks never faded. The pain went away as soon as I applied an aloe ointment, so it wasn't as horrible as it could have been." She shivered, as if remembering the whole incident. "What do you think? I know you're good with locator spells and that means looking at maps. I wondered if you could, simply by looking at it, decide whether or not it might be a map."

I found the map intriguing, if indeed it was one. "I

wish I had my dowsing stuff. I could hold the pendulum over it and see if it was pointing to something."

"I already tried that. Although, it's a good thought."

"So what happened when you tried it?"

"I didn't find much of anything, at least not without knowing what I was looking for. It's just random lines without a reference point, but recently I was looking at an Atlas, specifically of the Superstition Mountains area where I was planning a trip, it seemed familiar somehow. I took a selfie of my back, and compared the two. It looked as if it could be a satellite view of the Verde River in the Tonto National Forest. However, I'm not sure."

That was interesting, but not for the reason you may think. "I know you live there now, but what led you to the Superstition Mountains in the first place?"

She chuckled. "It was a getaway with a man." She shrugged one shoulder. "What can I say? He promised me a great spa weekend."

I rolled my eyes. "So, go back to this Atlas thing? What is it? I have the feeling you don't mean the strong Greek Titan who's supposedly holding up the celestial heavens until the end of time…"

She laughed. "An Atlas is a book of maps—usually with every region's geography, topography, temperature and time zones. You can find them online now. There was this large book of maps in his house, and there were also maps of each state. While I was waiting for him to pack I leafed through it. I guess I was bored. When I came to the map of Arizona I paid a little more attention, since that's where we were headed."

"Sounds like a fascinating guy. I hope your weekend was more fun."

She laughed. "Well, we all do things we hope will be fun, but aren't from time to time. The spa was wonderful. Top-notch. So I moved there, but not with the guy."

My jaw dropped. "You moved to the spa? What? So you can get pampered every day?"

She grinned. "Not exactly. I work at the place as a massage therapist, and I tend the herb and vegetable gardens. I have a cabin on the grounds, but it's private and separate from the guests."

"Do you cook your own meals or eat in the guest's dining room?" I pictured our staff eating in the cafeteria with us instead of in the teacher's lounge. It just didn't look right.

"I have a little kitchenette, and I can cook."

"Oh, I know you can cook. You've made some yummy things for me."

She smiled. "Thank you. Although, I thought you were going to turn as green as my zucchini bread when I told you it was made with vegetables…"

I giggled. "What was I, five? Six?"

"Seven. But I probably shouldn't have told you it was made with zucchini."

"Yeah, I was quite the vegetable hater when I was younger. I'm still not crazy about most vegetables."

"Are they feeding you decently here?"

"Up until last weekend. We all got sick and then they gave us the brat diet. It means—"

"I know what that means. They would've been better off giving you a clear liquid diet with a touch of apple cider vinegar, if they needed to detox your bodies."

"Vinegar? Yuck." *Detox.* It sounded again like we'd been poisoned, but why just the witches? It made as much sense as anything else did. "Yeah. It was hard to make a meal out of bananas, rice, applesauce, and toast."

"I would have recommended a combination of clear fruit and vegetable juices which would have cleansed your systems and been more nutritious. The apple cider vinegar taste could have been masked. What did they say you had?"

"Illness wise?"

"Yes. What did you all come down with?"

"I have no idea. They said it was something that only affected witches."

"Really. I haven't heard of anything like that. Usually witches can boost their immunity and fight off any mortal illness."

"That's what I thought too. But it was weirdly the other way around. The fuggles were fine."

"Interesting… You're okay now?"

"Totally. But anyway, getting back to that spa…"

She smiled. "I was going to talk to you about that, how would you like to come live with me in Arizona when you get out of here?"

I gasped. I couldn't speak for a couple of seconds. "Seriously? You would really do that for me?"

She grinned. "Of course I would."

I threw myself into her arms and gave her a huge hug. She was happily giggling and returning it.

"Aren't you afraid I'll cramp your style? I know you like to date."

She shrugged. "I wouldn't worry about it. I rarely find anyone worth dating these days. But if I do, you're old enough to understand, right?"

"You're not going 'to do' it in my room, are you?" I used air quotes rather than saying the words, have sex, out loud.

She burst out laughing. "Not even if you're away for the weekend."

"Then I'm fine with it."

I was so engrossed in my conversation with my aunt I never looked up to see who else had come into the room. At least, not until I heard a loud squeal and saw some kind of lavender fabric flash by my face.

The cardigan sweater that flew past me was worn by Alien. By the time I turned around she was already jumping into a suited gentleman's arms.

"Daddy! Daddy you came!" She looked around him and seemed genuinely confused. "Where are the lawyers?"

"What lawyers, honey?"

She got this look on her face that was truly terrifying. She spoke through her teeth and said, "The lawyers you've hired to get me out of here. I'm not staying in this shithole."

The gentleman straightened to his full height and cleared his throat. "We should talk in a more private place. Where can we go?"

Alien slumped and folded her arms. "Nowhere. This is it." She gestured to the room with her arm outstretched. "This dump is where we visit with our loved ones."

Her father strolled over to one of the guards. He leaned in and whispered something to him. The guy just shook his head.

Now I see where Alien got that facial expression. Her daddy was not happy.

I suppose I should have offered to give them the couch, but I just couldn't manage to feel sorry for them. It was clear they were used to getting their way, and used to people making exceptions for them. Maybe it would be good for her to live like the rest of us for a while.

I tried to continue my conversation with my aunt, but my attention kept getting dragged into the Costas' rather loud conversation at a table near us.

"Daddy, get me out of here! You have to be able to get me out of here! I don't understand why you can't."

"It's court ordered, honey. I tried talking to the judge. My lawyers tried talking to the judge. Apparently he feels it's for the safety of the community and your own good that you stay here, and I have to say I can't disagree with the assessment that your behavior has been unacceptable. Perhaps if you learn to—"

Alien bolted up so fast her chair fell over. "Do not say what you were about to say, Daddy!"

"You don't know what I was about to say."

"Yes I do. You were going to say I should stay here, learn my lesson and serve my time. That would be convenient for you wouldn't it?"

He shook his head. "'I would never be so harsh. You're my darling daughter, but you can't do the things that draw attention to us as a family. We have some sensitive business deals going on..."

Alien slammed her fist on the table. "I knew it. You want me out of the way. If I embarrass you, whoever wants your favors, or whatever you're pedaling, won't do business with you. Is that right?"

"I want you safe," he tried to whisper.

"Oh, so your enemies won't hold me at knifepoint while they extort you, or whatever…again?"

He sighed. "It's not that simple. But you are probably safer here until this blows over."

"Speaking of blowing things over, you never thanked me for getting us out of that situation." Alien had had enough apparently and stormed out. Her father stood slowly, like he was beaten and exhausted. I could only imagine what dealing with a spoiled brat like her was like. I'll bet having her in here was a vacation for him.

When the Costas were gone and the room returned to normal, I got back to my aunt's question. I had to wonder if her telling me about this plan now was a way of letting me know I wasn't going to be here much longer. That would be awesome!

"Aunt Hilary, is there something that made you ask me to come live with you today as opposed to the first time you came? In other words, am I about to get out?"

She cupped my arm with her warm hand and said, "Oh, no, honey. I didn't mean to mislead you. I just wanted to gauge how you'd feel about it when the time came. I honestly don't know when you'll be released."

"They said I was supposed to be here for six months, and then I screwed up and one of the teachers added another six months, then I was told she'd been too harsh and the administrator said she'd modify it, but that was a while ago. It sounds like I could get out now or have another few weeks or months. I'm confused and no one will enlighten me."

"I thought it was a year, or six months for good behavior," she said.

"Yeah, it was. Then this dumb-shit teacher set me up, and I failed her little test."

Her eyes widened. "What kind of test?"

"It's something a few of the staff do from time to time—but she did it *all* the time. They act like they're not watching while they lift the suppression on our powers. Not quite like that teacher did though. She tried to bait us, and I swear she wanted us to fail."

"Bait you?"

"Yeah push our buttons. Find out what really hurts us emotionally and go for the jugular."

"What did they do to you that pushed your buttons to the point where you couldn't just ignore them?" She looked disappointed.

I had plenty of time to be disappointed with myself, believe me. But this was the first she was hearing of it. I took a deep breath. I didn't really want to admit I could be so dumb, but this was Aunt Hilary. I think she'd understand if anyone would.

"My teacher was talking about our parental units."

Aunt Hilary tipped her head and just waited for me to fill in the rest.

"Okay, so she wanted to know why my parents never came to visit. She suggested they didn't love me. I was able to ignore that. Then it was suggested that they couldn't control me. And I managed to blow that off. And then…" I couldn't quite finish.

Aunt Hilary nodded. "I can guess. Did she say they were scared of you?"

I let out a deep breath and nodded. I could feel tears burning the back of my eyes, but I refused to shed them. I just took a few deep breaths and waited for the emotions to settle. Aunt Hilary gave my arm a comforting squeeze then let go.

"It's a weird thing, being a witch. We don't always know how, when, or why we come into our powers. Some of us are born from two witches, and that's easy enough to understand. But some of us aren't. And some are more powerful than others. I've been in your shoes. I wasn't the only witch in our family, but I was certainly the strongest. My parents were just better at denial than yours are."

She was giving me that half smile. What did she know that I didn't know? She was actually telling me she and I experienced the same kind of thing—but I wasn't smiling.

"So, you're saying my grandparents knew you were a powerful witch, but they were just able to ignore it and pretend it wasn't true?"

"Pretty much. I got the sense that I wouldn't be getting much help from them in that department, so I looked for guidance elsewhere. And that's why I know you need it too."

I nodded enthusiastically. "I do. I need guidance from someone who knows what I'm going through and what I need. Not my parents. Not one of the teachers. In here I don't know who I can trust, but I know I can trust you."

She gave me a side hug. "Yes, you can. So…" she leaned back and her eyes twinkled, "do you want to come to Arizona and live with me there? Do you think you can find something to do to help out at the spa?"

"You mean like a job?"

She chuckled. "Yes, like a job."

"I'm only 16 years old. Okay, almost 17, but still…"

"That's old enough to take a job in the state of Arizona. You can work part time and get your G.E.D. then take college courses online, if that's what's bothering you."

"No, it's not bothering me. It's just…I guess I haven't thought about alternatives. My future had always seemed to follow a nebulous straight line. I'd finish high school, go to college, and at some point I'd figure out what I wanted to do with my life."

*But could I do that now? Right now?*

"I think your idea sounds like a decent plan. Maybe better than the other one," I added, quickly. "I guess I could get a job washing dishes or cleaning the facility. I really don't know what else I could do without some kind of higher education. And since nobody else knows what to do with me..."

Aunt Hilary let out a long breath. "I was afraid you'd feel that way, but don't. A job is just so you have a reason to be there. We can find something you can do temporarily which you might like. A lot of us don't know what to do with ourselves at your age. Hopefully, in time you'll discover your passion, and you'll know what direction to take in life."

That sounded good to me. But what if I wasn't out of here by the time I turned eighteen? One major setback and I'd be going to Hell—the adult version of Haven. Witches don't believe in a literal Hell. Figuratively, I could only guess why they called it that.

# CHAPTER 6

Later at dinner, Alien was pouting. What else is new? The only difference was it was pouring outside. Coincidence? With our powers stripped, it must have been. At least Just Jen was in a goodish mood and Lake Pirate was his always optimistic self. I was trying to hide my hope, because I didn't want to jinx it.

Thankfully, Lake Pirate brought up a whole new subject.

"You know, I heard a rumor that Lawless Logan got out because he broke into the library and found a spell to lift the ban on his powers."

"Why didn't he do that for all of us?" Alien whined.

I mentally rolled my eyes. She hadn't even been here when it happened.

"I imagine he didn't want to get caught," Just Jen said.

"How would he get caught, if we were *all* out of here? There would be nobody left to rat on him."

*Whoa.* Alien used that old-timey expression. Was it innocent? Maybe something she'd heard her parents say? Or did she have her powers all along? Maybe she was a plant. Meaning, she was put here to spy on us… not a plant like a Ficus or Gardenia. She definitely wouldn't be a Gardenia. More like a version of Bossy Rando's Venus Fly Trap. *Are we the flies?*

"Um, I don't think that's possible, LP. You know that place is warded up tighter than Fort Knox," I said.

"No, it isn't," he said, excitedly. "I saw Simmons go in there with just a key. He couldn't break a ward with an axe."

"Well, I'm still not convinced it would be that easy," Just Jen said.

Lake Pirate shrugged. "I could try it…"

"Try what?" I exclaimed. A few kids from the next table turned around and stared at us. I should have kept my voice down, but I couldn't help worrying about what reckless chance Lake Pirate might take.

"Mind your own business," Alien snapped at the next table.

As soon as the others turned back to their own conversations, he grinned. "I could steal it. After all, Lake Pirate's gotta *pirate*, right?" Using his name as a verb was pretty clever…for him.

"Don't. Seriously. Do. Not."

He sighed. "Look, I doubt I'll ever get out of here, even if I am… Well, what I mean is, I could at least do it for you guys."

He left out the part about his having no powers. His shoulders drooped slightly and his smile disappeared altogether.

"It's a nice thought, but let's focus on what *is* possible." I said.

"Like Bossy Rando getting canned," Just Jen said, cheerfully.

"Yeah, I heard about her," Alien said. "Why do you think they fired her?"

Lake Pirate groaned. "There are so many reasons to choose from. Mostly she hated us. She set us up to fail whatever tests she gave us. Like giving us the wrong answers when she was lecturing, then saying we should have figured out it was wrong and answered it right."

"And those other kinds of tests," Just Jen said. "She'd lift our powers enough to prove we could do a spell responsibly, then shut them down before we were finished. Sometimes that caused them to backfire."

"Really? She was that bad?"

"Trust us," Just Jen said. "She was that bad and worse."

*Trust.* That's the part that had been bothering me. I didn't know how much we could trust Alien. "I think I'm done here. How about you, Jenika?"

"Yeah, but there's nothing to do. We can't go outside today."

"We can walk around the building. Get a little exercise…" I managed to give her a wink the others couldn't see.

"Okay. I guess they wouldn't think much about a couple of kids walking the halls. It's not like a gang of us are prowling around, looking for trouble."

"Right," I said, grateful that she'd subtly uninvited the others.

"Let's go." I took my tray and gave her a quick smile as I placed it on the collection table and watched it go poof.

The following day we had a class with our new teacher. I didn't know Ms. Maddox well, but she seemed a whole lot more reasonable than Bossy Rando. I was actually looking forward to this class.

"Hello, everyone "I'm Miss Maddox," she said in a sweet southern drawl. "I'm aware this class has been difficult for you, and that some of those difficulties may not have been your fault."

The murmuring among the student inmates suggested strong agreement with that statement.

"So, let's start fresh, shall we?"

"Yeah!" one of the older boys exclaimed as he pumped his fist.

Miss Maddox smiled. Hey, she might not earn a nickname. The obvious would be Mad Dog, but I'd reserve judgement for now.

"Today, I will lift your powers, one at a time, to allow you a short visit with your familiars."

*Hooray! This teacher rocks!* I missed my black and white cat. His name is Oreo, and he's as sweet as the cookie.

"Now, as you know, the Goddess enjoys spells set to rhymes. I will give you a few minutes to compose a simple spell to summon your familiar, with at least one rhyme in it. State your intention clearly, because I'm sure you also realize the powers-that-be can be very literal. When you're ready, simply raise your hands."

Everyone, with heads down, started scribbling like mad. We were all anxious to visit with our furry besties.

I had to think a minute. What rhymes with Oreo? Borneo? No, that would send him somewhere in the South Pacific… *Coreo? Doreo? Foreo? Goreo?* Screw it. I can't use his name. I'll just have to describe him.

My black and white fur baby? Oh, no. That might result in a hairy infant.

Hands were going up all over the place. I didn't want to be last. Okay…black and white pet. Yeah, that might do it. I raised my hand before I was actually ready.

I figured she'd go in order of readiness. Or alphabetically.

Nope. She called on Paul Washington to go first, so I could rule out alphabetical order. And I don't think he was the first to finish. He was the first kid in the first row, so I imagine she was going by our seating assignment. Awesome. I sat right behind him, so I might be second—or fifth.

Paul called out in a clear confident voice, "Goddess, well met. I miss my little pet. Bring me my familiar. Her name is Quillier."

*Quillier the familiar? You've got to be kidding me.*

A moment later, a porcupine appeared on Paul's desk. "Quillier!" Paul grinned and wisely didn't try to hug the thing. "How are things back at home?"

"Oh, you know. I eat. I sleep. But it's lonely without you to talk to. And I spend all day in my cage."

"I sympathize, Quill. It's the same here."

Miss Maddox who had been smiling from ear to ear, cleared her throat. "I'm sorry to cut it short, but I want to give everyone time to say hello to their beloved guardians."

It's funny. I had never thought of Oreo as my guardian. Our relationship seemed more like the other way around. My cat was a lazy slug who slept in any patch of sun he could find and occasionally lifted his head to offer an opinion, *if* I asked for it. Oh, he would just love Florida! So much sun. I actually couldn't wait to see him…lazy or not. I loved the little bugger.

Paul gave his porcupine a sad wave and sent her home.

"Genevieve. You may go next."

*Yay!* I hoped I'd get this right since I was kind of flying by the seat of my pants. "To Gods and Goddesses please take heed, send me the black and white pet I need."

When a skunk appeared in front of me, the whole class burst out laughing. I gasped. Unfortunately, the spooked animal chose that moment to spray his displeasure, and I sucked in a lungful.

Choking, coughing and sputtering while my classmates held their noses, I tried to wave away the offending smell.

"Is that really your familiar, Fish Face?" Alien asked, nasally, due to her pinched nose.

"No! I—" I coughed some more and couldn't finish.

Miss Maddox opened the door. "Everyone, please go outside until Genevieve and I get this contained."

There was a stampede for the door.

"We will continue class outside in a few moments," she called out.

Miss Maddox turned her hands palms-up in supplication, "Goddess of all, reverse this spell. Please send back the skunk and purge the smell."

The skunk vanished and the scent, which held on a little longer eventually dissipated too. By now, my mortification had multiplied ten-fold.

"There. All better."

If it was that easy, why did she have to send everyone outside?

"I wanted to talk to you alone for a moment anyway, Genevieve," she said as if she'd heard my thought.

"Oh?" She was probably going to send me to Mrs. Black Hole for disciplinary action.

"I understand you've been having some trouble with your spells."

"Yeah, you can say that again…but don't! I know I'm a screw-up."

She smiled sadly. "You're too hard on yourself."

"Am I? I can't get the words right and focusing my thoughts is hard too." I sighed deeply. "In other words, I'm having trouble with everything."

She tipped her head. "Not everything. You seem to know right from wrong. That's a huge part of magic *and* growing up. The rest is just learning and practice."

"I—I guess."

"I can tutor you, if you need some extra help with spells."

"Really?" It sounded as if she believed in me. Bossy Rando would have called me hopeless and slapped another month or two onto my sentence.

"Absolutely. Think it over. For now, would you like to go to your room and brush your teeth—just to feel a little fresher?" she asked.

"Yeah, and gargle a gallon of mouthwash."

She chuckled, then shook her head. "I'm sorry. I didn't mean to laugh at your misfortune. Perhaps we can work on your wording and concentration later this week."

I rose and thanked her, then made a beeline for my room.

On the way to my room I decided, what the heck, I'd try the library door. No one I had seen go in or out of there ever got electrocuted from touching the door. I reached out, grabbed the handle, and—as if I belonged there, pulled it open!

The door opened!

I set one toe inside waiting for some kind of lightning bolt, but none came. Oh, this was wonderful.

Slipping into the library, I realized I had maybe five minutes before I was missed. Now if only I could find the right book in five minutes. I had never even been in this room before, so I edged my way in peeked around the corner. Fortunately I didn't see another soul. However, I did see stacks and stacks of books. Some on shelves, some just piled in corners. Who treats books like that? Especially magical books!

We're taught to revere magic. It's odd how some people just don't have any respect for things. Okay, enough. I didn't have time for outrage. I needed to find the right book. I leaned against a wall just to think.

"Hey, get off of me."

I jumped about three feet away. Staring at the wall wide-eyed, I asked, "Wall? Was that you speaking?" I'd feel really stupid if it wasn't. It could have been someone who was cloaked and watching me or something…

There was a strange undulating movement behind the wall and then it answered me. "Yes, girl. The wall is speaking. What do you want?"

It obviously didn't know my name. So, maybe even if somebody asked who came in and requested a book, it wouldn't know who to blame. I decided to take the chance.

"I'm looking for a book that Lawless—I mean Logan Holderness took out."

"I'm not familiar with someone named Logan Hold-erness. Can you describe him?"

"Yes. He has blue eyes and sandy blonde hair that's kind of long in the front. It doesn't get in his eyes, but it brushes his eyebrows. He's about 5 feet 10 inches tall. He has the nicest smile with straight white teeth. I think he's eighteen years old or so? No, he can't be older than seventeen." If he were eighteen, he would've been out of here.

"Yes, I know the youth of which you speak. He may have been the youngest person ever to enter this library."

*Until me,* I thought.

"Until you," it said.

*Busted.* At least I looked fairly nondescript. Even if it described me as a sixteen year-old female, 5 foot 5, with straight dark brown hair, that could apply to other girls here.

"So, which book did the boy take?"

"Go down to the third row of shelves. It's the fourth book from the end on the top shelf."

I ran down the hallway and followed directions, then quickly pulled out a fairly thin book. It looked quite old, but it wasn't falling apart or anything. At least this one had been well cared for.

"Is this it?" I asked.

"That is the book he requested," the wall said.

Again I thought of the saying, *if walls could talk...* Nobody ever said what they would say, but now I knew. They were rather helpful.

I had to cut my conversation with the wall short so I could get this book back to my room and then join everyone outside for the rest of class. I shoved the book up under my shirt, mumbled a quick, "Thank you, and please don't tell anyone else I was here." Then I shuffled down the stacks, around the corner, peeked out the glass in the doors, and when I didn't see anyone I quickly exited the library and rushed to my room.

Nobody saw me, thank goodness. As soon as I got there, I had to either look at the book quickly or hide it. Maybe I had time to do both. Wait a minute if I had an eidetic, or photographic, memory I could just scan the book, have it all in my head, then replace it. I wouldn't even need to have the book in my room. I'm sure if I were caught with it, I'd be in big trouble.

"Now think," I said to myself. "How do I turn that into a spell? What rhymes with eidetic? I know. Pathetic." *Groan.* Clearly I would have to think about this one, it was important.

I tucked the book under my pillow and ran toward the outside door. As I was just about to leave the building, I realized I should've changed my clothes. They didn't smell anymore but if I wasn't wearing the sprayed stuff, Ms. Maddox wouldn't question where I'd been if she thought I took too long just to brush my teeth.

I leaned against the wall and said, "I like these clothes, but not for now. Place them back in my room and clothe me in cow."

I closed my eyes and quickly imagined leather. Not an actual cow. That would've been tragic.

I opened one eye and peeked down at myself. Thank goodness I was now wearing a leather jacket and leather pants. Wait, no shirt? Well, I didn't ask for one, did I?

*Shirt. What rhymes was shirt?* Bert? Kurt? Dirt? Flirt? Okay. Lots of stuff rhymes with shirt. "Goddess of all, hear my call. In order to flirt, I need a cute shirt." I shrugged. It was a stupid sounding spell, but if it got the job done...

My favorite purple shirt appeared in my hand.

"No... I need to be *wearing* the shirt."

It disappeared and reappeared on my body.

*Hey... That was pretty cool, and it didn't even rhyme.* At least it was comfortable. I don't know how the leather was going to feel outside in the sun though. It might be winter in Florida, but the temperatures could fluctuate from forty to eighty here. Maybe I could change my jacket and pants quickly too.

"Goddess this leather is hot, is that all you've got? I'd love some jeans or shorts and a jacket of sorts."

Now I was wearing nice blue jeans and a black hoodie along with my purple shirt.

"And sneakers..." I added a bit late.

I mentally crossed my fingers and looked down at myself. I was wearing blue jeans and white sneakers while still wearing the purple top and black hoodie. It worked! I wasn't a total failure!

Running outside to join the class, I was overjoyed. Not only had I performed a couple of spells in a row that hadn't backfired, I also had the book I needed tucked under my pillow for later. Since we had to make our own beds, I couldn't see anybody discovering it. I just had to hope that Lake Pirate would stay out of my room. I couldn't even trust my most trustworthy friends with this.

# CHAPTER 7

I NO SOONER GOT OUTSIDE THAN I WAS CAREFULLY approached by my peers. Paul Washington sniffed the air. "Oh, good. You don't smell disgusting. It's a good thing I didn't get sprayed by your skunk…"

"Or what?"

"Or I'd be stinky too. Is that really your familiar?"

"No. I have a black and white cat. I don't suppose you have a leg to stand on criticizing my familiar since yours is a porcupine named Quillier."

A few kids standing around chuckled.

Surprisingly, Alien was the one who came over and stuck up for me, although I had it well in hand. "What's it to you? You have a porcupine as a familiar," she said, haughtily. "You can't hug it. It didn't seem especially intelligent. What's it good for?"

Paul reared back and glared at her as if he she had

slapped him. "*She* is my friend. I don't suppose you have any of those, so you wouldn't know."

One of his buddies said, "Why don't you go back to North None-o-yo-business, Alien?"

Paul folded his arms, but didn't seem upset. Or maybe that's the New England version of upset. It's hard to tell. "Look, we don't choose our familiars. They choose us," he said. "I had no control over a porcupine wandering into my neighborhood in rural New England. They live there."

Alien just shrugged. "We went to a pet store and this adorable little puppy came up to me and I was immediately in love with it. So I picked it. It didn't pick me."

Paul laughed. "You just said it came up to you and you fell in love with it. That's *it* picking *you*."

I was just happy not to be the subject of discussion any longer. So I faded into the background and spotted Jenika a few feet away. She looked over at me and we met in the middle. "Are you okay?" she asked.

"Yes, thank you for asking. None of these idiots care about anything except insulting each other—and not in a funny teasing way."

She put her arm around my shoulders. "Well, I care. That was a nasty blast you took. How did Miss Maddox get rid of the stink?"

"I was pretty amazed. She rattled off a beautiful spell like she had practiced it, but I don't think she had.

She's just that good. She said she'd tutor me if I wanted her to."

Just Jen's brows rose. "Really? That's pretty special. I've never heard of a teacher offering to tutor us delinquents before."

I gave her a sly smile. "What can I say? I must be special."

She snorted and laughed. "Oh, you're special all right."

"So, where is she? I thought she was going to continue class out here?"

Jen shrugged. "She hasn't shown up yet. I thought she and you were probably down at the admin's office talking about having you scrub the classroom with a toothbrush as punishment."

"I'm happy to report that's not the case. She let me go to my room, brush my teeth and change my clothes. I don't know where she went from there."

I suddenly remembered the alibi I needed to ask Jenika for. I was tempted to tell her about the library, the walls, and the book. I knew I could trust her, but if she was ever questioned, she would get in trouble for withholding information. So I really wouldn't be doing her a favor by telling her most of it.

Miss Maddox came out to the exercise yard clapping her hands. The students gathered around.

"I'm sorry for the wait. Let's continue practicing spells to conjure and visit with your familiars. I know you're all anxious to see them. Those of you who have already had your turn, please sit up against the building and that way I can keep track of who still needs to try."

I strolled over to the side of the building, but didn't sit. I wasn't sure if I was going to get another chance or not. If I were Miss Maddox, I'd probably want me to spend some time rewriting the spell.

She went along and let each person conjure their familiar one at a time. They got about a five second visit, but it was better than nothing. Everyone was happy to see their beloved pet, and it seemed that most of the familiars were also happy. Maybe it was better if they didn't see my lazy slug of a cat ignore me.

Most of the familiars were cats. Just Jen had told me about her familiar. She had a beautiful Persian cat with long white hair and blue eyes. She had said she was always nervous about her being stolen.

"Jenika, it's your turn," Miss Maddox said.

"Goddess near and Goddess far, bring to me my familiar, Star."

I never knew her cat's name, but obviously, it was Star. The gorgeous feline appeared right in her arms.

She hugged and kissed her and it was obvious that witch and familiar were thrilled to see each other. They spoke in hushed whispers. Jen turned her body a bit and pointed to me. Her pretty kitty nodded her head once.

Then she had to put her on the ground and bid Star

goodbye. I don't know if this exercise was a good idea or not. Jenika had a tear in her eye and looked like she had to wrestle herself under control pretty quickly. If you didn't know her, you would think she was tough as nails and never cried. But on the inside she's made of mush. She steeled her shoulders and walked over to the wall near me and slid down.

"Beautiful cat, Jen."

"She is, isn't she? I usually kept her in the house, but sometimes the two of us would go up to the roof, look at the stars and talk. Those are the times I miss the most."

"Yeah, I don't know if I'll get to see Oreo or not."

Paul looked up. "Your familiar's name is Oreo? And you're giving me a hard time about Quillier?"

I had to laugh. "I guess they both make sense in a way. My familiar is a black and white cat."

He rolled his eyes. "Yeah, I can see how a skunk could be confused with a black and white cat. I think I saw a cartoon like that once." He looked away with a sly smile as if he were remembering it.

"The kid next to Paul was named George, and he asked, "Why didn't you just ask the Goddess for Oreo? At least if you didn't get your cat, you'd get a cookie."

"Yeah, and you could eat it," Paul added.

They laughed and I finally understood the term, *sophomoric humor.*

Most of the kids had had their visit with their

familiars and they strolled over and sat next to the wall, except me. I bit my lip and looked over to Miss Maddox. The look she gave me wasn't even a little ambiguous. Pity. It made me sad, but what could I do?

I guess I could ask for that tutoring session she'd offered. I didn't dare screw up again. Of course, I'll probably never hear the end of the skunk story anyway. It'll be all over the jail by dinnertime. I could only hope I wouldn't get a new nickname even worse than Fish Face.

One of the girls we didn't socialize with looked over at me and said, "What did you do with the disgusting clothes you were wearing?"

I shrugged. I couldn't tell her that I'd just poofed them away, then poofed more on. She'd know my powers were accidentally left in place. That's the last thing I wanted anyone to know. I might need them sometime.

The girl next to her elbowed her and said, "I bet she burned them."

The first girl gave her a sly grin and said, "Yeah, if those were my clothes I'd burn them too. Such tragic fashion!" The two girls laughed and I remembered why I didn't associate with them.

Not everyone has the same priorities. If their priorities are cute clothes then more power to them. They can have all the designer styles they want. I didn't know exactly what my priorities were. But when it comes to clothes, I like comfort. Is that so wrong?

I turned my back on them and resumed my conversation with Just Jen. "There's something I need you to back me up on."

She smiled. "Oh? Are you going to trip one of them and say it was an accident? I'll swear it was."

I laughed. "No, although I'll keep that in mind for later. I was just hoping you would back up a different story I concocted earlier. Don't mention this unless you're asked, but the other day when Logan disappeared…"

Her eyes grew wider. "Yeah?"

"Oh, I'm sorry. I didn't mean to get you excited. I don't know anything about that. Nothing real anyway. I just want you to say I was waiting for you near the library, but across the hall on the corner."

She seemed disappointed. "That's it?"

"Yup. That's it. And please don't ask why."

She frowned, then said. "Sure. You just said you were waiting for me and we were going to study together. Right? Study what?"

"Oh, yeah. Maybe we should decide what the details are. Algebra?"

"That sounds plausible. I should study more math."

"Me too. But I wonder if we'll ever need algebra in the real world."

"I doubt it. I remember my older brother, saying

he'd never need it for his job as a bus driver, but who knows… I think I might want to become a police officer. They need to figure out trajectories at accident scenes, and that might use math."

"Seriously? After being in here, will they let you become a cop?"

She shrugged. "If our records are sealed and I don't screw up again…"

"Wow. That would be—interesting. I don't know what I want to do. It looks like I may be going to live with my aunt and she works in a spa. Maybe I could learn to be a massage therapist. I'm pretty sure I don't need algebra for that."

"Yeah, but you will need anatomy and physiology. At least that's what I heard a masseuse say when she was accused of picking a fluff job."

"A what now?"

"Fluff. Look, I didn't make that expression up, someone else did."

"Okay. Well, I guess I have to come up with some sort of a snappy comeback in case someone accuses me of being a fluff brain or something."

Miss Maddox had gathered us all together again and said, "Class is just about over, why don't you go ahead and get ready for the next one. Class dismissed."

Just Jen and I went in together. We both had study hall in the auditorium.

"Want to study algebra?" she asked, smirking.

We both burst out laughing.

Then Miss Maddox said, "Oh, Genevieve…"

*Shoot. I knew it was too good to be true.*

<hr>

It was almost as I feared. I was sent to the administrative office, but there was no toothbrush in Miss Maddox's hand, so I didn't think I would have to actually scrub the classroom. However, I imagine they could think of some other means to torture me.

By the time I arrived at the office, I had invented half a dozen scenarios in my head, none of which were good. The secretary peeked over her shoulder at me and shook her head, then walked away. Okay, this couldn't be good at all.

The door to the administrator's office opened before I took a seat. Mrs. Black Hole motioned me inside. "Genevieve, I'm glad you came so quickly. I need to speak with you."

I figured I'd get ahead of the thing rather than play dumb. "I'm sorry about the skunk incident, it really was an accident. I certainly wouldn't do that on purpose."

Mrs. Black Hole turned around and looked at me over her shoulder. "That's what you think this is about? Actually, no, I let your teachers handle things like that. I'm sure it was a mistake."

If she was sure it was a mistake, what was I doing here?

"It's come to my attention that you've been in the library. The *off limits* library." She said the words 'off limits' as if they needed to be emphasized.

"Um, yeah. I was just checking the door and it opened."

"Why were you checking the door?"

I shrugged. "Just curious. I guess someone left it unlocked once before, so I thought I'd check. And, you know how it is… If something is off limits people want to know why."

"I see."

I don't know if she did see or not, but it was the best grain of truth I had at the moment.

"What did you find? Or did you just satisfy your curiosity and leave?"

"I saw books…nothing special, so I left."

She stared at me as if expecting more. I couldn't help wondering how she found out. Did they have cameras in there? Did the walls tell her? I didn't see anyone around—unless someone was practicing an invisibility spell at the time. If any of those were true, I was in deep doodoo. I still had the book in my room.

She was just staring at me and it was weirding me out. I couldn't cave though. If I started babbling about how poorly the books were treated, some in piles on the floor, or any details at all, she'd know for sure I'd gone further into the stacks. I just had to outlast her.

Finally she leaned back in her chair with a huff. "Fine. Why don't you go back to class? Meanwhile, think about what else you may have seen—or done, while you were in there."

*Or done.* Did she know I had smuggled a book out under my shirt?

I rose. "Am I dismissed?"

She simply waved her hand as if she were shooing away a fly, then picked up some papers on her desk and whirled her chair away from me to read them.

I hate that feeling that I get when I've disappointed someone. But in this case, I could only take it as a positive sign. She had hoped I'd confess to more. She really had only one thing against me—curiosity. And that is a hard thing to punish a kid for.

I scurried down the hall, checking for people, cameras, and even trying to sense spirits. Chances are there was some kind of silent alarm on the library door. I'd have to figure out how to magically disable it when I put the book back—and oh, yes... I had to put the book back ASAP.

There were no cameras in our rooms or bathrooms, thanks to some civil liberties or human rights thing. Instead of going on to study hall, I stopped at my room. No one saw me slip inside, so I figured I might be able to hang out and read a while. Too bad I didn't have a photographic memory. I could scan the book, put it back, and…wait a minute. Maybe I could whip up a spell to give me one, temporarily. I wouldn't want to remember everything always and forever. What a pain that would be.

So, what do I ask for? Calling it photographic would probably install a camera in my brain. There's a correct term, but I'm not positive what it is. I think it's *eidetic* memory. If I had one, I'd know the right word.

Damn. I didn't dare screw up another spell, especially one involving the inside of my head. Those were notoriously tricky. Only fools and criminals attempt mind control. Okay, so I might be walking that fine line, but I wanted to stay on the safe side.

Setting up my pillow to block anyone's view of the book from the window inset in my door, I could read it and cover it quickly should someone—Lake Pirate, probably—pop in unexpectedly. I didn't know which class he might have right now. He was in a whole different track and our paths didn't cross except at meals, some behavioral classes, and whenever he took it upon himself to find me—which was often.

I wished there were a table of contents in this book. It was old, handwritten, and seemed barely organized. It could have been some ancient witch's *Book of Shadows* or grimoire. I'd just have to plow through the whole thing.

Healing spells, love spells, fertility spells, astral

projection...yawn. So far it seemed pretty basic. Eventually I found some more unique spells. One to insult someone and make them take it as a compliment. That might be fun. One to unlock a chastity belt. I just shook my head at that. One to make a troublesome neighbor move away. One to set a trap for vermin, and then transport them to a neighbor's house. Transport! This had to be the right section.

Travel spells followed. Safety when riding an ox cart... Determining the distance to one's destination... Hmmm. Must be an early form of GPS.

Where are the spells to transport oneself? Logan didn't have a Star Trek transporter. Someone would have noticed that.

I kept reading.

Suddenly I came upon a spell that sent shock waves through me. *How to visit Summerland.* Summerland is what the fuggles call Heaven. Not Haven.

*Actual Heaven.*

Yes, witches go to heaven—sort of. There aren't angels playing harps and sitting around on clouds. It's more of a peaceful place for souls to rest and reflect, and according to wiccans it's not a one-way trip. It takes about a hundred years, but eventually when an individual has reviewed their past life and knows what they need to learn in the next one, reincarnation takes place.

So... Was this a suicide spell? I think not. It specifically talks about *visiting.* That infers returning, right? As I read the fine print—aka, the details of the spell, I saw there was a companion spell in order to return.

Why hadn't Logan returned? Did he forget the return spell? Was he stuck there? Did he choose to stay? Did he find a way to fast-forward his reincarnation and now he's on earth as an infant or something else, like a bird?

Oh, frig. Who knows? The only people I could ask would add another six months to my sentence for withholding information. That's just not an option. I want to get out of here!

I'll bet Logan felt the same way. So did he hate it here so much he preferred the land of the dead? So many questions! And the longer I kept the book the more it was apt to be missed.

I simply had to read faster.

## CHAPTER 8

BY THE NEXT MEAL, I STILL HADN'T FINISHED THE BOOK. I was almost through it, but there were no other spells to transport a human anywhere. Could he have performed that Summerland spell? It really didn't look like a great possibility unless a person was desperate.

I had to figure out something else, and do it quickly. I shoved the book under my pillow and was just getting ready to head to the cafeteria when I bumped—literally — into Lake Pirate.

"I was just coming to get you."

"I can find the cafeteria on my own, you know."

He laughed. "I know that, I was just being a good friend. I thought you might like some company as you walk down there. So, how was your day?"

What could I tell him? I had conjured a skunk, been sprayed in the face, found a secret book in the off-limits library, lied to the administrator, found a spell that might or might not be the one Logan used to get out of here… "Nothing much. How was your day?"

He shrugged. "Oh, you know, the usual. I'm really struggling with some of my academic classes."

"What kind of classes do they have you taking?"

He shrugged. "Math. English. You know, the boring stuff."

I couldn't help making a little inside joke. "History?"

He laughed. "That's the class where you hit your teacher in the face with a fish, right?"

I sighed. "I still swear it was an accident."

"Oh, I know it was. I believe you."

By this time we had arrived at the caf and got in line for our nightly slop. It wasn't always terrible. But tonight it was fish.

"Yuck. Fish. There's only so much they can do with fish to make it palatable. Even breaded and fried it's still fish."

"Hey, I love fish." Lake Pirate elbowed me. "Just don't hit me in the face with it."

"Keep talking like that, and I might."

He grinned and grabbed his fried fish and onion rings. We also had a small cup of coleslaw and some fruit. It looked like it came right out of the can. This was about the most disgusting meal anyone could have put together. If I had been in charge of the menu… But alas, they didn't ask me.

I looked around the cafeteria and didn't see our usual table. Rather, I saw it but there were other kids sitting there. I searched the faces all around. "Where is Just Jen?"

He turned and looked, then shrugged. "I don't know, but somebody's sitting in our place."

I had just finished filling the last spot on my dinner tray, including dessert, which was bland white cake with white frosting. The most tasteless version of something that should have been good. Anyway, I finally saw Jenika come in with a teacher.

"Oh no, I wonder what she did to be escorted to the caf by a teacher?"

Lake Pirate was silent but his expression said it all. He was just as surprised as I was.

"Just Jen is usually the quiet one," I mused. "How could she get in trouble?"

"I guess there's a reason they say, 'You gotta watch out for the quiet ones,'" Lake Pirate muttered.

As we wandered around the caf looking for a suitable place to land rather than challenging the people who took our spot, he said, "What do you think she did?"

"I have no idea. I can't imagine her doing anything. We all want to get out of here, and she knows because of the seriousness of her screw-up she's being watched closely. She's been trying to keep herself out of trouble since day one."

"I wish there was some way we could talk to her," he said.

I wondered if I could communicate telepathically. It seemed like they had forgotten all about shutting down my ability. I wondered if Jenika could still hear me if I called out to her in my mind.

"Jen? Just Jen? Genevieve to Jenika!"

Nothing. Either she was afraid the teacher would intercept our communication or she really couldn't hear me. I'd vote for either one. Maybe if I knew the name of that teacher, I could try and hail her, but what would I say? 'What are you doing with my friend?' That wouldn't help. I wasn't exactly persona non grata, but I wasn't anyone's favorite student right at the moment, either.

Lake Pirate had found an open spot so I sat with him there. "Do you think it's about you?" he asked.

"I already said I don't know. I just tried reaching out to her telepathically, thinking that maybe our powers hadn't been suppressed, but yeah they are. She didn't react at all. Even if she didn't want to talk, she would have given me a quick glance and a headshake or something. I'm guessing we're not able to communicate that way anymore."

He had a funny look on his face then turned away. "Yeah, that must be cool."

I had almost forgotten that Lake Pirate was actually a fuggle. I still couldn't understand how he didn't know that to begin with…and when he wound up here, what must he have thought? But Lake Pirate wasn't one to think a lot. When things got hard, he just sort of moved on.

I tried not to stare, but I kept Jenika in my peripheral vision as she went through the line. When she was done she didn't look for a table. She looked toward her teacher and the two of them went back out the door they'd come in.

*Oh no. This cannot be good.*

I wondered if it really was about me. No. I was just being paranoid. Speaking of which, Mrs. Black Hole questioning me was like a recording replaying in my head. Yeah, they lost Logan, but that was days ago. If he's not here, he's not here. Do they really think one of us is going to crack if they keep pounding away at us?

Come to think of it, that's what they show on cop shows all the time. The detectives ask the same questions a dozen different ways until the bad guy yells, "It was me! I confess! I did it!"

*Yeah, right.* Clearly the teachers picked the wrong kids to intimidate.

"Finally! I've been waiting to see you after your dinner with a teacher. What was that about?" I asked Just Jen when I finally saw her in the TV room later.

"Sorry. I knew you were there, but I didn't even dare look at you. She was fishing for dirt."

"On me?"

"Not you in particular. At least I don't think so."

"Did you hear me trying to communicate with you, telepathically?"

She looked surprised. "No. Why would you? Our telepathy was only temporary."

"Are you sure?"

"Yeah. They suppressed it about half an hour after the assembly. Do you still have yours?"

"Probably not. I haven't even bothered trying to use my powers for the most part, but occasionally something makes me think they might have missed me when they were taking them away."

"Like what?"

"I…" *Shoot. What could I say without giving her a big piece of information they could wrestle out of her?* "I don't know what I'm talking about. Just ignore me."

She laughed. "Okaaay. But if you think you might still have some of your powers you could try a simple spell."

"If I do that, I'll wait until I'm alone. No sense tipping anybody off."

"Sure. You can tell me, of course."

"I can, but I shouldn't."

"Why not? Mrs. Grayson already grilled me. I doubt she'll do it again. I really didn't have any information for her."

"What kind of information was she looking for?"

"Stuff about Bossy Rando, mostly. I guess she must be suing to get her job back."

"She is?" I was shocked. I thought we'd gotten rid of her once and for all.

"I don't know. I'm just guessing. I think Mrs. Grayson's more than an English teacher. I remember someone saying she's a lawyer too."

"What kind of questions did she ask about her?"

"Was she a fair teacher? Did she play favorites? Did we see her doing anything illegal?"

"Illegal? Like what? Like dealing meth on the side?"

Just Jen shrugged. "That's what made me think they might be defending their decision to fire her."

That sounded about right. First determine if the kid was fond of the teacher or not, then grill the ones who didn't like her. Ha. That will take a few months.

"She only asked about you once."

My ears perked up, but I didn't have to coax her.

"She asked if we often met in the hall to walk to the auditorium together. I remembered what you said about waiting for me near the library, so I just said, 'Yeah,' and acted like it was no big deal."

I was relieved—but only partially. The more I thought about that book under my pillow the more I wanted to get back to it. Lake Pirate was riveted to the TV and I imagined he wouldn't miss me. "Okay. That's good. You know what? I'm kind of tired. I think I'd like to lie down for a while."

"Really? Are you okay?"

"Yeah, I'm fine. I just need a nap. It's been a crazy day."

She grinned. "Sure has—even for here. Go ahead. I'll see you later."

"Probably tomorrow at breakfast."

"G'night, then."

I hightailed it out of there, hoping I might have enough private time to figure out if I had some or all of my powers back. If so, I needed to try a spell on the book to put itself back where it came from. I didn't dare breach the library doors again.

As soon as I got back to my room, I flopped down on my back and shoved a hand under my pillow. I tried to make it look natural, as if I was just going to cup my head. Thank goodness the book was still there. I scanned the room and didn't see any new devices that might have been installed to spy on me. The place looked the same.

Okay. It was go-time. Grabbing the pen and paper I had secreted in the bottom of my laundry basket under a pair of permanently ruined panties from my period. I knew better than to put any contraband in the top dresser drawer under clean panties—that's the first place guards look...perverts) I figured I should write down any spell I tried. After all, I'd proven the wisdom of that practice simply by seeing what happens when I try to wing it.

Thinking in rhyme, I came up with a few simple words I could adapt to send the book back to its spot in the library. But first I would try to send my pen back to its spot in the basket. If it failed, I'd have to come up with something else.

"Dear Goddess, everything has its place to wait until it's needed. Return this pen to its space, may my words be heeded."

The pen disappeared from my hand. When I checked my laundry basket it was back under the pile of clothes and the dirty panties at the bottom. *Yippeee! I did it!* I wanted to shout it from the rooftops, but I had to settle for a silent party in my own head.

So, okay. This proved two things. First, I had my powers back. That in itself was cause for celebration. But even more importantly, I could probably replace the book without getting caught.

Now—I needed to decide whether or not I was going to use that Summerland spell before they figured out they'd somehow missed me with their suppression spell. I didn't know a lot of people who had died. Would I see my goldfish again? Probably not. But my grandparents on my father's side should be there. It hadn't been a hundred years yet. If I saw them, would I recognize their spirits?

I didn't know them well. Would they remember

me? Could I even find them? I wasn't really sure I wanted to. They might just be mad at me for trying such a stupid spell.

So…why did I want to go there? Be honest Genevieve. To see Logan? Okay, yeah. There was a chance I might see the cute boy I wish I'd gotten to know better. Was that such a bad thing? Was it the only reason?

No. I had to admit I was curious as heck about what lay ahead of us…all of us. Wouldn't it be cool to know that? Maybe I could give comfort to people on their death beds. Maybe I could describe it to children who'd lost a parent or friend. Maybe I could write a book about it someday, and hit a bestseller list, and get interviewed on TV… On second thought, I didn't want the attention that would draw. I'm kind of an introvert. I mainly wanted to know to satisfy my own curiosity.

I took a last look around my bleak room. Okay, it was go time. I was going to try this.

I breathed in deeply and aligned my mind with the divine. Then breathed out and pictured that breath going all the way down my body and out through my toes, anchoring me to mother earth.

Again, I dragged my breath all the way up from my toes, through my lungs and out the top of the crown of my head, reaching for the heavens, then exhaled down through my entire body, out my feet, through the floor and down into the ground.

Okay, I know that sounds weird since I'm not standing on the ground and there's a ceiling over my head, but it's amazing how just dragging deep breaths in and mentally directing them in deep waves seems to ground and free a person at the same time. It's called Pranic breathing. Hindus do it. Many witches do it before a ritual.

So I took some deep pranic breaths, aligned myself with the divine and the earth, became calm and recalled the words from the book—but I didn't say them aloud. *We all go to Summerland some day in time. My time is not now, but I seek the divine. I will not stay, if it's not my time. I'd like a day, that's only mine.*

I didn't dare change the words of the spell, but it seemed odd. I might be gone for a whole day—or longer if Summerland decided it was my time after all. I couldn't think about that or I'd chicken out. I hoped I could just take a peek; maybe find Logan and ask him a few questions since he'd been there longer. If I couldn't or didn't want to return I'd be in the same kind of trouble as Lawless Logan... Taking another deep oxygenating breath, I decided to deal with one problem at a time.

First of all I had to put the book back into its spot in the library, so I repeated the spell I had used with the pen and the next thing I knew the book was gone. *Woo Hoo!* One big problem avoided.

I'd committed the return spell to memory, so now I was ready to state my 'travel itinerary' aloud.

I was grounded. I was ready. Closing my eyes, raising my hands, palms up, I called upon the Goddess and her God. I entreated them both to send me *temporarily* to Summerland. I repeated the spell three times, speaking clearly. When I opened my eyes I was stunned.

# CHAPTER 9

I STOOD IN A BRILLIANT MEADOW. BRIGHT WILDFLOWERS fluttered in the floral scented breeze. The sun's warmth soaked into my shoulders and scalp. An overwhelming sense of peace relaxed me even though I was facing the unknown.

As far as I could see, no one else was around. Even so, I didn't feel alone. I felt safe. Loved. In the distance I saw woods and beyond those, mountains. It was one of the most vividly beautiful spots I've ever been to, but I had definitely not seen it before. I would've remembered this. It was not conjured by a memory.

I wondered where everyone was. And then I almost slapped myself upside the head when I remembered, *oh yeah, everyone usually comes here in spirit form.* I'm probably the only body walking around unless…

I reached out with my mind and called, *Logan?*

When there was no response, I decided to yell out loud. If he was here and not in spirit form, I hoped he would hear me and do whatever people did…just appear or float or whatever to show me that I was right. This is where he went.

I took a deep breath and called out as loud as I could. "Loooooggaaaaaannnnnnn…"

I was just about to take another deep breath and call again when behind me I heard the words, "Is that you Fish Face?"

I whirled around and saw the super-cute surfer-blond boy with his hands in his pockets and a sly grin on his face. I wanted to launch myself into his arms and hug him, but I didn't know him well enough to do that. I would just have to let words suffice. "I found you! I can't believe it. You're here!"

He chuckled and sauntered over to me. "Want to touch me?"

My brows shot up. *Was that an invitation?* I think it was just his way of joking around. But what the heck I was actually curious to know if he was real or just a figment of my imagination.

I reached out with my index finger and touched his upper arm. In response, he flexed his muscle and I laughed. He seemed pretty fit for a kid. Maybe he worked out.

"So you're real. And alive?"

He nodded. "You are too, apparently."

I looked all around and said, "Is anyone else here?"

His face fell. "No. I was hoping to find my mom. But..."

I gentled my voice. "I'm sorry. I didn't realize you lost your mom."

He nodded slowly. "I was only seven. I don't remember her real well, but I had the feeling she would always protect me—even from here. I was hoping she could get me out of Haven."

"How?"

He shrugged. "I don't know, maybe backing up time? Letting me do something differently? If anybody could do the impossible it would be a God or Goddess, right? Maybe she knows them. Anyway... I figured *if* it would take a miracle, I would need someone on this side to help."

"Was Haven really that terrible for you? Couldn't you just do your time and get out?"

He sighed. "Let's take a walk."

I looked around and gestured to the large open space. "To where?"

His grin reappeared. "There are some nice places that you haven't seen yet. Let me show you around. We can talk while we're walking, right?"

"As long as I'm not chewing gum..." I said as a joke.

Happily, he laughed. "I didn't realize you had a sense of humor, Fish Face."

He started strolling and turned back, waiting for me to come along.

I eventually did. "Would you mind doing me a favor?"

"Sure, if I can. What is it?"

"Can you call me Genevieve, instead of Fish Face, please?"

He chuckled. "Yeah, I think I can do that."

He looked at me, grinning, and I noticed his eyes were a clear sparkling blue. I think all colors were more vivid here. The purple, pink and yellow wildflowers seemed brighter. The green vegetation was lusher…or more lush. I'm not sure which is the right adjective, but you know what? Here it doesn't seem to matter. The sky was bluer than a robin's egg. I couldn't help continuing to stare in every direction.

"Pretty, isn't it?"

"It's stunning. Is that why you decided to stay here?"

He let out a long deep breath. "You asked why I didn't want to return to Haven. I guess I can answer that question for you, as unpleasant as it is."

We continued walking toward the woods. The mountain air reached me and I took a deep breath of freshness I had never known in the Pittsburgh area. At least I didn't live in Centralia, Pennsylvania. That town is deserted because of a coal fire that's been burning underground since nineteen sixty-two and they say it could burn for two hundred and fifty years!

At last he stopped and crossed his arms. I halted too.

"I was in for something pretty serious," he said. "I really hurt someone."

"Was it an accident?"

He made an odd expression and tipped his head back and forth as if considering the question before he answered. "Technically."

"You can tell me whatever it is. I won't tell anyone else. I mean look around, who would I tell?"

He laughed and said, "True. There's no one to tell here except me, and I've already heard the story. In fact, I've replayed it in my mind over and over."

I waited and let him compose the words any way he wished. If I asked questions I might get the whole story, or I might not. I was waiting for him to tell it his way.

"It was all about this girl…"

I remember Just Jen saying that her uncle, a Detroit cop, told her when there's a bar fight, it's almost always about a girl. Before I pictured Logan in a bar fight, which I couldn't do, I had to ask a question.

"There's one thing I have to know. Did you hurt a girl?"

He took a step away from me. Holding up his hands, he said, "No! No, no, no. I would never do that. I was raised to respect and protect women."

Since he came looking for his mother, I guessed

he'd had at least one good relationship with a woman and must have had something to do with how he was taught to treat women and girls.

"No, Dora was like a little sister to me. She'd been friends with my little brother since they were in diapers and spent a lot of time at our house. One day she came over, crying her eyes out. When she could speak, she begged me to hide her. She had a huge black eye and was rubbing her arm. When I asked her what happened she said her step-father had beaten her."

"That's awful!"

"Yeah. He was a big brute. First he knocked her down, then dragged her by her hair. After that he held onto her arm so she couldn't get away and whipped her with his belt. When she told me this, I flipped out. How a grown man could do that to a little girl was beyond me.

"Anyway, I asked her where he was at that moment. She wouldn't say at first. Finally, I coaxed it out of her. He was still home, right down the street. I marched down to their house. I was just going to talk to him. The whole time she was yanking on my arm and telling me not to, but I just had to do what I had to do."

I waited through another long pause.

At last he looked me right in the eye and said, "I killed him."

I tried not to act shocked. I was definitely acting. The shock vibrated around inside me.

"But you said, it might've been an accident?"

"Oh, yeah. I didn't mean for him to die. When I delivered my speech, he laughed. I punched him. He laughed even harder. I was furious. I wanted him to get the message that he couldn't beat up twelve year-old girls and get away with it. That somewhere someone would stick up for them.

"When I hit him again, he went after me. He was much bigger and stronger. Probably six-foot-three and two-hundred-fifty pounds. I might have been stronger with all the adrenaline pulsing through my body—or it might have been my magical abilities. Even *I'm* not sure if I used them or not. I picked him up over my head and threw him. He landed on the paved sidewalk. His head was bleeding. When he tried to get up, I kicked him in the chest. That time when he went down, he didn't get back up.

"The blood gushed from his head wound. Dora was screaming. Her mother came out of the house and she started screaming too. Finally, somebody called 911, probably a concerned neighbor. I was actually thinking about calling them myself as soon as I had calmed down. And you can guess the rest. He didn't recover. I was brought before a savvy judge. I had a good lawyer to get me out of first degree murder charges, but that's the best he could do. I wound up in Haven, for manslaughter."

I nodded. It made sense. First I was sad that this had

happened at all, and second that he hadn't found a better way to deal with the situation. It sounded like he wished he had now.

"Was her mother going to report the abuse?"

He sighed.

"I guess you didn't get that far in the conversation? You just heard what happened and had to confront him?"

"No. Dora said when it happened before her mother promised the asshole she wouldn't report it, and later when Dora begged her to get the guy some help, she just refused. I didn't want that asshole to get off Scott-free and able to do it again."

"I get that." And I did. It seemed almost noble. But did that make him a violent criminal? Was this just an isolated incident that could've happened to anyone? Are we all capable of being pushed beyond our limits? These are things I've wondered before. Maybe I was getting an answer.

"So you're looking at more than just Juvie. They were going to lock you up for life or something?"

"Not exactly. Life sentences for juveniles was ruled unconstitutional. But that didn't mean I wouldn't be an old man by the time I got out of an adult facility. I'd go straight from Haven to Hell. And even with legal help there seems to be no way out. I needed a miracle, so I came to Summerland looking for that miracle."

He shrugged. "At least I get fresh air, and for some reason I'm never hungry, so I don't have to worry about eating. I can sleep if I want to or stay up all night and stare at the beautiful stars over my head. The only thing wrong with this place is it's lonely."

I felt bad for him. What kind of choice was that for a seventeen year-old kid? Spending your prime in prison—maybe parole after a bunch of years. Or some kind of solitary life surrounded by beauty, but no one to talk to and nothing to strive for. No hopes and dreams to achieve.

I had to lighten the mood. "Hey, you said you didn't need to eat, but what if you wanted to? Could you eat all the desserts you could conjure and never gain weight?"

He laughed.

*Good.* I liked the sound of his laugh. It was a fully committed throaty laugh. Nothing hesitant about it. And his grin... Oh, my. He oozed charm when he smiled with all his pearly white teeth.

"I never thought about that. Want to try it?"

"Heck, yeah!"

Witches didn't say 'Hell' very often. They didn't believe in it. For magicals in Juvie it meant something just as bad. An adult prison with scarier magicals.

Logan gestured at the ground and said, "Have a seat."

I looked down and saw a red checkered tablecloth on the grass. "Cool!"

I guessed he had his powers back. That was the other thing the kids missed in Juvie. Not just freedom, but their magic too. I don't know why I still had mine, but if I didn't, I wouldn't be here now.

"So, what would you like? Pastry? Ice cream? Cake?"

"Yes, please," I said, grinning.

He laughed and said, "Your wish is my command."

A whole dessert buffet appeared in front of us. I grabbed the Ice cream Sundae before it melted. Then I wondered if it *would* melt here.

"So it looks as if you not only have the power to do spells with words, you can manifest things with your mind."

"Yeah. Isn't that what you did, Fish Face?"

I gave him the stink eye, than realized he was referring to *the incident*. "Yes. I just thought about a fish and was suddenly wrestling with one."

He nodded and sat on the checkered tablecloth facing me, reaching for a chocolate éclair. "These are so good. Thanks for thinking about conjuring dessert. To be honest, I've been a little depressed since trying to contact my mother with no luck."

"Where do you think she is?" I asked around a cold mouthful of vanilla ice cream, dripping with warm chocolate.

He shrugged. "I was pretty sure this was the place, but maybe there's more than one."

"More than one Summerland?"

He shrugged. "Maybe."

"Or maybe we're someplace high in the Rockies called Summerland. No, wait. It's winter. We could be in New Zealand, I guess…"

"That would be nice, but I don't think so. No place on Earth is this…dazzling is the only word I can think of to describe it," he said.

"True. Maybe they're all here and we can't see them, because they're spirits?"

"Or… They say we come back in groups. Maybe this is the place our group is supposed to meet up later, but no one is here yet."

"You mean there are no people our age who have died?"

"I don't know of anyone close to me who has. No siblings or cousins. Do you?"

"No."

"Well, maybe that's it."

I shrugged. "Do you have any other siblings? Not just your little brother and the girl who's like a sister. Any more sisters or brothers?"

"Just two brothers. One older and one younger."

"Ah, so you're the middle child. What do they say about middle children? They're rebels or something?"

"I don't know. If so, I wasn't much of a rebel. Didn't skip school—often. Didn't break curfew—much."

I laughed. "It sounds like maybe you were a half-hearted rebel."

"More like half-assed. How about you? Any brothers or sisters?"

"Nope. I'm the one and only. I used to fantasize that I had a sister out there somewhere."

"Why a sister?"

"Dunno. Maybe I just felt like a sister would be closer." I put down the frozen sweetness that was my partially consumed Sundae and picked up a chocolate chip cookie. "Do you miss your brothers? Or do you think they miss you?"

He nodded slowly. "Yeah. A little bit. We had different interests, but we basically liked each other."

I wondered what they thought happened to him. Even if they weren't especially close and only liked each other I'm sure they'd want to know where he was —if they knew he was missing. "So, you should know… the faculty is desperate to find out where you went."

His brows shot up. "You didn't tell them, did you?"

"Of course not. What kind of inmate do you think I am?"

He looked at me sideways. "I don't know. You seemed to be friendly with Lake Pirate. You can't trust him as far as you can throw him you know."

"What do you mean? Is it because he's a fuggle?"

"A fuggle? I didn't know he was a fuggle. How the heck… Never mind. I think I can figure it out."

I straightened my back. "What do you mean?"

He sighed. "You know that dumb farm boy act he puts on?"

"Um…I guess."

"That's what it is. An act. He's smart as hell, but for some reason he's decided it's smart to play dumb."

I didn't know what to say. Lake Pirate smart? "Why would he play dumb?" *Especially around me.* It's true I didn't let my guard down completely, but I could have. I *did* trust him, but what could he gain by letting me believe he was…what? Too dumb to understand things? Maybe he felt he could get more details that way?

"That's weird. How did you know he was smart, but not know he was a fuggle?"

"I overheard him talking with teachers. He didn't just understand the lessons, he was always one step ahead. He asked for time off whenever he could test out and prove he already knew the material. They let him take midterms and finals months before the rest of us."

It suddenly dawned on me… "That's how he was able to look in on me so often. I thought he was in remedial classes that were for shorter attention spans or something." *Oh, man. Now who feels dumb? Hint: I do!*

Logan laid his hand over mine. "Genevieve?"

"Yeah?"

"Will you come back and visit me?"

Would I? I wanted to say, *of course I will!* But how many times could I get away with this? I had to be honest with him. "I want to." *Boy did I want to!* "But I don't know."

# CHAPTER 10

Eventually I had to say goodbye and go back to Haven. I gave Logan a hug, and he actually kissed me on the cheek! My cheek tingled. It wasn't the best kiss I'd ever had, but it wasn't the most pathetic either.

I stepped away with my head down and had to mumble the spell quickly or I wouldn't have left at all. Upon reciting the return spell three times as instructed, I opened my eyes and found myself standing in my drab room, in Haven. *Bummer.*

Everything looked the same as it had before I left, except the clock on the wall. The hour had moved one space and it looked as if the minute hand had moved a few spaces, so I may have been gone an hour and some minutes. Or maybe I was gone all day plus an hour.

I glanced out the high transom window and it seemed to be dark out. That was a good indication that

I hadn't been gone thirteen and a half hours. So there was that.

I poked my head out the door. Nobody was searching the place frantically, so it seemed like I wasn't missed. Whew! I was supposed to be there taking a nap, so I flopped down on my bed and my head hit something a little firm. Reaching under my pillow, I found the book. *I thought I put that back in the library!*

After reviewing the written spell all I'd said was for it to go back to its place until I needed it. Apparently it thinks its place is under my pillow. *Or maybe I still need it.*

With my pillow blocking anyone's view who was peeking in my window from the hall, I looked for something that might help me figure out if Lake Pirate...er James was really who he said he was.

Glancing through more useless spells, I finally came across something that might do the trick. It was a spell to find out what your neighbors thought of you. I guess that would work, if he could be considered my neighbor—especially if I added his name to the spell.

I memorized the spell and again thought how nice it would be to have a photographic memory. There was a cool spell in here to erase someone's memory simply by putting a spell on an object and then giving them the object. As long as they kept the object they wouldn't remember whatever it was you wanted them to forget.

I wondered if I could try it without losing my own memory. Probably not. With my luck I'd put a spell on a piece of jewelry to give away, then take one look and say, "Oh, pretty!" and put it on myself. But now I need my memory more than ever, so I committed that 'what your neighbor is thinking' spell to my somewhat limited memory and said it aloud three times.

Nothing happened. Suddenly I had the urge to go for a walk. I tucked the book back under my pillow and left my room to wander the halls. I didn't see anyone except the janitor who was sweeping a corridor facing away from me and Simmons, standing nearby. Not being in the mood to chat, I hurried on.

Eventually I wound up near the office. It should have been completely dark, everyone having gone home for the day. But there was a light on in Mrs. Black Hole's office. Strolling by, casually, I noticed the blinds were mostly shut but there were a couple that seemed kind of stuck open. From there I could peek in and see the administrator sitting behind her desk. She was chatting with someone who looked like a young man comfortably seated opposite her with his hands clasped behind his neck and his left ankle crossed over his right knee. A very casual stance for a student meeting with the administrator.

I whispered the spell again and suddenly I could hear their conversation clearly.

"I don't know, Mrs. Whitehall. I tried to become more than her friend, but she didn't go for it."

Black Hole shrugged. "Some girls aren't ready for male attention so early. You can just continue to be her friend. I didn't think we'd get much information out of her that way anyway."

Lake Pirate laughed. Yep, it was him, most definitely.

"That's what you think," he said. "All girls her age are very interested in male attention. They may not want to go where it leads, but they want to feel desirable."

'Desirable' didn't seem like a dumb farm boy word. It looked as if Logan was right. It made me sad to think one of my two friendships wasn't real.

"Any girlfriend/boyfriend relationships don't have much chance to mature beyond friendship here," he continued, "but she's more apt to confide in a boyfriend than just a friend."

Admin Black Hole looked like she was thinking and eventually nodded. "I understand what you're saying. But you can't force her to want to be your girlfriend. I thought by choosing someone her own age who was good looking, she would *want* to be your girlfriend regardless of any other issues."

James said, "Apparently she has standards. I wish you hadn't told me to act so dumb. That may be what's turning her off."

"It was important at the time that she not feel threatened. Just thinking you were a witch who wasn't particularly bright wouldn't tip her off."

*Hmmm... Well I guess I can tell what he thinks of me from this. But what is it they're trying to get me to confide to him. I have no idea.*

"She hasn't used her powers for you has she?"

"Not at all. I haven't asked her to. Do you think I should?"

"Oh, no. Definitely not. We don't want her to realize how much power she has. We're hoping if she thinks she has none, she won't even try. That's what we've been counting on from the beginning. And if she doesn't try using her powers maybe she won't figure out what she is."

*What* I am? *What?* I'm not just an unwilling student/inmate at Haven? A certain Genevieve Howe, accidental conjurer of fish? If not, what the heck could I be?

Listening further didn't give me much to go on. I wondered if I could turn the tables on Jim and get him to confess something to me. But how would I do that? I wish I knew what secret they were trying to keep me from discovering. It sounded like they knew I had my powers, but they didn't know I knew. So now I know they don't know that I know...something. Oh please. I'm giving myself a headache.

"Hey, Fish Face! I've been looking everywhere for you!" Lake Pirate exclaimed when he entered my room without knocking.

I was lounging on my bed, trying to look casual, but thinking, *Oh, crap. I was missed after all.* "Oh? Well, here I am." It was hard to keep the chill out of my voice.

"No, really. It was like you just up and disappeared or something."

I laughed. "If only I could. I was just in the bathroom for a while." *He wouldn't have opened the door to my bathroom, would he?*

He tipped his head and studied me for a moment. Then he set one hip on my bed and I pushed him off.

He hit the floor with a shocked "Ack!" Getting up, he rubbed his hip. "What the heck, Genevieve? Are you okay?"

I glared at him. "I'm fine. You're the one who's out of place. You don't belong in my room, much less on my bed."

"Oh." He just stood there.

I don't know if he was waiting for me to tell him to leave or just playing dumb again.

"Are you on your period?"

"WHAT?" Apparently he was neither of the above. He was suicidal! I gritted my teeth. "Get. Out."

"Okay, okay..." He inched his way to the door, carefully. "I'm sorry if I said anything to..."

"OUT!"

He ran out of the room and I could hear his footsteps fading down the corridor. I have to admit there's a certain satisfaction in making someone bigger than you quake in their boots. Of course, I'm magical and I don't know if he is, so the odds might not be in his favor.

I think I shut down that conversation well enough though.

I needed to sneak the book back into the library before it was missed. I tried to do it magically but it wouldn't go. Apparently I do have my powers...but if so, why couldn't I get the damn thing to go back to the library like it's supposed to?

During the night, I tried an unlocking spell on my bedroom door and it worked! Now I had to avoid the night security guard who checks on the worst inmates every fifteen minutes. Some that are doing well and are soon to be discharged were housed in another wing. They only get checked every half hour. I, on the other hand, am in the incorrigible quarters, and when I asked Simmons why, I received no answer. Thus, I have fifteen minute checks. That means I have less than fifteen minutes to get the book in its place and sneak back into bed—meanwhile entering and leaving the library without getting caught.

So I strapped on my watch and had to wait until the night security guard had checked my room and saw me in bed, supposedly asleep. As soon as I was sure he had turned the corner, I jumped out of bed fully dressed and shot down the corridor to the library. I figured I could try the same unlocking spell that I used on my door. If it wasn't warded up the ass and alarmed, I might be able to sneak the book back on the shelf where it was supposed to be before it was missed.

I'd kept to the shadows. My stocking feet insured my movements would remain Ninja quiet. I tried the door without the spell and surprisingly, it opened for me. Just like last time. I wondered why but didn't have time to ponder it.

I dashed inside around the corner down the stacks until I found the exact place I had taken the book from. I tried to put it back, but the dang thing was like a boomerang. The book pushed itself right back into my hands.

"Oh no you don't. You don't belong with me, you belong here. Right in this spot on this bookshelf in this library. Do you understand me?"

I halfway expected the book to respond, but of course it didn't. I pushed it back in, and it shot right back out. I wondered if the wall could explain this phenomenon.

I leaned against the wall and asked, "Why won't this book go back on the shelf?"

The wall didn't respond this time. "What the heck? Hello… Genevieve to Wall. Come in, Wall."

No one was talking to me, or rather no *thing* was talking to me. I checked my watch and realized I didn't have much time. I needed to get back to my room and in bed with my door closed and locked. That would take at least five minutes.

Frustrated, I tried to outrun it. Cramming the book back into its spot, I turned to dash away, but it flew off the shelf and hit me in the back. "What the heck…"

I picked up the little sucker from where it had ricocheted onto the floor. Suddenly another book jumped off the shelf and hit me in the ass.

"WHAT THE… Okay, Friggin-book, show me why I need you too."

The words hadn't rhymed, but the book seemed to be okay with that. The pages flipped until it landed on a particular section, which was all about relationships. "Why do I need a book about relationships? Book? Wall? Anybody?"

Naturally I didn't get an answer. By this time I was seriously pissed off. Glancing at my watch I realized I didn't have time to futz around in the library. I had to get back to my room.

With both books tucked under my shirt and hoping no more jumped out at me, I hurried to my room. The door closed with a click that sounded as loud as a gunshot in my paranoid mind. As I dove into bed, I murmured the door locking spell and pulled the covers up to my chin.

About a minute later I saw filtered light through my eyelids. All the night guards had to watch our blankets rise and fall to know we were breathing. So they shined a flashlight on us. *Oh, no. Are the books making my chest flat?* I guess I didn't have to worry about that looking odd. At least not on me. I'd begun developing my boobage late and didn't have a whole lot to notice yet. Maybe someday when I get out of here, I'll get one of those push-up bras. For now, I didn't care.

They were supposed to aim it below our faces so they wouldn't disturb our sleep, but some guards couldn't care less if we slept or not. This time I was actually glad I could tell the guard was watching me. When the room went dark again, I let out a sigh of relief and tucked both books under my pillow.

A few minutes later my room was bathed in filtered light again. But the light was different. Faintly yellow-orange and flickering.

*Fire!*

There were no smoke alarms going off yet. Had they been disabled? What if the guards couldn't get all the doors unlocked in time when they finally discovered what was happening?

I had no time to think—only react. I pulled on my door without saying the unlocking spell and it opened as easily as the library door had. Again, there was no time to puzzle that out now. I dashed to the fire alarm and pulled it. The warning blared throughout the building.

Then I ran down the corridors and yanked open each kid's door as if they weren't locked at all—and they weren't—at least not to me.

By the time everyone was out on the lawn the front of the building was going up in flames. The fire department couldn't possibly get here in time to save any of it. *The books! Why didn't I grab the books?*

Glancing over at Alien I remembered she could manipulate the weather. But her powers were probably suppressed like everyone else's. Or...almost everyone's.

I had seen the teachers use hand gestures when they lifted the grounding of our powers and reinstated them. They didn't even have to say a spell. I found Alien and called out to her over the chaos, "Make it rain!"

"What?"

"Rain! Put the fire out!"

"I can't."

"Yes, you can." I concentrated on lifting an invisible curtain over her head, making the gesture I had seen the teachers do as Alien's eyes grew wide. "Do it!"

Alien closed her eyes and muttered some words I couldn't quite catch, but it worked. Suddenly a pouring rain beat down on the building, the yard, and all of us. I was never so happy to be soaking wet in my entire life.

# CHAPTER 11

SOME OF THE KIDS WERE FURIOUS WHEN THEY FOUND out that a witch had made it rain and ruined their fun of watching Haven burn to the ground. But in the good old Haven tradition, I wasn't going to 'rat out' Alien and she wasn't going to tell anyone I had helped her. Both of us would stay silent about the whole fiasco.

I tried to explain to the loudest complainers at lunch the next day that if our whole building had been destroyed, we'd all be sent to Haven West which would result in overcrowding, lack of supplies, and who knows what else.

They grumbled, but I think eventually they saw the wisdom in saving what parts of Haven East were left. In truth a few less dangerous inmates would probably have their sentences commuted. So the fire might help a few get out early.

But the rest of us would've been in less than desirable circumstances if we'd had to transfer. As I understood it, Haven West was somewhere up in the Rocky Mountains. Anybody evacuating in the middle of the night in central Florida has probably never frozen to death. I can't say that for people at or above 14,000 feet in the upper Western states.

So thanks to Alien's quick action our classrooms were saved, our cafeteria was saved, and *thank the Goddess*, our bedrooms were saved.

Apparently only the administrative wing had burned. That brought on all kinds of speculation. If someone had meant to destroy records, that was probably an inefficient way to do it. I'm sure they had backups online somewhere.

But who knows how the fire started? I had my guesses, but so did everyone else. Nothing made a heck of a lot of sense—except for one theory—that it might be the actions of a certain disgruntled magical teacher who was fired recently.

I couldn't believe that Alien and I were getting to be actual friends, but that seemed to have been the result of our one and only shared heroic action. I wasn't quite ready to declare us BFF's though. She might leave me in the dust at the first whiff of a Kate Spade bag.

Emergency meetings with teachers and administrative staff resulted in our getting more recreation time. During one of these periods, Alien and I took a long walk around the perimeter. Just Jen was doing something in her room for a project and I didn't know where Lake Pirate was.

It still hurt to realize he wasn't an actual friend. I hadn't wanted to be boyfriend and girlfriend, but that was because I thought we were intellectually incompatible. I would hope my first real boyfriend was an acceptable conversationalist and someone I could admire for their values, thoughts, and actions. As well as someone *I could actually trust.* Being taken in like that made me feel gullible and that sucked as much as the betrayal.

So Alien a.k.a. Francine and I were strolling outdoors along the invisible fence. Part of me felt like testing this sudden lack of magical suppression by 'accidentally' stepping one toe over the line. However, I don't know if that's a smart thing to do with a witness.

At some point I might try it on my own, but do I really want people to know I can leave here at any time? I didn't even know if I wanted to. Not until I knew if a jail break would change my circumstances for the better. Now that Bossy Rando was no longer sabotaging us, I could let my sentence progress to its natural conclusion.

I thought about Lawless Logan. He didn't seem all that happy to be in Summerland. I guess it was better than looking at life in magical prisons, but if it weren't for that alternative I don't think he'd still be there. Maybe the books, which were still under my lumpy pillow, meant for me to help Logan somehow. Could that be the relationship it wanted me to look at? I sighed and gazed over at the trucks rolling onto the property.

Construction started shortly after the fire. I'm guessing it took no more than a couple days to file for insurance, and magicals might be able to cut the red tape, getting approval right away. Then—the trickiest part for a magical prison—they had to lift the invisible fence to let construction vehicles in. A magical teacher was always at the entrance during working hours.

That gave some of the students tempting ideas. One idiot even tried rushing the perimeter. We all heard a loud crack around the side of the building. When Alien and I rounded the corner, he was sprawled in the dirt—unconscious with his clothes smoking.

But he served as a cautionary tale. Besides, nobody knew if their powers would or would not be restored after they left the property. How would they get along out there in the world without them?

Independence seemed like an impossible situation. In any community nowadays, magical or not, to think you could just disappear and have nobody find you was absurd. There's always a paper trail, a camera, or some kind of trace you leave like breadcrumbs for the FBI to come and find you.

For all I knew there was probably a whole branch of the FBI entrusted with magical criminals. I wouldn't doubt it one bit. Alien might know more about things like that. She was from a powerful family in a big city. Maybe she had overheard informative conversations.

So I decided to ask her, "Hey, do you know anything about the national magical community and the powers governing it?"

She looked at me like I had two heads. "What?"

"You know. Like if there are secret branches of government dealing with the law enforcement of magicals."

"Like on some TV shows?"

I shrugged. "I thought maybe since you're around some influential people, you might know more about how the magical community governs its own."

"Oh." She chuckled, then proceeded to laugh outright. "Oh, Fish Face. I guess you don't know who my family is… Believe me they're about as far from law enforcement as you can get."

*Far from law enforcement? How far? The complete opposite would imply they're criminals.*

She tossed her arm casually over my shoulder. "Did you know you're now friends with a daughter of one of the biggest crime families on the east coast?"

"Um… No. I did not know that." *Oh, shit.* "Does that mean anything?"

"Does it *mean* anything?"

"Yeah. That's what I asked."

She halted and placed her hand on her hip. "If you

want it to mean something it can. If you don't want it to, it doesn't. I wouldn't blame you if you wanted to stay as far away from me as possible. As soon as the kids at my private school figured out who my family was they steered clear."

"Oh." *Now what?* I just shrugged. "Can we be friends with no strings attached?"

She reared back and stared at me in disbelief. Eventually a sly smile crept across her face. "I guess that depends."

"On what?"

"On if I do you a favor or not." She lowered her voice to sound like Marlon Brando. "Someday, I may need a favor…"

I realized she was just kidding. "Yeah. I'll try not to ask for anything." At least I *hoped* she was kidding.

Remembering her first day and the administrator saying something about being nice to her and her being traumatized, I tried to make the connection using this new information. Maybe she had witnessed a gangland execution? Maybe some enemy enforcer killed a relative right in front of her. Yeah, that would do it for me. I shivered inwardly.

She didn't ask to be born into a crime family. I couldn't help feeling a little sorry for her. Unless she had participated in picking out this family, maybe for their money…

I know, I know. I sound confused. That's because I

am. Actually there are some witches who believe we get to preview a few possible next lives and pick the one that may help us learn the lessons we still have to learn. Why would she have picked this life?

For that matter, why had I picked the life I was living? What was I still meant to learn? It would be nice if the powers that be allowed us to keep our memories, but noooo... Our minds are wiped in infancy. We have to fly blind all over again. At some point, if we learn all our lessons and don't repeat our mistakes we're allowed to stay dead—or something.

Hmmm... Maybe my lesson is to learn to be less sarcastic. If that's the case I'm doomed to keep reincarnating.

---

Later that day I saw Lake Pirate in the cafeteria. I felt semi-bad about throwing him out of my room, and had later thought maybe it's best to 'keep your enemies close,' or however that saying goes. So maybe I could turn the tables on him and find out what he knows, instead of *him* trying to find out what *I* know.

I walked up to our table and sat next to him. "I'm sorry Jim. I didn't mean to yell at you before."

He smiled tentatively. "That's okay. I know... Well, we all lose patience sometimes." He shrugged.

I'm glad he didn't mention anything about my

period again, or I'd probably have to pull Alien off of him. I'm sure he was just playing dumb, but how dumb is a guy who points out the joys of PMS to a magical witch?

Maybe he was testing me and my powers. He was taking quite a chance, considering I could explode —literally.

He thought maybe I had disappeared. I knew that was possible, but he didn't or did he? I'd just have to play along.

"Do you forgive me?"

He put an arm around my shoulder and said, "Of course I do."

A guard came over and said, "Hey, no fraternizing."

"Fraternizing… That means touching, right? Why don't you just say touching?" he asked the guard.

The guy just shrugged and walked away. Would he do that with any other inmate? Or did everyone know Lake Pirate was a plant?

I just smiled at him and said, "I'm going to go get my lunch. Do you want me to get you anything while I'm up there?"

He raised his eyebrows. "Can you? I mean, you know. We get what we get."

I smiled. "I might be able to ask for a little more of something. I think the kids there like me. It depends."

"Okay, if you can get me another Jell-O that would be awesome."

"You like Jell-O? You can have mine," Just Jen pushed her 'dessert' over to him.

I laughed and went to get my lunch. As I went through the line, I peeked over my shoulder a couple of times. Both times he was watching me. I'd have to be extra careful now. "So, can I have an extra Jell-O?" I asked one of the guys behind the counter.

He just laughed. "Uh…no. Move along."

When I went back to the table, I sat beside Jim again. "Sorry, I tried." I handed him my Jell-O.

"Why did you even ask if you were going to give me your own? Now I have three."

"I just wondered if they might make an exception, and then you'd have lots of desserts. I have to make up for being such a bitch earlier."

He smiled. "I already forgave you. You don't need to make up for anything."

Just Jen was watching the interaction with one eyebrow raised. Finally she asked, "What happened between you two?"

I just shrugged. "I kinda yelled at him to get out of my room."

Alien sat up straighter. "He goes into your room?"

"Yeah, I don't know why. If he gets caught again it'll probably add time to his sentence."

Lake Pirate just shrugged one shoulder. "I like some alone time with a friend, that's all. We can talk more openly that way," he said, looking at me.

"Sure. But, Alien's right to be concerned. You could get more time added, if you get caught. You really shouldn't try it anymore."

He looked hurt. It was that same hurt puppy look he gave me when I'd thrown him out. He must've perfected that one in the mirror.

Just Jen folded her arms. "I would probably yell at you if you were in my room too. She's just trying to help you."

"It's true," I said. This conversation might help a lot. Getting him to stay out of my room where he could accidentally discover some of my secrets would really help my cause.

He looked right at me and said, "She's worth a few extra months."

"You— you're kidding me, right? Nobody is worth extra months in Juvie. Seriously, I don't want you coming to my room anymore. That's really a stupid risk to take. We can talk right here in the cafeteria."

His shoulders sagged. This time he didn't look like a sad puppy, he looked like a defeated soldier. He had to know he was failing in his attempts to get information out of me for Mrs. Black Hole.

I wish I knew what that was all about. *'What'* I am. Quote unquote. That was so weird. How could I find out? *I wonder if my parents know what that means.* But how could I ask them? They never come to visit. That made me both sad and angry.

I wasn't in the best of moods anyway, and obsessing over this mystery made it worse. Thankfully Just Jen picked up Jim's aluminum Jell-O container top and folded it. "Who wants to play football?" she asked.

"Oh! I do." I took advantage of the distraction and grabbed back the Jell-O I gave Lake Pirate and folded the cover into my own makeshift football. Then I held up my fingers as a goalpost and she flicked hers right over them. "Nice one!"

I knew if I missed, it might look like I had no powers. And yet if I didn't miss it would look like I did have powers, but I could act like I still didn't know it. Since that was what I was going for, I might as well do that.

She put her fingers up as the goalie and I flicked my football right through them. "Yay, the score is one to one."

Alien got bored and sighed. "If that's all you guys are doing to amuse yourselves, I think I'll go watch grass grow."

Lake Pirate waved. "See you." He didn't look up from our little game. Evidence gathering, probably.

We played this game back and forth with Just Jen missing two goals. Meanwhile I missed none, but I acted surprised and triumphant when we declared the game over and me the winner. "I can't believe I got a perfect score!"

Just Jen winked at me. "You must be pretty good. Either that or pretty powerful. What's your secret?"

*Dammit, Jenika.* I laughed. "Ha, I'm just that much better than you. Isn't that what all the athletes say without coming right out and saying it?" Then I lowered my voice to mimic a football player. 'It was a good game. We scored more points than the other team. That's why we won'.'"

She rolled her eyes and we both laughed. I just ate my lunch and tried to stay as quiet as I could with Lake Pirate sitting right next to me where he could bombard me with questions. It was time I came up with a few for him.

"Have you found out anything more about why you're here instead of in a regular Juvie?"

He shrank back and looked nervous. "No, you're not gonna say anything, are you?"

I shrugged. "Probably not."

"Probably?" He looked extra nervous now.

I chuckled. "No. Of course not. What do I have to gain by that?"

He let out a sigh of relief. "Exactly. This is probably a lot better than regular Juvie. At least here they've got easy classes. And some of them are even fun. Like me saying I could smell your mother's farts from my house."

We both burst out laughing. It was nice to enjoy

that kind of genuine laughter again. However, it made me sad to know I still had to stay on guard with him.

Just Jen was another matter. She had no clue my powers hadn't been suppressed, and I wanted to keep it that way. If she did figure it out, I'd hate to have to wipe her memory. Messing with people's minds is scary stuff. We're told not to even attempt it. I don't want to hurt my friend, so I just hoped she would stay clueless.

"I guess I'd better go too," Just Jen said. "We have algebra next and you know how much I love my algebra."

I groaned. "Crap. Algebra next? I forgot."

"I'm glad I don't have to take algebra," Lake Pirate said.

Just Jen smiled. "I can't wait for the weekend."

"It's kind of boring, but at least we can relax," Lake Pirate picked his teeth with his fingernail.

We had different guards on rotation and most of them took turns on weekends. Only the administration and senior teachers got every Saturday and Sunday off.

"Well, I'll see you later," Just Jen said and rose from her chair.

"Okay, I'll eat fast and join you later."

"What took you so long to get to lunch anyway?" Lake Pirate asked.

I jammed a lot of food in my mouth and started

chewing slowly. I shrugged as if I couldn't really talk, and pointed to my full mouth.

If he was going to wait me out, he was going to sit a while. I was going to chew every bite one hundred times like they tell you to. Eventually he sighed and said, "Okay, I guess I better get going too. I have remedial math. It's so stupid."

I nodded, but I was thinking, *yeah. Unlike you.*

# CHAPTER 12

Back in my room that evening I was able to take a long look at the other book under my pillow. The book, with its faded ink and crispy brown pages had a penciled in caveat saying it had been translated from Old English, then Middle English, spoken long before Shakespeare—and everyone knows how confusing *his* English was.

Back then, Latin was the usual written language, especially by the clergy, but a crazy kind of Frenglish was spoken by regular people after the Norman conquest of England. Yeah, I read about that in European history class.

The person who originally wrote this spell book may have been trying to keep it secret from the clergy, like writing in code. Since peasants couldn't read or write at all, it may have been a scholar trying to record words passed down verbally.

It seemed as if romantic love was first on the list. The words began with *Love is best left to peasants and surfs, for nobility will arrange marriages based on political alliances...*

Suddenly the words I was reading rearranged their letters and became, *Love is one of the most profound emotions known to human beings. There are many kinds of love, but most people seek its expression in a romantic relationship with a compatible partner.*

Was this another bizarre power of mine? Or was it built into the book by magic? Cool if it was the book updating itself, but I had the feeling it was me. I wanted to understand it in today's terms, therefore I could. I was noticing that things I wanted most didn't seem to need a spell. It was as if wishing made it so. And how many times had I heard that wishing *would not* make it so. Ah, fuggles...

Continuing on with the book...

*For many, romantic relationships comprise one of the most meaningful aspects of life. The need for human connection appears to be innate—but the ability to form healthy, loving relationships is learned.*

As I read, I wondered if anything had been lost in translation or if relationships had changed over millennia. Certainly the status of women was very different. And from what we learned about the treatment of witches back then, to own a book like this must have been extremely dangerous.

Yet it had survived. Someone had to have guarded it and passed it down for generations. Now the library being off limits to students made more sense. If someone with chocolate on their fingers picked it up without gloves, a thousand years of knowledge could be obliterated.

So, handling the book more carefully than I had been, I read the words which continued to change until they made sense to me.

*Evidence suggests that the ability to form a stable relationship starts in infancy, in a child's earliest experiences with a caregiver who reliably meets the infant's needs for food, care, warmth, protection, and social contact. Such relationships are not destiny, but parenting establishes deeply ingrained patterns of relating to others.*

Oookay. My parents fed me and clothed me. I guess I wasn't totally neglected. But there was definitely something lacking. Probably the warmth…not the physical kind.

*Failed relationships happen for many reasons, and the failure of a relationship is often a source of great psychological anguish*

Yeah. Tell me something I don't know, Book.

*Strong relationships are continually nurtured with care and communication. Although relationships can take many forms, certain traits have been shown to be especially important for all healthy relationships.*

Finally, we're getting to something I can use now, not ten or twenty years from now.

*Both individuals should feel confident that their partner is willing to devote time and attention to the other.*

I remembered a time when my mom complained that my dad was ignoring her and taking her for granted. I think they went to counseling for a while.

*In good relationships, each try to afford their partner the benefit of the doubt, which creates a sense of being on the same team in life. That feeling, maintained over the long term, can help couples overcome many difficulties.*

Back to couples again. Well, there goes any hope of a relationship with the smarter version of Lake Pirate. I don't think we're on the same team at all.

I decided to skip ahead.

*Reading your partner's mind...* Oh! Interesting topic! This I can get into. Skimming, I started in the middle of a sentence.

*...one may conclude being empathic is generally a good thing. But some think empathic accuracy is also associated with negative outcomes, such as reductions in relationship closeness if one guards thoughts from the other...*

Am I not supposed to guard my thoughts? This doesn't pertain to me, does it? I was getting bored, and I had to wonder why the book insisted on my taking it. The guards could discover it easily...especially with the book lying open on my sleeping face. I forced my eyes open and continued reading.

*There are a number of situations in which empathic accuracy is good for relationships. One is when romantic partners have to co-ordinate their behaviors to achieve important goals as a team.*

Yeah, okay. If my partner and I become master thieves, we'll have to coordinate our efforts to pull off every heist. Come on, book. Where's the good stuff? And why all this couples advice? Am I half of a couple? Not if I don't know about it. Right?

*Empathy also helps relationship functioning by putting a partner's "bad behavior" into perspective by understanding why they behaved in a negative way. This in turn allows them to constructively deal with it.*

Okay, I was about done with this bull-shite. What could the book have wanted to show me? I didn't even have a partner to empathize with. I was about to close it when the topic changed.

*Parental relationships:*

Oh! Here we go…

*Parental warmth, or love, seems to be the dominant factor in raising successful children. Splitting parenting styles into categories, those who use warmth and discipline (authoritative style) had the best child-rearing results.*

*The next best category is a style of warmth, but low discipline (the permissive style) and they did considerably better than those raised with low warmth and high discipline (authoritarian style). Not surprisingly, low warmth, low discipline (neglectful style) fared poorest.*

Oh, crap. My parents were kind of neglectful. They weren't uncaring—exactly. They were just more wrapped up in their work, causes, and each other... more than worrying about me.

I remember how shocked they looked when the school said I had to be expelled. They just stared at each other, as if thinking, *"What do we do with her now?"* I think they were perfectly content to let the school and public television raise me. I wasn't sure I wanted to read any more of this.

I was just stuffing the stupid book back under my pillow when I heard a knock on my door.

"Who's there and what do you want?"

Simmons opened the door just enough to peek in. "Your parents are here."

It was as if I'd conjured them.

⸻ ✳ ⸻

My parents sat in the visitors lounge, alone. Visiting hours were over at seven p.m. and here it was almost nine.

They rose when they saw me and didn't hold out their arms or come towards me. They just waited for me to go to them. My father and I embraced loosely, and then that bit about warmth stuck in my brain. I decided to give harder hugs than usual. So I grasped him and squeezed. He reacted slowly, eventually patting me on the back as if to say, 'There, there.' When I hugged my mom like that, she said, "Oomph."

"Why are you here so late?" I asked. That had a double meaning…

"I'm sorry honey, did we wake you?" my mother asked.

"We took two planes and drove four hours to get here." My father's tone was what the book called authoritative. Not usually his style. He only sounded like that when he was ticked off.

"Uh, thank you?"

"Let's sit down." My father gestured to one of the comfortable couches. He waited for my mother and I to sit, then pulled a plastic chair over and looked at it with distaste, but sat in it anyway.

"Something must be really wrong for you to be here."

My parents glanced at each other. "No, no. We just wanted to see you, and it was recommended that we come now."

"Recommended? By whom?"

My father's lip twitched up for second. It was like the professor was going to smile at my correct use of the English language, but the rest of his face didn't quite make it.

"Mrs. Whitehall said we hadn't been here for quite a while and that you were wondering why."

Hmmm. I *was* wondering that, but how did she

know? I hadn't said anything... Oh, wait. I hadn't said anything to *her*. But Lake Pirate got an earful and must have given her that information.

"Well, thank you for driving all this way to see me. I'm fine, by the way."

"I can see that." My father leaned back in his chair, extended his legs and crossed his ankles.

If they forgot to ask how I was, they weren't going to admit it. Well, perhaps I could role model some better behavior. That might be fun.

"So, how are you two?"

They glanced at each other. I picked up some kind of uncomfortable vibe.

"Oh, no. Something's wrong."

My mother cleared her throat, then stammered out, "We are... We're kind of —"

"What your mother is trying to say," my father interrupted, "is that we're about to go abroad, to teach English in Africa."

My jaw dropped. "Africa? And how long will you be gone?"

My mother bit her lip and looked to my dad to fill me in—again. "We'll be teaching over there for at least a year."

"And what about me? Am I going to Africa when I get out of here in a couple of months?"

My mother suddenly found her voice. "No, of

course not. You'll finish high school in the States. We'll be writing to you from wherever they station us, but you'll be staying with your father's sister, Hilary."

Inwardly I was doing a happy dance. However, I had to look appropriately sad when thinking about my parents being on the other side of the Atlantic Ocean. "Well, I'll miss you, but no more than I miss you now." *Whoops.* That just sort of slipped out.

Again, my parents stared at each other. I thought about that part in the book that talked about reading minds. It looked like they were doing it. I wondered if it would work between me and them. There was something about empathy in there. I didn't know if I could empathize with them, but I could try.

"It's really nice of you to teach in Africa. What made you decide to do that?"

As my father babbled about the Third World getting most of their used textbooks from English speaking countries and how useless they were, unless the readers were appropriately educated yada, yada, yada, I prodded his mind gently for the truth.

I wasn't getting much of anywhere until I looked at my mother. Her mind was speaking loud and clear. *We need to be as far away as possible when she realizes... It's still hard to believe what Mrs. Whitehall told us... I just can't wrap my mind around it. I feel badly sticking Hilary with this.*

I couldn't help looking at her with wide eyes. She immediately shut down and leaned away from me. She looked scared.

*What the heck is going on? What is wrong with me?*

"Mom? Why do you look afraid of me?"

My mother laughed nervously, then leaned forward and placed her hand over mine on the couch. "We're not afraid of you, dear. We love you. What a silly idea."

I tried to prod her mind again, but she had firmly closed the door. So I looked at my dad for a while. He had stopped talking so maybe he was thinking.

Whatever was going through his mind wasn't easy to read. I caught some fear relating to control. Is that what they are afraid of? That they can't control me? Or I can't control my powers? After all this time here, I was pretty sure I was getting better at that.

Do they think I would do something heinous to them? And what could I possibly do? Neither one of them has a fish face.

"Well…" My father rose from his seat. "We'd better be on our way. We booked a late check-in at the nearest hotel, about an hour from here."

I guess I was supposed to sympathize with their long drive and late check-in, but I couldn't bring myself to do it. Empathy had to go both ways. My mother rose too.

My father wrapped his arm around my mother and

escorted her to the door. The guard, who had been waiting opened it as they approached, and they left without a backward glance.

I just sat there, feeling like I had been dropped off at daycare and hadn't even been given a hug goodbye.

Back in my room, I was driving myself nuts, trying to figure out what everything meant. I thought about Aunt Hilary. Did she know what she was 'getting herself into?' If so, maybe she could clue me in.

It was late. I couldn't ask to use the phone. I wondered if I could reach her mentally. I didn't know if you had to be right next to somebody to be able to read their minds or not.

Chances are it wouldn't be easy, but I could try. I didn't want to bother looking through the books or I could get sidetracked—easily—and probably never find the spell I wanted. Why couldn't they put indexes in these things?

I sat on the edge of my bed, still dressed and ready to host her, if she decided to pop in. I hoped to the Goddess she could.

Closing my eyes, I concentrated really hard. *Aunt Hilary? Aunt Hilary? Come in Aunt Hilary.* Hard, hard, hard concentration followed.

Eventually there was some kind of answer, but it was very, very faint. "Genevieve?" I was a little surprised, but more thrilled than anything. I closed my eyes and concentrated again. "Yes! It's Genevieve. Aunt Hilary? Is that you?"

"Genevieve. I can barely hear you. Come here."

"You want me to come there? Aren't you in Arizona?" Could I do that? How? Then I remembered I had a spell to get to Summerland. "I don't think I can do it without a spell. Do you have one to take me to you?"

"No." She said something else, but I couldn't quite hear what it was.

*Maybe I can adapt that Summerland spell to go to my auntie?*

As I was puzzling that out, I heard her repeat what she'd said before. It sounded as if she'd said, "You don't need a spell."

That sounded really *really* hard. Probably above my pay grade. "Aunt Hilary… Can't you come here? I'm in my room at Haven. I don't know exactly where you are."

"Concentrate on my voice…" I could hear her a tiny bit better now. "See me as if I'm right in front of you. Visualize everything you can from the hair on my head to the straps on my sandals."

That seemed like a lot, but sure… I'd give anything a

try right now. Closing my eyes, I said, "Can you keep talking to me? Tell me what you're wearing."

I heard a barely-there tinkling laugh. Then, still coming from far-away, she said, "Okay, I'm wearing my hair long and loose. I have a white cotton top on and it's sleeveless."

*Of course. What else would you wear in a hot Arizona desert?*

She continued her description. "I have on a pair of cut offs. Not short-shorts. They go to mid-thigh. Blue jeans that have been washed about a million times, and ripped, like the ones you buy already that way? Only mine are the genuine article."

Now I was getting an actual picture. I could see her wearing those clothes with her hair long, loose and wavy. I could see her long arms and legs with a nice tan. And as far as the straps on her sandals? I could only see her wearing flip-flops. "Aunt Hilary? What are your sandals like?"

She giggled again. "They're hard to describe. Why don't you come and see for yourself?

"Oh, sure. I'll just pop over there now," I thought sarcastically.

"Yes. You've got it! Now concentrate on my energy as if you're standing right in front of me."

I wasn't standing, I was sitting and that may have been part of the problem, because the next thing I knew I was falling…right on my butt.

*Bam.* I opened my eyes abruptly. I saw a pair of strappy leather sandals and an outstretched hand to help me up. My gaze traveled upward and I saw Aunt Hilary's tan, smiling face.

# CHAPTER 13

I gasped. "Am I there? I mean, are you really here? Am I just imagining this?"

Aunt Hilary yanked me to my feet, then grabbed me and hugged me hard, laughing the whole time. Then she held me at arms-length and took a good look at me. "I don't know. You don't seem very imaginary." Then she yanked on a handful of my hair.

"Ouch."

"Yup. I don't think you would've felt that if you were just imagining it." She grinned mischievously.

"Okay, okay. I'm still kind of stunned, but I guess I'm really here. By the way, where is here?"

"You are in the Superstition Mountains of Arizona. Our spa is right over that hill."

I gazed past the dirt road, the cactus, the few succulents lining the driveway, more cactus... Finally I saw a roof. It was one of those Spanish roofs with wavy tiles.

Okay. I guess I traveled three thousand miles, and looking at the sunset I would say it's earlier than nine o'clock, like it was when I left Florida.

I glanced at her and asked, "What time is it? And for that matter what day is it?" She laughed again. "What day was it when you left?

"Friday. And it was about nine-fifteen. Maybe nine thirty."

Aunt Hilary took her phone out of her back pocket and smiled. "Yup. It's Friday, almost seven thirty."

"Wha...? Oh! The time zones makes the difference."

"You got it. Seven-thirty here, eight-thirty in the next time zone, nine-thirty where you were in Eastern Time."

"That's why it's still light out here."

She smiled. "So, now that we've established the date and time, give me another hug." She grabbed me and hugged me really tight. This was the kind of hug I needed. I hugged her back just as hard.

"Aunt Hilary, I need to talk with you. There's something wrong with me, and no one is telling me what it is."

She cocked her head. "Wrong with you? What the heck could be wrong with you?"

I shrugged. "I was hoping you would know. My parents are going to Africa, and they were worried about saddling you with me. Did you know about that?"

"*Saddling* me with you? Honey, I was delighted when they asked me to take you in when you were released."

*Well, that's a relief. At least they asked.*

"When they came for about a thirty second visit I read my mother's mind, and she was worried about something having to do with taking care of me. Maybe it was just about me being a handful or something, but it felt like more than that."

When Hilary didn't comment, I continued. "Both Mom and Dad looked like they were afraid of me. And I found out that one of my classmates has been spying on me. From the brief scan of my mother's mind I learned it was the administrator who told them to come, and hinted that there was something wrong with me."

Aunt Hilary threw an arm around my shoulder and guided me down a path away from the main building toward some cabins. "No, honey. There's nothing wrong with you. If anything, you're more right than a lot of people."

"I've always felt different—even from other witches, but I don't know why. Do you?"

She nodded. "We have something in common, you and me. We're both the outcasts of our families. I scared my parents, because they guessed that I was more powerful than they were. And they were right.

My brother was also scared of me, so I felt shut out. They all kept me at arms-length."

"I know what you mean. That's how I feel too. Like an outcast. Except I don't have a sibling to feel abandoned by. Just my parents."

Hilary went silent. She let her arms drop to her sides as we walked. Eventually, we came to what must've been her cabin, even though they all looked alike. Hers had a clunky wind chime. I knew she loved horses and there were horseshoes on this particular one. Apparently she wasn't going for the tinkling glass sounds.

"If you're worried about me feeling saddled with you, don't. Just saddle your own horse and giddy-up. We can ride off into the sunset together."

I groaned. "You won't be doing a lot of punning will you?"

She laughed. "No promises."

We had arrived at Aunt Hilary's cabin. Opening the door wide, she said, "Welcome home."

My kitty came running toward me and I scooped up my sweet familiar in my arms. "Oreo! I missed you so much!"

He meowed and head butted my chin. As I scratched under his jaw, I looked around and didn't see much room for myself. On one wall there was a cute little bistro table and three mismatched chairs, and on the opposite wall was a couch that may have folded out into a bed, plus a small TV on top of an equally small dresser. My view continued to the back wall where a basic kitchen was laid out in an L shape. There were two doors off the kitchen area. I assumed one was a bedroom and one was a bathroom.

"Are you sure you have room for me?"

She winked, picked up a well-worn wooden wand and aimed it at the only free spot on the back wall. "Guestroom please." *Zap*. Another door appeared. "Go see your new room."

"Wait, did you just create a whole new room off the back of your cabin?"

She shrugged one shoulder. "Maaaybe." She looked like the Cheshire cat from Alice in Wonderland.

*I* was definitely *Alice*.

Striding to the end wall and opening the door, I was gobsmacked! An adorable guestroom with a white storage bed which looked to be a queen-size, and night stand with a few books on it and a lamp—all in my favorite colors, white and light purple. The dresser on the opposite side was huge and displayed a vase of flowers plus a large TV. When I set down Oreo my wand popped out of the flower vase and sailed toward me. As I plucked it out of the air it felt so right in my hand I twirled it like a baton.

I wanted to ask where she got all this stuff, but I didn't want to accuse her of stealing. At least not until she understood I wasn't going to rat on her. *Oh, God. Now I'm doing it.*

Another question needed to be asked, however. "Aren't you worried that people might notice this sudden expansion?"

"You mean fuggles?"

My eyes widened. "You know that term?"

She laughed. "Did you think you're the one who invented it?"

"No. But who did?"

She shook her head. "I'm not sure where it came from originally, but it wasn't your current inmates who thought of it."

"Wait, does that mean…"

She nodded. "You're looking at a member of the class of 1999."

"Wait a minute. Are you telling me you were incarcerated at Haven East?"

"Only for three months. And I did something worse than you. I don't understand how they've kept you this long."

I wasn't going to ask what she did, at least not right away. I was curious as hell, but I was more concerned about why I was being treated differently than everyone else at Haven.

"Yeah. That may have had something to do with an

ex-teacher who seemed to have it in for all of us. She kept finding excuses to add to our time." I couldn't stop staring at her. "Haven huh? So I guess we have something else in common."

"Oh yes. There are a lot of things we have in common that you'll discover a little at a time."

I made a sweeping gesture of my adorable new room. "And this? You still never told me if the fuggles were going to notice. Unless there are no fuggles here."

"Oh, there are plenty of fuggles. Most guests are non-magical. But there's nothing behind us but woods and I have the expansion cloaked. Nobody will know it's there unless they walk right into it. Hmmm. I think I'll put a couple vegetable gardens out there to block it off."

"Cool. Can I help you plant the garden?"

She smiled. "You sure can. We can make it one of our first bonding experiences."

I laughed. "I think we bonded a long time ago."

She gave me another hug. "You're so right.

Eventually we had dinner, or was it breakfast? I was kind of confused about the time, or at least my stomach was.

"So, here is the burning question…" I said between bites of French toast.

"Yes?"

"Why are people afraid of us? What's different about us, even from other witches?"

Aunt Hilary worried her lip.

"If you're wondering how much to tell me, tell me everything," I added. "I certainly won't repeat it. I have the feeling no one would believe me anyway."

She laughed. "That's the truth. To be honest, I'm not exactly sure if I know the whole answer. But here's what I do know. Some call us minor goddesses. I'm not really comfortable with that term, but you and I don't need spells. What we do need is mental discipline and concentration."

*No shit?* was my first reaction. But as I processed what she said about needing to develop the very things I sadly lacked, I understood why my parents might worry. "Um… About the goddess thing. I doubt anyone would *or should* worship me."

She laughed again. "That's why I don't like to use that term. Here's the thing… Like I said, we don't need spells—for most outcomes. There are a few really diffi-cult things that maybe we shouldn't even try, and those would need a spell. I think it's *The* Goddess's way of giving us a chance to think twice about what we might do."

"Okay, I get that. My classes are big on discipline, concentration, ethics…"

"Mine were too. As it turns out the lessons I

received there have been invaluable. We can continue working on anything you're not comfortable with when you get here."

My face fell. "I'm not staying?"

She paused with her fork midway to her mouth, syrup dripping off her toast. "Oh, I'm sorry, honey. You'll have to go back and finish your sentence. Otherwise, they'll come looking for you. We don't want that. We need to be free to do what we will without looking over our shoulders."

I totally agreed with her. I didn't want to worry about being followed and spied on. I wasn't crazy about what was happening with Lake Pirate back at Haven.

"Are you cool with going back in a few minutes? I don't want you to be missed."

"It's probably too late for that," I said. "The guards do checks on me every fifteen minutes."

"They have you on the frequent checks side?"

"Yeah, that should have been one of the tipoffs that something is wrong with me, or extra right with me." *Sigh.* "I'm still confused."

She placed her hand over mine. "First of all, don't worry. You can turn back time when you return. But only a couple hours, tops."

"Wow. Are you sure? That must take a lot of practice. I wouldn't have the first clue how to do that yet."

She smiled. "There are a lot of things you can do,

but they don't want you to know that. They told you that your powers were suppressed, right?"

"Yes. How did you know? Did they do that to you?"

"Of course. Or they tried to."

"I guess that explains why I've been able to do things even though my powers were *supposedly* suppressed."

"Exactly. They just hoped you wouldn't try anything magical, thinking you were going to fail anyway."

"Good gamble. That's exactly what I thought—at first. When I found out there were still things I could do, I just thought they forgot to re-suppress my powers...or were testing me to see what I would do with them."

She nodded. "So, what have you done? Besides calling out to me tonight."

Did I dare tell her about my trip to Summerland? Would she be furious? Impressed? Or would she just yawn and say, 'I've done that...'

"Um, Aunt Hilary, there is one thing I had to do with a spell, and you might not like it."

"Try me."

"I'll have to back up a bit so you understand the whole thing."

"Okay..."

"There was this boy..."

"Ah!" she said with a knowing smile.

"No, it's not what you think." *Probably not anyway.*

"It's a long story. There was this boy who had been there for about a year when he escaped."

Her brows shot up, but she didn't say anything. Now that I knew some witches could do more than others, I wondered if Logan might be one of us—a minor god—or a wizard like Merlin...or whatever. But before I got too side-tracked I pulled myself back to the timeline as I understood it.

"Anyway, they wanted anyone with information on his whereabouts and how he managed the prison break to come forward, so they called an emergency assembly."

"Makes sense so far. Keep going," she said.

"Yeah, so here we are, all assembled in the cafeteria, and the administrator tells us what he did and says she understands that we might not come forward in front of our peers. She knew we wouldn't break the inmate code, the one where you don't tell on each other."

Aunt Hilary just nodded and kept listening.

"So what they did was lift the suppression on our ability to communicate telepathically, just temporarily. They felt if we could contact one of the teachers silently, mind to mind, someone might offer the information they were looking for. That way no one would be the wiser about who tipped them off."

Aunt Hilary cocked her head as if she were curious about what was coming next.

"Anyway. When they lifted the suppression I was

able to chat with my best friend there, Just Jen. I know...it's a weird nickname, but her real name is Jenika. That doesn't matter right now. What matters is that when they didn't get the information they wanted they shut down our ability to communicate telepathically again.

"Only I wasn't shut down. I guess now I know they *couldn't* shut me down. Still, I didn't try to use that power or any other for a while. I thought I tested it. I tried talking to a guy friend that we hung out with, but nothing happened. I found out later he might actually be a fuggle."

"What?"

"Sorry, I'm getting sidetracked again. Anyway, I *did* know something. This guy Logan was coming out of the off-limits library one night. I saw him, and he just winked at me and left. He didn't have a book under his arm or anything, so it didn't look as if he were stealing."

Aunt Hilary sat up straighter. "Brazen little bugger, isn't he?"

I chuckled. "Well, he's self-confident anyway. I've gotten to know him a little better since... But again I don't want to get ahead of myself. So, yeah, I knew something. But I didn't want to tell on him, so I shielded my thoughts from the teachers, and apparently I got away with that. They didn't know about his getting into the library or the book he must have memorized.

"I couldn't help being curious though. I wanted to get out of there too, even temporarily. Just to, you know, find a nice beach where I could get a tan and maybe a tall glass of iced tea."

Aunt Hilary smiled, but didn't interrupt. I'm sure she understood that feeling quite well.

"So, anyway, I was talking to my friends about wanting to get into the library, but none of us knew how, and I didn't tell them about Logan. I was just hoping they might have some sort of clue. The only clue Jim had was to sort of borrow the keys…okay steal them, from one of the guards."

"You didn't let him, did you?" she asked.

"Of course not. I wouldn't put anyone in that position. In fact, I told him not to."

"But you got in there on your own, didn't you?"

"Yeah. And it wasn't even hard. I just opened the door."

She laughed. "If only I had known back then what I know now…" Then she waved her hand as if banishing the thought. "That doesn't mean you should go back there and read all the off-limits books. I hear there are some very controversial titles in there."

"I just took one…that time."

She leaned back in her chair and crossed her arms. "You've been in there more than once?"

"Yeah, just a couple times. I didn't know what book I was looking for. I wanted the one that Logan had, so I leaned against the wall and *surprise, surprise,* the wall talked to me!"

Aunt Hilary laughed. "Are you serious?"

"Yes. And the wall told me where I'd find the book he used, so it directed me to the right stack and when I found the book, I hid it under my shirt and managed to get back to my room without being seen."

Aunt Hilary leaned forward and rested her elbow on the table and her chin in her hand. "Keep going…"

"So anyway, I had the book under my pillow and studied it when I could. There was a whole lot of information, but none of it seemed relevant. Until… "

Having second thoughts again, I hesitated.

"Come on. Spill!"

I guess I had to tell her now. "The only travel spell he could have used was one to visit Summerland."

Her jaw dropped. The fork she had been holding clattered to her plate.

"Tell me you didn't try that."

I gulped. "Well, if I told you that, I would be lying."

She covered her mouth with both hands. Her eyes were huge.

I didn't expect her reaction to be so shocked. It looked like there were tears in her eyes for a moment and then she cleared her throat.

"Genevieve, you're never to try that again. Do you hear me?"

I hadn't expected her to get all parental on me. She

would probably like to know more. Maybe when she calmed down, she'd stop freaking out. I was kinda dying to tell somebody about it.

"It was really beautiful, Hilary." That was the first time I ever used her name without calling her Aunt or Auntie first. I wanted us to get on a more equal footing.

She looked from her plate, to me, to her lap, to the ceiling. "What were you thinking?" she finally asked.

"I was thinking that maybe that's how Logan got out, and where he went. And I was right."

She folded her hands in her lap. "You found him? In Summerland?"

"Yeah. We were the only two there. And it was gorgeous. I wound up in this big meadow, filled with colorful wildflowers, and there were pine woods around that, and in the distance beautiful mountains with snowcapped peaks. The colors were so brilliant! I don't think I've ever seen any place like that, even in pictures."

She nodded. "Okay, I'll take your word for it."

"I guess you've never tried anything like that spell?"

"I never knew there was such a spell." Her voice shook a little bit.

I quickly pressed on. "So, anyway, Logan was looking for his mom. She died when he was seven. He wanted to know if there was a way she could help him. He wanted out of Haven."

"Like everybody does. So he went to Summerland?

Couldn't he just reach out to his mom from wherever he was, like a Medium? Oh, wait. Power suppression would prevent that. I get it."

"Plus I think he felt safer in Summerland. The spell we both used was for a round-trip from our original location to Summerland and back. He wanted his mom to help him return to a different destination."

"So, I guess he was looking for a beach and an iced tea too?"

"More like a cold beer."

She laughed. "It sounds like this Logan is a bad influence."

"No, he's really not. He got in trouble for standing up for a young girl who was badly beaten by her step-dad."

Aunt Hilary slapped her hand over her heart. "Oh, dear. And how did he stand up to this criminal?"

"He killed him, but it wasn't on purpose. They were fighting, and the guy was really strong. Logan was just defending himself. He finally knocked the guy down on the concrete sidewalk."

"How much time did he get in Haven?"

"I don't know, but he thought he was never getting out. They planned to send him to the adult facility after he turned eighteen."

She narrowed her eyes. "Really? For self-defense? It doesn't sound like he's telling you the whole story."

"No, I'm sure he did. I'm just not telling *you* the

whole story. Apparently he kind of lost it and threw the guy onto the pavement—then the guy hit his head. I'm not sure if it was completely accidental, and I don't think Logan knows for sure either."

"Oh. That makes more sense now. Still, Genevieve, this isn't a good boy to get mixed up with. I hope you're not ever going to see him again."

I couldn't say one way or the other yet. So I kept my mouth shut.

She gave me the stink eye. "Genevieve? You're not going there again, are you? Promise me you won't."

I let out a deep sigh. "I don't know. I think I just figured something out, and I want to tell him so he can try it."

Aunt Hilary rose and began pacing. "Don't you think he could figure it out on his own? It sounds like he's smart..." She stopped pacing and looked at me intensely. "And powerful."

"Yeah, maybe. But we were talking about it and neither one of us could come up with any explanation."

"Explanation for what?"

"Why he couldn't find his mom. There was nobody up there. No one. The place was totally empty other than the two of us."

"Well, that's disconcerting," she said.

"I know, right?"

"I'm sure there's a good explanation, but it's not up to you to find it. Leave him alone, Genevieve." She got tears in her eyes. "I can't lose you." She came over and put her hand on my shoulder, looking down at me. Her eyes still shimmered. I guess I never realized I was as important to her as she was to me.

"Okay, okay. I'll do my best not to upset or disappoint you. I rose and gave her one of our long, warm hugs. "I should be getting back now."

"Yes. We can always talk about this later, *if* you can wait before doing anything rash."

"Uh… Sure."

Doing something I had already done successfully wasn't rash, was it? Maybe it was rash the first time. Okay, it was definitely rash the first time.

"Well, you can call me anytime," she was saying. "If it's late, that's okay. I'm here for you, kiddo."

And we're back to auntie and niece. I guess that's more realistic than expecting us to be sisters with twenty years separating us.

She took both my hands in hers and kissed me on both cheeks. "Au Revoir, Cherie."

"Hey, I never thought about learning another language magically. Can we do that?"

"Mais oui!"

"Cool! You'll have to teach me how to do that sometime—if you still want me."

"Of course!" She grinned. "We have a lot of things to look forward to."

"I love you, Aunt Hilary."

"Love you too, Fish Face." She winked.

I groaned. "Hey! Did you have a nickname when you were in Haven?"

"No. That's a fairly new development."

"Darn."

# CHAPTER 14

I had almost told Aunt Hilary I was making a second trip to Summerland. But I stopped myself because she would just try harder to talk me out of going again, and I really had to see Logan...especially now. I had an idea how I might be able to help him.

When I arrived back at my room I glanced at my clock and it was ten. I'd been gone an hour. But no one was running around looking for me...at least I didn't think so. I could just lay in bed and pretend I'd been in the bathroom all that time, or I could try turning back time.

Guess which one I chose? Hey, who could resist something as cool as fixing time? At least I hesitated long enough to realize I needed a clear plan before I screwed up the date or the year.

I thought about what I should say and do to turn back time for just one hour. I remembered my aunt speaking her intention aloud, without rhyming or writing anything. She looked at the spot where she wanted the guest room to appear and pointed at it with her wand. I didn't have my wand. None of us did. We'd been told to leave them at home. To be honest, wands were kind of old fashioned accessories, like decorative hats and long gloves. Witches gathered more power in a circle with hands held, and wands would only get in the way.

I studied my clock. They had to be battery operated since they didn't want anyone to have a long cord. Yeah, I shivered when I realized why they came up with that rule. Anyway, my clock is one of those analog ones with hands that go around in a circle. I could move the hands or…

I sat on the edge of my bed and stared intensely at the hands, willing them to light up in the dark. When they did, I had ceased to be surprised. Pleased, but not surprised. Concentrating really hard on those hands and time itself, I spoke aloud as I pointed to the minute hand. "Turn back time one hour, please." Then I made a complete counterclockwise circle with my finger.

The minute hand moved precisely with my finger movement. And the hour hand moved much more slowly, stopping at nine. I was raised to be polite, so I said, "Thank you".

I still didn't know much about where my powers came from, but it seemed as if I was getting an assist from somewhere or someone else. A simple please and thank you might mean a lot to the powers-that-be.

I wondered if I could just wish myself to Summerland. That seemed dangerous, and one of those things that needed a spell. Since I used one successfully before, I had no need to mess around with it. I would just do the same thing. My only question was, should I go now, or wait? I lay down on my bed and reached under my pillow for the book I needed.

Shock set in when I realized both books were gone!

"Oh, crap. Where did they go?" Had somebody found them? Is that what happens when you're not in bed and they check on you with the flashlight? I should have stuffed some clothes under my blanket so it looked like I was there. But noooo. My bed was neatly made. Had they come in and turned my room upside down—but then remade my bed and put everything back in place? Or did they know what they were looking for and as soon as they had the contraband just left with it?

*What should I do?*

I thought about what Aunt Hilary had told me about being a minor goddess. That really blew my mind. But maybe I could sense or *just know* what happened to the books, if I concentrated. Kind of like psychic second sight. I had never really developed that part of myself, but I sensed it was there, waiting to be amplified.

I rose and concentrated on the books. I pictured them in my mind in perfect detail just like I had my Aunt Hilary. Then I spoke aloud. "Where are you, books?"

When I opened my eyes, I was standing in the library. I'm glad I stood up first and didn't make the mistake of falling on my butt again.

*So, the books must be back in their place?* I went to the aisle where I found them before. Sure enough, both books were filed properly, as if they had never left their spots. *That's weird.* As far as I knew, no magicals were around at this hour. If the books transported themselves, that would be kind of wonderful. That meant I didn't need them anymore.

But what if I did? I almost hit myself upside the head. *Of course. I could just summon them and they would appear.* Maybe. This would take some getting used to.

Meanwhile I had a date in Summerland.

⁎ ⁎

"Loooggaannn…" I yelled when I got there.

Rushing toward me from the trees, he yelled, "Fish Face! Er…I mean, Genevieve! You came back!" He stopped short of knocking me over and gave me a warm hug.

"So I did. I wasn't sure if you'd still be here or not."

A sad smile replaced his initial grin. "Where else would I go?"

"Have you been able to contact your mom?"

"No." His smile disappeared altogether.

"I had an idea…"

"Really?" His brows rose and hope brightened his face. For a guy, his emotions were surprisingly easy to read. Or maybe I'm stereotyping.

"So, here's the thing… I've just found out there's a slew of stuff I can do without a spell. Things I never even thought about trying."

"Like?"

"Like, well… I don't know yet."

"Huh?"

"It's a long story, and I don't have time to explain. Anyway, I'd like to try some mediumship. I realized that since only the *souls* of our dear departed are here, naturally we couldn't see them. But their spirits are probably all around us. Have you tried to contact your mom through a medium?"

"You mean here? Where would I find a medium? Are *you* a medium?"

"I don't know. I've never tried it."

"Do you think that might work?"

I shrugged. "It's worth a try."

"Have you contacted the dead before?"

"Um, no, but as I said, there are a lot of things I can do just by concentrating and asking nicely."

He looked skeptical. "Hmmm... Yeah, I guess we could try. What do we have to lose? Wait. You couldn't get hurt by doing this could you?"

I mulled that over for a moment. "I don't think so. It's not like I'm going to join them in spirit form. I'm just going to ask them to speak to you through me."

"Who's 'them'?"

"I don't know. Whoever shows up, I guess... I'll try your mom first. From what I've heard, sometimes other spirits come through too. People you weren't expecting."

"Oh. Yeah, I guess my grandfather might show up. That's okay. He's cool."

"All right. So I have your permission to try to contact your mother?"

"Yes. Absolutely!"

"Okay, but since I don't know her it might help if you concentrate on her and let me into your mind."

He took a step back. "Whoa. You can read my mind?"

"Not without your permission. I'm not a peeping Genevieve."

He chuckled. "Yeah, okay. But just for a minute."

I held my hands out to him. I didn't think holding his hands would be necessary. I just wanted to. So, sue me.

He took my hands in his warm grasp. I closed my

eyes and said, "Concentrate on your mom. See her in your mind's eye just as you remember her."

He didn't say anything, but he must have been doing as I asked because the picture of a smiling blonde woman popped into my head. At first it seemed as if he was remembering a photograph, but then the woman moved. She laid her hand on Logan's shoulder. "Hello, son. I'm here."

*Whoa.* That was MY voice, calling him 'son'. Well, I guess that's the only voice he could hear, so she had to use my vocal chords.

"Mom? Is that really you?"

"Test me," *she* said. She must mean for him to state something only she would know.

"Okay. How did your blue glass lamp get broken?"

She laughed. "It happened on Christmas. You and Brian were tossing your new football across the living room. You both apologized and offered to buy a new one with your yard work money."

He actually jumped up and down. "That's it. It's really you!" As soon as he'd caught his breath he asked, "What can you tell us about the afterlife?"

"What? And ruin the surprise?"

"Mom..."

"I'm sorry, honey. We're not allowed to tell you much. You already know more than most corporeal beings."

*It must be her. I'm not even sure what 'corporeal' means.*

"That's okay," he said. "I actually have a more important question. Do you know what's been happening in my life? Can you help me?"

She let out a long sigh. "There's only so much we can do, or I already would have done it. We *can't* turn back your timeline or transport you to another location on your plane of existence. We can watch over you and make subtle suggestions, and I have. Do you remember Dad taking you all to Lake George as a kind of reset vacation about three months after I died?"

"Yeah. That was kind of cool. We all slept in a teepee. You came with us?"

"I didn't ride along in the car, and I can't hang around for long periods of time, but I knew you went there and watched all of you. I think you were happiest in the boat your father rented. You caught the biggest fish one of those days."

He grinned. "Yup. So, other than watching us, what *can* you do?"

"Well, have you heard about people waking up from a sound sleep when their house was on fire? It's not always because they smell smoke or hear the noise of an alarm or a roaring fire. Someone from the other side may have woken them."

"Cool."

*Very cool.* I had a few questions of my own now, but I didn't want to interfere with the time Logan was enjoying with his mother.

"I have to go now, son."

"Go? Go where? It's not like you have a class to get to or something, is it?"

She chuckled. "Actually it's very much like that. I'm learning some of the lessons I missed during my time on earth."

"What lessons could you have missed? You were an awesome mother!"

"I'm happy to hear you say that, but there's so much more to know. The universe is a very big place."

"The universe? You're learning about the whole universe?"

"I'm afraid I may have said too much. I'd better go, hon. Just know I'll always love you and watch over you."

I felt like a heel when I let her go, but it's not like I could kidnap her and keep her soul tied to a tree. Logan's eyes watered but no tears escaped. I can't stand watching people cry when no one comforts them. I know what that feels like. So, I pulled him into a hug.

He kind of sagged onto my shoulder and let out a long sigh. "Thank you."

Eventually, he pulled his head back so he could look at my face, without letting go of my back. His gaze drifted to my lips, and I wondered if he was going to…

He kissed me. Long, and slow, until my toes curled. You know how some people say something feels Heavenly? Well, here I was in Heaven experiencing the most

Heavenly kiss I could imagine. I wouldn't forget this moment. Ever.

Back in my room, I couldn't help worrying about him. I wondered if I might be able to channel spirits from anywhere. Like here, and now.

I didn't really know anybody over there, but I wanted to talk to his mother some more. I did have my own questions, and like I said it would be nice to know in order to tell people that Summerland was a really great place, but she got me thinking…

Learning about the whole universe? That sounded amazing. I don't know how much she could tell me, but maybe she knew someone who could talk to me more. A witch's elder or something. I know she was kind of nervous. It seemed like she thought she might get caught, and I wouldn't want to get her in trouble.

As I lay there thinking, I realized I'm not usually the mulling-it-over *type*. I'm more the let's do it before I talk myself out of it type. *Hey! I'm actually mulling! That's growth.* I think I must be maturing…a bit.

I waited another couple of minutes, and to be honest I didn't think anything was going to happen. I thought maybe I'd have to find a spell for spirit communication, and then I heard a voice in the back of my head.

"Genevieve? You wanted to speak to me?"

"Mrs. Holderness? Is that you?"

"Yes. Is there something about Logan you wanted to tell me?"

I was kind of ashamed of myself for just wanting to know all the secrets of the universe without talking to her about her son first. I know it seems like she knew everything that was going on with him, but what if she didn't? "Logan is in real trouble, you know that, right?"

I heard her sigh. "Yes. I know. And he has to learn his lesson. I'm worried that he won't."

"I think he's certainly learning his lesson now. He's got nothing to do but think about what he did and how much he regrets it."

"Regret isn't the lesson," she said. "He can't unkill that man. He has to accept responsibility for what he's done…and learn to *live* with it. It's not his time to go to Summerland. He's hiding there."

She hesitated, and I didn't know what she was trying to say or not say. Obviously there were rules. Eventually she sort of shimmered in front of me, so I could see her. That was really cool!

"I know you can't tell me everything," I began, "but what can you tell me? I mean, especially about learning our lessons here on earth."

"That's a big part of what we're all supposed to do. Learn our lessons while on earth, and if we do an amazing job in fifteen or twenty lifetimes, we might

not have to go back and repeat and repeat and repeat…
Ad nauseam."

"I understand, I think. It sounds kind of like the Hindu philosophy of reincarnation. Coming back in a higher caste if you do well in your current life. But do our ancestors really come back as cows?"

She smiled indulgently. "Most religions have a piece of the puzzle. If only human beings could sift through it all and put together the best philosophies, you'd have it."

"So what you're telling me is that Logan is kind of doomed to repeat this lesson until he gets it right…"

"I don't want to use the word doom. No one is doomed. You either do your best or you don't. Logan has a lot of life left, and there is still plenty of time to turn it around, but he can't do that in Summerland. He's just avoiding his truth. Stalling, as it were."

"I see." And I did, kind of. "But if he comes back here, he's gonna be in a load of trouble. Is there anything I can do to help the administration understand? Should I even tell anybody where he went?"

"This isn't your test, Genevieve. It's his. You can offer your thoughts, but any decisions he makes are his and his alone."

"Okay, I guess I understand that, but can I let him know what you've explained to me? I think he really needs a little guidance from you."

I was pretty sure she was smiling.

"You can tell him anything we talk about. In fact, I hope you will. He just isn't asking the right questions."

"But I am?"

She chuckled. "Your questions are better."

"Then how about this question? How do you know when your loved ones need you? Do you peek in on them randomly, and sometimes catch them in the shower?"

She laughed out loud. The same kind of fully committed throaty laugh Logan had. "It's not like that. We have a sort of spiritual tether to our loved ones. We can sense when they need us by tension on the tether."

"You must have been feeling a lot of tension on his tether. Why didn't you go to him, and how did you know to come to me?"

She sighed. "To answer your first question, there's only so much I can do as a spirit. Of course I tried to help him, but people have free will and can ignore our signs and suggestions. The outcome is still up to him and others who think they hold the power over him. I'd be terribly upset if things went badly for Logan because of something another person decides, but that's always a risk. No one can control other people's actions or reactions."

"But you said spirits can suggest things... Can you talk to the administrator's loved ones and ask them to suggest leniency—or whatever will help him, not just make it worse?"

"One hopes they'll listen to their conscience. Sprits often comes across as still small voices within."

"I know what you mean. I've heard it, but I don't know of any relatives I have over there."

"And that brings me to your second question. How did I know to come to you just now?"

"Yeah, especially since we're not related."

"Everybody over here loves you. You don't have to worry about contacting someone you knew. In fact, one of the best things about Summerland is the love and peace that's available to all souls. But I sensed you would be important to my son, so I tethered to you too."

That got my attention, but she wasn't through talking. I had to focus my attention on what she was saying since I didn't know when she'd be called away.

"Most of us let go of resentments once we realize there's nothing we can or should do about them anymore. Unless we're needed, we don't interfere."

"So any of you can make a suggestion to a... an earthling?" I had no idea what to call us anymore... Humans? Corporeals? The living?

"Yes."

"What about a mass protest?"

She looked confused. "I'm not sure what you're asking, Genevieve."

"If a thousand of you ganged up on one influential

figure and told them not to do something stupid, could you? Would you?"

She laughed. "No, probably not. There are things that have to happen down there. Your world is shaped by events both good and bad. There are times you might wonder how anyone can let bad things occur, but… *Oh!* I'm being summoned back."

"Wait, one more question. Is The Goddess real?"

"I'm sorry, Genevieve. I have to go…"

Her spirit faded. She had just enough time to wave goodbye.

She seemed genuinely helpful and like there was more she wanted to say, but there were those darn rules. I forgot to ask what they were. Maybe next time…or not. Something told me I just shouldn't ask certain things or she'd disappear again.

I liked the part about finding peace and love. Most people would like to know that, but should I tell them? Argh. I still had so many questions. I remembered something my mother told me once… 'Genevieve, when you don't know what to do, don't do anything.'

I was really, really bad at doing nothing. Maybe that was one of my lessons. I had to figure that out for myself, I guess. Fortunately, Mrs. Holderness didn't mind my talking to Logan and sharing his lesson to be learned.

It was now very late, and I was tired. I didn't feel like resetting time again. I just had to close my eyes and give my brain some much needed rest. All this spiritual communication might be the reason for my exhaustion. I had heard it could be draining. At any rate, there was always tomorrow to puzzle out the crap-bag Logan's life had become—and what to do about it, if anything.

## CHAPTER 15

I TRIED TO GET BACK TO MY NORMAL LIFE AT HAVEN—OR as normal as it could be. I had classes and I went to them. I hung out with Just Jen and Alien, keeping my distance from Lake Pirate. Now that I knew he was a spy, I was not going to give him any inside information. And I had a lot of it.

It was reassuring to know he was a fuggle, and couldn't read my mind. I think. The only reason I had to believe he was non-magical was the lack of vomiting and diarrhea, so I still had to be careful. Maybe he just had a strong stomach.

I didn't even have to block my thoughts from my friends whose powers were suppressed. I did wonder about being around certain teachers though. I kept my brain on strict lockdown as much as I could.

If nothing else, disciplining my mind this way was even better than the classes designed to teach us to control our thoughts. There are plenty of different ways to learn things, I guess.

So, it was time for another one of our *fun* classes. I say fun sarcastically. This one was more about learning not to mess with people. Basically, how to walk away.

You'd think that would be the whole class... Just walk away. But, no. There were some kids who just had to deliver a parting shot, and that was no good. Especially if they used magic to do it.

There were other times when you'd come off as inadequate or unable to defend your opinion, if you walked away without addressing a situation. And then you had to be sure to do it assertively, not aggressively.

So we had to learn when to hold 'em, when to fold 'em, when to walk away, and when to run. There's a song about that. I guess the trick is learning what to do when.

I had a hard time concentrating that day. My mind kept drifting to Logan and what I should or could do to help him. Should I walk away? Run? Folding him might not be a good idea, but holding him seemed like something I could do. And to be honest, I couldn't stop thinking about doing just that.

I didn't leave things with him in a way that led him to believe I'd return, but I wanted to. I wanted to tell him the things his mother told me. She was making a lot of sense and his hiding out in Summerland forever didn't make sense at all. No matter how much Haven sucked, I think he needed to hear the hard truth.

I was so preoccupied, I barely made it through the day without getting caught spacing out. After dinner I begged off socializing. Most kids went to the game room or watched TV. I just said I was tired and needed to rest, *alone.* I gave Lake Pirate the death stare, daring him to invade my privacy.

He held up his hands and said, "I get it. You don't want me to drop in and bother you."

I didn't even try to spare his feelings by telling him he wasn't a bother. I just nodded, got up and took my tray to the 'poof deck'. That's what we'd taken to calling the trash handler.

Just Jen looked at me with concern and quickly followed behind me as I walked down the corridor.

"Fish Face… I mean, Genevieve," she said.

I had to turn around when she used my proper name. I waited for her and hoped she'd understand my need for some alone time. When she caught up to me, she came right out and asked, "Are you all right?"

"Yeah, I'm fine. Just tired."

She nodded. "I've had a hard time sleeping too. I get the sense there's something going on. Do you feel it?"

I tried not to show any emotion, but I couldn't help wondering what she was picking up on. I had been so preoccupied, there might be something else going on in Haven and I wouldn't have even realized it.

I shrugged and said, "I don't know. I haven't sensed anything in particular. Are you feeling an odd essence or a disturbance?"

"It's hard to say since our powers are suppressed, but I've always been an empath. I can sense when things are wrong. It's like ripples in the energy. Recently, the energy ripples are feeling more like waves."

I couldn't help wondering if she was picking up on all the crazy spiritual stuff I had been involved in, or if it wasn't about me at all. Hopefully it wasn't. However, if there was something else going on, I'd want to know about it.

Just to protect my backside, I tried to reassure her that I hadn't experienced anything unusual in the energy, or whatever, and we parted with a simple, "See you tomorrow."

Once I was back in my room. I was able to stop pretending I was tired and start planning what I would say to Logan when I saw him. I was still using the spell to travel back and forth, but I thought maybe I could do it with just a thought now that I had been there a couple of times. So I rumpled up my covers, making it look like I was asleep and stood behind my closed door. I concentrated on where I wanted to be. When I opened my eyes I was still in my room.

Okay, this was one of those things that Aunt Hilary told me I should think twice about. Yeah, okay. I thought twice and faced the ceiling with my hands upraised, recited the spell with my eyes closed, picturing Summerland and Logan. After saying the words for the third time, I felt rather than saw my destination. It smelled of flowers, and I felt warm sunshine on my shoulders and my scalp. I smiled as I open my eyes and saw Logan right in front of me.

He grinned and said, "I was hoping you'd come back. But I thought you might come sooner."

I bit my lip and wondered how to start this conversation. "Walk with me," I said. He reached for my hand. I hadn't expected that, but maybe he was feeling the same attraction to me that I was to him. That would be nice, but I had to ask… "Is it just because I'm the only girl in town?"

He reared back and laughed heartily.

I held his hand, noticing it was warm, and…cushy. A nice feeling came over me. We walked through the grass slowly, admiring the view. Eventually I had to tell him, and I had to start somewhere.

"I had a nice talk with your mom."

He stopped in his tracks and faced me with wide eyes. "You did? What did she say?"

"She said a lot of things." I started walking again, but he let go of my hand and put his hands in his pockets. The loss of contact saddened me, but I'd live. "She said you weren't asking the right questions. Instead of asking how she could get you out of Haven, she thought you really needed to face the truth."

"The truth, of what? That I killed a man? It was unintentional. I hate that the whole thing happened, but there's nothing I can do about it now."

"She said it had nothing to do with regrets. That you had to learn not to hide out here. I was thinking that even though you might have to go back to Haven, you could talk to the administrator about all the extenuating circumstances…maybe even get a new hearing and have your sentence reduced."

He snorted. "Yeah, like that's gonna happen."

"I don't know for sure, but your mom seemed to think it might help. I guess it depends on you and others involved in your incarceration. I think if you turn yourself in and beg forgiveness, cooperate anyway you can, that might go a long way toward being freed sooner."

"Did she say that? Did she say my sentence would get reduced if I did all that?"

"No, she didn't."

His posture sagged. "Why tell me then? You got my hopes up."

"But she's right. You can't hide out here forever. It's not your time."

He took a deep breath and let it out slowly. "I know. But I also know of a place I can hide out down there. I just need to get to it. Can you help me, Genevieve?" He took his hands out of his pockets and reached for me.

I hesitated, but took his hands in mine. Both of them. "I'm not sure what I'm capable of. I would hate to say I can do it and not be able to. I'd also be helping you ignore your mom's advice—doing the opposite of what she said you should do. She said we all have lessons to learn on earth, and your lesson has something to do with facing the truth. It sounds like you just want to hide from it and never go through with your sentence, whatever it may be."

He dropped my hands and looked angry. "Of course I don't want to go through with the sentence, it's unfair."

"I agree, it's unfair. And maybe you can get a new trial."

"Do you really think they're going to trust the escapee with a trip to the courthouse again? They'll have so many magicals surrounding me, I won't be able to go to the bathroom without somebody watching my every move."

I shrugged. I didn't know what to say to that. He was probably right.

Something occurred to me that I hadn't thought of before. "Your mother said something about tethering to people who needed them. That they felt some tension on the tether—and she's tethered to you. She'll know when you need her and will come to you, but not in the way you may want. Apparently she has whispered this advice to you before, and you've disregarded it. She said you have free will, of course, but ignoring her suggestions isn't helping."

He worried his lip. Then looked at the sky and said, "I know. I've thought about doing exactly that. Turning myself in, throwing myself on the mercy of the court, the whole thing. I just don't see the results going my way."

"Nothing will change if you don't even try."

He raked his hands through his hair. "I would like this to be over, but I don't know how to make that happen. I don't know what to do."

I shrugged. "It's up to you, ultimately. Whatever happens, it has to be your decision. I don't want to tell you what to do and be responsible if things don't turn out well, *but* I wouldn't be able to live with myself if I didn't at least communicate your mom's advice. She said she hoped I would tell you."

"She did? You didn't just come here because you wanted to, but because she asked you to?"

"No, she didn't ask me to. But she said it was all right if I told you everything we talked about."

"Is that everything?"

I thought about it. "Pretty much. I asked some general questions about the other side, because I was curious. She couldn't tell me much without violating some kind of rule, I think. Just know her concern for you…that was on her mind. It doesn't matter when you come back. You're going to face the same problems."

At that point he just plopped onto the ground. With his head in his hands, he remained there quietly.

"Look, I'm helping you however I can. I don't want to get you into more trouble than you're already in, so I'm not telling you what to do. I'm just relaying the message."

He looked up at me. "I know. And you've given me a lot to think about. This tether thing, that's new, but it does answer a couple questions I had."

I sat down next to him. "Me too. I asked how she knew when she was needed, because she came to me when I was alone in my room and thinking about you."

"So she knew when you needed her?"

Should I tell him about the tether she put on me? Maybe that was okay, but I didn't want to say I'd be important to him. If that was gonna happen, it would happen on its own. I didn't want to influence it and always wonder.

"Yeah, she came to me, because she put a tether on me too. I guess anybody can tether to anybody, if they have some kind of investment in what they're doing. She said they ignore a lot of what's happening down here, because some things, even bad things have to happen."

He leaned back on his hands. "All of this is major stuff. It's a lot to take in."

"I know, right? I'm getting an education from her too."

"Look, I'm not ready to give up on finding a way to get to that cabin I know about. I can hunt and fish and everything I need is right there. I'd rather live out my life, enjoying the great outdoors, than cooped up in the awful indoors of Haven and Hell."

I totally understood his point. And maybe he was right. I didn't know if his mother knew about that place and his alternate idea, or not.

"Would you mind if I talked to someone else about this? I'm thinking my aunt might know more. She's cool, like me." I grinned, hoping to cheer him up.

He smirked. "You are cool, Genevieve. I like you."

"I like you too."

He leaned over and I leaned in and we shared an innocent kiss. There was no way I was ready for more, especially with the guy who hangs out in a place for dead people. How do you explain you have a boyfriend no one can meet? Ever.

Besides, who knows if I'll always be allowed to transport back and forth...or if at some point maybe my luck will run out.

<br>

The next visiting day was a week away, and I wanted to see my aunt sooner than that. I couldn't help being nervous about telling her I'd gone back to Summerland. She'd told me not to. I wasn't especially good at doing what I was told, and if she didn't already know that, maybe she should.

To my surprise she reached out to me first. I thought about that tether thing and wondered if witches could attach to a loved one even before they died. I wouldn't be surprised. Aunt Hilary seemed to think there were a lot of things we could do that regular witches couldn't.

I didn't have time to get nervous about our whole Summerland conversation. She popped in on me in my room and said, "I think I've figured out something about that map!"

"Your tramp stamp?"

She snickered. "Yeah. That."

"Tell me."

"First you have to sit down."

I'd already sat down. "Maybe you should sit too?"

"Oh, yeah." She lowered herself beside me and took my hand. "This might come as a shock. I was never supposed to tell you…"

I steeled myself against whatever news was coming. "Go ahead."

She took a deep breath. "You have a twin sister."

"I have a… Wait. What?"

"Your parents knew you were both much more powerful than they were—especially together. You both walked and talked at six months old. You two could float out of your cribs and play together any time you wanted to. They tried to suppress your powers, but before they could finish with one, the other had undone their efforts. Nobody had seen anything like it, and they were worried that word would get out."

I thought about how I'd always felt like I had a sister. How I sensed there was a girl out there, about my age, and we were close. Maybe it wasn't just wishful thinking.

"I know you worried that they might be guarded because they're scared of you. That's not it. They've been protecting this secret because they're worried what would happen if you two were together again."

"Like 'twinning' up on them?"

"Yes, I'm sure that's part of it. They may have worried they didn't have the ability to raise you as carefully as you needed to be. They're both full-time teachers, needing both salaries to pay the bills."

"I guess Mary Poppins wasn't available."

She tousled my hair. "Very few can afford a supernatural nanny. I'd offered, but I was barely an adult at the time. Each of you needed caretakers with a home and good steady jobs."

"Okaaayyy… What does this have to do with the map?"

"First, I want to reassure you that your parents

loved you both and giving one of you up was probably the hardest thing they ever had to do."

Yeah, sure. My stalwart parents must have wrestled with the decision for about five whole minutes.

She worried her lip and when I didn't comment she said, "Really. I don't know how they decided which of you to keep and which to put up for adoption."

"So my sister was adopted? By fuggles?"

"I don't know, but I doubt it. I wasn't privy to that whole decision making process and they refused to tell me much. But recently it occurred to me that perhaps Joy found me and placed a map to her location on my back."

"That's her name? Joy?"

"It was until she was adopted. It may have been changed."

"Why you? I mean, don't get me wrong—you're probably the best adult in our family, but why not reach out to my parents—or me?"

"I don't know."

"And why did it take her so long?"

"I'm not sure. She may have just learned she was adopted."

"What *do* you know?"

She sighed. "Nothing. Only theories. Possibly the lightning strike happened four years ago, because witches often have a power spike during puberty."

*Oh, yeah. I remember it well. Zits be gone! I was using*

*that spell every other day.* "So, four years ago would have made her twelve, and that's when I got my —um..."

"Your period? You can talk to me about stuff like that. I'm not squeamish."

"I know. I'm glad of that, but it's still a little weird to talk about it at all."

She shrugged. "Whatever."

I looked at her askance. "Did you and my father really come out of the same womb?"

She laughed. "As far as I know… Anyway, I tried to find a spot that might look like an X—you know, X marks the spot? Unfortunately there's nothing like that on the map. I drove around the area and hoped I could 'sense' my way toward her. That didn't work either. I just kept driving around these dirt roads up in the mountains, but there were no homes there. Anyway, I thought maybe *you* could find her."

"I understand why you might think that, but I'm in kind of an inconvenient place."

"I know."

"Why do you want to find her right now?"

"Because the scars are itching like crazy. I've spread aloe all over them, made tinctures with essential oils, taken mint baths, baking soda baths, I even used Benadryl cream. It isn't natural, but it treats allergic reactions…" Nothing has helped. If it's her and she wants my attention, she has it!"

"What about a spell? Did you try to stop the itching with a spell?"

She rolled her eyes. "Of course. That was the first thing I tried."

My eyes widened. "It didn't work?"

"No. And it won't, if it's not supposed to. Every witch knows the Witches Rede…"

"An' if it harm none, do what ye will," I quoted. "Do you think not finding her will cause harm somehow?"

"Yeah, I do. Sometimes my spells weren't answered in the way I wanted or expected them to be, but I've never had one completely ignored like this. That must mean something."

I was getting kind of overwhelmed at this point and decided not to talk to her about Summerland and Logan. I had a new crusade. *Find my sister!*

# CHAPTER 16

THE CRUSADE WOULD HAVE TO WAIT. MY ITCHY AUNT tried talking to Mrs. Black Hole and nothing she said could get me out of Haven any earlier. In frustration I took long walks around the perimeter by myself every evening.

I told Just Jen and Alien I had a lot on my mind. Lake Pirate would try to accompany me until I gave him the 'drop dead' stare. Then he scurried off, waving and calling out that he'd see me later.

"Not if I see you first" meant something else entirely now. I wanted to dodge everyone and everything while I obsessed over all this new information I'd gathered since I've been here.

On one of my rounds I saw something suspicious behind the trees. Having to investigate, because I was the curious sort and couldn't let things go, I tried to hide myself behind a post. That was kind of useless.

I had to become invisible—something I'd never tried before, or skinnier—something every witch has tried with varying success. So I sucked it in. With the tall grass partially hiding my feet and legs, I remained as still as I could and hoped the rest of me wouldn't pop out a little bit around the pole as I scanned for whatever caused the movement.

It wasn't a bird or an animal. It was human sized. And as much as it tried to hide behind the trees and approach stealthily, I knew I was looking at someone familiar.

*Bossy Rando!* She neared the back gate, and one of the guards came forward. I thought he was going to ask what her business was there but instead he seemed to move stiffly and slowly toward her, without blinking. It was almost as if he were—oh Goddess—*mind controlled!*

He unlocked the padlock and opened the back gate just enough to take a package from her. He didn't appear to be speaking to her at all, but she spoke to him. He relocked the emergency exit, turned and walked slowly back toward the building, holding the box in front of him. I spotted the smirk on Bossy Rando's face before she turned and ran off into the trees again.

This couldn't be good.

I followed the guard and when it looked like he was about to take the box inside I said "Hey... Hey..."

He didn't turn around. He didn't even acknowledge

my existence. I would've expected some kind of remark like, 'You don't belong here,' or 'Go back to the front entrance' or something. But it was as if I wasn't even there.

He held the box under his arm like a football, opened the door balancing the box against his hip, and entered, letting the door go. I managed to slip inside before the door closed and latched behind us.

"Hey, what you got there?" I danced around him and walked backward facing him as he continued to walk like a zombie. Well he wasn't shuffling or groaning or anything. He just looked straight ahead without responding or even blinking.

"Hey!" I called out. I put my hand on his chest to stop him, and he just kept going, pushing me backward. I had to scramble to keep from falling and being trampled. He was definitely mind controlled or under a spell.

I had a bad feeling about this box. If Bossy Rando sent it in, it wasn't a fruit basket. Maybe a snake basket…or something much worse.

"Let me see that box."

He didn't hold onto it harder or anything, so I just tried lunging at it to push it out of his grip. Surprisingly, it flew out behind him. I grabbed it and ran out the back door, setting off the alarm. *Good.* I had the feeling this box needed some emergency attention.

Running all the way to the fence with it, I tried

opening the back gate, but it was locked with a padlock on a chain wrapped around the gate posts. The architects made sure it wasn't easy to open—even with magic. It sure wasn't the kind of thing any bozo could open with a credit card.

The guard came after me, but with the same slow steps. I opened the box and gasped when I saw what had to be a bomb.

*Oh, great.* She couldn't burn the place down. So she was going to blow it up. As the guard came closer to me. I tried to push him away. "Go! Get out of here." He just kept coming.

Some of the kids heard me screaming at him and saw me trying to grab him and pull him away. Of course they came to look at the scuffle.

I tried to wave them away, yelling, "Don't come near here. Get away. Run. Tell someone to call 911. There's a bomb." It wasn't until I said the word 'bomb' that they turned and ran back toward the front entrance.

I just couldn't get the guard away from the damn thing. He kept walking until he reached it, despite my yanking him with what would look like human strength. No inmate had more than that here.

He kept trying to pick it up. Finally, I didn't care who saw me... I picked *him* up and threw him as far as I could. I was pretty amazed with myself, actually. You know how they say, 'You can't trust some people as far as you can throw them?' Well, I guess I can trust people about 50 yards.

I peered inside the box again and spotted the red digital numbers counting down. It was getting close 18, 17, 16…

If I had a brain in my head, I would've been running for the opposite side of the yard, but part of me wanted to pick it up and hurl it over the fence. 14, 13, 12… The dickhead guard had picked himself up and was coming toward me again. *Dammit.* If I threw it, he'd just go after it.

10, 9, 8, 7… The guard was going to arrive at precisely one second before this damn thing went off. I ran toward him, picked him up, and had just enough time to throw him back to the same fifty yard line, then grab the box, hurling it with all my might over the fence.

But it bounced off a tree and ricocheted back at me. "Shiiiii…"

I heard Bossy Rando laughing. Then the box exploded.

I felt myself flying through the air. The loud bang and ringing in my ears deafened me. Smoke blinded me and stung my eyes. I inhaled and started choking. For some reason I kept flying, without landing…

Eventually the air cleared and I open my eyes, shocked to see Summerland. Or kind of…I was fading in and out of what I recognized as Summerland from my previous visits. I was gliding over the grass. Extending my hands in front of me, I saw the grass right through them.

It was like I was half there and half not there. At that moment, I really would have welcomed a hard landing and whatever pain would ensue. I'm pretty sure I should be in pain, but I wasn't. I was very afraid that meant I had died.

The blast was probably meant to blow up the whole school. I didn't know anything about C4 or anything like that, but there was a big brick of something that looked like clay with some wires coming out of it. The whole thing was duct taped to a digital clock.

I remembered the countdown. *I hope that stupid guard lived.* I imagine he did, I didn't see anyone else around me…not even Logan.

*No, wait. There he is!*

Logan peered over his shoulder and looked shocked.

"Genevieve?"

I was slowing down, and soon I wasn't flying anymore but just kind of hanging in the air. He came rushing toward me and reached for my arms. Even jumping up, he couldn't quite grasp me. So he went to my feet and jumped up trying to catch one of those.

"Lower your legs so I can grab you!"

I was still semitransparent and didn't know if his hands would go right through me or not. Was this what death was like? Did a spirit come through here kind of transparent before turning into pure spiritual energy?

Then Summerland began to change, fading in and out of my vision. Sometimes I could see it completely, and other times the landscape and Logan became cloudy.

I didn't see any other spirits. It wasn't like anybody was there to meet me. Not that I expected anyone, except maybe the grandparents I had never met.

Logan's mother must be feeling one heck of a yank on our tether.

But there was no one. No one even to tell me it was time to go back. What the heck?

Finally everything faded from view. I heard voices shouting, and that horrible smell of burning bomb blast which invaded my nostrils and lungs again.

*Crap, am I?*

I couldn't open my eyes. I felt my body being jostled and pain shot through me. I let out a groan.

"She's alive! She's alive!" There were many voices and I couldn't tell where they were coming from or who they were. Finally, I just sort of blacked out.

I woke up in a hospital. Aunt Hilary was in a chair beside my bed. I tried to say something, but it just came out as a croak.

She bolted upright and peered at me over the bedrail. "Genevieve!" She took my hand and held it gently, "Oh, my Goddess, I've been so worried."

I took a few deep breaths and tried to use my vocal cords again. "Am I…gonna be…okay?"

"Yes. I don't think anyone else could have survived that blast, but you are one tough cookie."

I smiled at that. Picturing her fabulous oatmeal cookies, I asked, "Can I have a cookie?"

She laughed. "As soon as the doctor says it's okay, you can have all the cookies you want."

"How long do I have to be here?"

"Are you that anxious to get back to Haven?"

"Heck no. Won't they allow me to go home now?" Then I remembered my parents were in Africa. "Or with you?"

She rubbed her temples as if she had a headache. "I've been working on the administrator. I think they might let you out early."

"Good. Because, you know, I saved the whole facility and everything."

"Very true."

"I think I almost died," I whispered.

"It was definitely touch and go for a while."

"I went to Summerland…no spell needed. And I was kind of transparent."

Her mouth dropped open, but nothing came out. Eventually she nodded and whispered, "Don't tell anyone else about that."

I wondered why not. Maybe they'd realize how close to death I'd come and they'd keep me in the hospital longer—or study me or something. I just know I wasn't in any mood to argue with my aunt about anything. I was bone tired and if I was asked to sit up, I wasn't sure I could do it.

While my aunt was so close I whispered, "Is this a hospital for magicals or is my doctor a fuggle?"

"Probably a fuggle. I wanted to arrange a healing circle, and lead a chant around your bed. She just smirked and said she didn't want to invite the possibility of someone bringing in a virus."

I sighed. "Well, I guess I didn't need the chant, but it was nice of you to think of it."

She shrugged. "I was desperate."

I didn't know where she'd find enough magical friends to surround my bed anyway. The few I had were locked up. Maybe she knew some at the spa.

"Are my parents coming?" I was almost afraid of either answer. If it was yes, I'd have to put up with their awkward visits. If she said no, it would confirm that they didn't care.

"They were going to, but I told them to stay where

they were—that you were healing well and expected to be fine."

I let out a grateful sigh. "You always know what to do. How did you learn that?"

She laughed. "*I wish* I always knew the right thing to do. All any of us can hope for is to guess right more often than we guess wrong." Then she dug her phone out of her purse. "That reminds me, I promised to call your parents as soon as you woke up."

I waited quietly while she spoke to an international operator, then spoke to someone else, then we both waited for what seemed like an eternity before she reached my mother.

"Yes. She's right here. Would you like to speak with her?"

A moment later Aunt Hilary placed the phone in my free hand and lifted it to my ear. The other hand sported the IV needle and a finger gizmo. I was able to hold it in my left hand okay, but it felt weird. I couldn't help wondering what I looked like.

"Hey, Mom."

"Hey yourself. How are you?"

"I'm okay," I lied. "How are you guys?"

"Really, really busy...but good." After a brief hesitation she asked, "Are you still in the hospital?"

I should tell her I just woke up...that my aunt had done her duty and called the minute I opened my eyes, but I just said, "Yes."

"Well, I'm sure you'll be out of there soon. You've always been a fast healer."

I wondered if anyone had told her what I was healing from. Did she know I was almost blown into next week? Wait a minute…maybe it was next week. I didn't know how long I'd been recovering.

A visitor knocked on the door and poked her head around. I was surprised to see the administrator, Mrs. Black-Hole…I mean Whitehall walking in, carrying a cardboard box. I asked my mom if we could cut the phone call short, and she didn't seem to mind. I told her I would call her again soon and let her know how I was doing. That seemed like the right thing to say, but who knows if it would happen.

"Well, you're looking better than the last time I saw you," Mrs. Whitehall said.

"I meant to ask, how long have I been here?" I glanced at Aunt Hilary.

She grimaced. "Two days."

"Two days! But I was only…" I quickly shut my mouth and remembered what she said about not telling anyone I had been to Summerland, however briefly. "So if I was asleep for two days, I guess that would make me comatose for a while?" I looked up at the bag of liquid hanging on a pole by the headboard. The fluids dripped into a tube, which was plugged into my hand. For some dumb reason I thought about why I didn't need to go to the bathroom and realized there was probably another tube taking the liquids away. Ewww… Remind me never to become a nurse.

At that moment a nurse came bustling in behind Mrs. Whitehall and said," You're awake!"

I didn't know what to say to that. *Isn't it obvious?* That wouldn't be very nice, now, would it? And she was probably the one emptying my pee bag.

So I just lay there, smiling, when she came over and checked the machine and the bag and nodded to my aunt. "It looks like everything is as it should be." Before the nurse excused herself she said, "I'll be back in a little while. Don't stay too long. I don't want to tax her."

"Tax me? Do they tax hospital visits now?"

Mrs. Whitehall laughed. "They would if they could."

I'd never thought of her as sarcastic, but seeing people out in the world instead of in the setting where you think you know them can be quite different.

Aunt Hilary walked around the bed and shook Mrs. Whitehall's hand. "Have you thought anymore about what we discussed?" she asked.

"Yes, in fact I was coming here to give you some news."

Sometimes news is good news, right?

Then she looked at me, even though she was still talking to Hilary. "When can she leave? Did the doctor say?"

My aunt shook her head. "She hasn't seen her doctor yet. At least not since she's been awake."

Maybe I could get out of here soon. "Has anyone told him or her that I woke up?"

"I'm sure the nurse will." Hilary took another step toward Mrs. Whitehall. "You said you had some news?"

"Ah, yes. Genevieve, you wanted to go home with your aunt at some point anyway, right?" she asked.

"Yes, that would be my wish." My fondest wish…my dearest wish… I didn't know how emphatic to be about it.

"I've spoken to the board, and they have no problem with it. Genevieve, we're grateful for what you did to save Haven and who knows how many lives." She placed the cardboard box she was carrying into my closet. "These are all the things from your room at Haven. You don't have to come back unless you want to say goodbye."

I couldn't help being a little surprised even though I was happy and proud that she recognized the sacrifice. I just didn't expect they would take that into consideration and let me leave early. It seemed like they only added time, never subtracted it.

I would miss Just Jen and maybe, in a weird way, even Alien. Lake Pirate not so much. I'd still like to say Goodbye to him though—and punch him in the face.

Then I remembered something important.

"Did you catch Bossy? I mean *Bessie* Randall? I saw her with the bomb, and she mesmerized the guards, or at least one of them."

Mrs. Whitehall sighed heavily. "We were pretty sure the fire was her doing. One of the guards saw her on his rounds, but didn't confront her because he recognized her as a teacher. He wasn't magical and knew he wouldn't be able to stop her anyway. He just stayed hidden, called 911 and reported her involvement later. That was probably the smartest thing he could have done."

"Except I don't recall him getting us all out of the building…but never mind that now. Why didn't you go after Mrs. Randall after he told you?"

"Oh, we did. Believe me, we did. She's a slippery one. But we have a more powerful organization going after her now, not just local police."

That meant FBI or something, I guessed. It might be federal because the facility was for several states, not just Florida. In fact, most of the kids were from everywhere else but Florida. Although I imagine there are plenty of kids who could screw up in the beautiful sunshine and balmy weather too.

"So, when I get out of here, I can go straight to my aunt's place?" I didn't know if they were aware she lived out in Arizona or not. I wasn't about to say anything that would jeopardize my release.

"Yes, she assures me there's a doctor and a nurse practitioner on site where she works and lives, as well as many natural healers. Of course you have a certain amount of ability to heal yourself too," she said.

"Thank you—for letting me out early." I didn't want her to make the mistake of thinking I was thanking her for the months I spent at Haven.

"No thanks necessary. You earned your early release. There's one final lesson you will miss that everyone needs to learn. I will leave you with that. It's about love and forgiveness." She took a deep breath as if about to launch into a lecture.

"Forgiveness means replacing ill-will with good-will toward another. That in itself is a form of love—perhaps the most important form, since human beings will disappoint you throughout your life."

"That's it?"

"You wanted more?"

"No! I mean, it's not necessary. I've got it."

She smiled and said, "Very good. Take care, Genevieve." With that she departed and I was alone with my aunt again.

"What do you think she meant by that?"

Aunt Hilary shrugged. "I think it was pretty straightforward."

"I mean, the one final lesson thing… Was there some kind of lesson plan I was unaware of?"

"Probably. If you didn't receive a syllabus, that's because inmates would make paper airplanes out of them."

I chuckled, figuring she was right.

## CHAPTER 17

I waited until my aunt and the bulk of the hospital staff left for the evening. When the night shift came on a nurse checked on me and then everything was much quieter. I knew that I had to make it look like I was still in my bed and fortunately there were extra pillows and a blanket in the closet. The box held clean clothes, so I changed into my favorite jeans and a purple t-shirt.

I grabbed the extra blanket and one pillow and stuffed my bed. I figured out how to turn off my machine and did that without setting off any alarms. Then I pulled back the gauze and bandage covering my IV, which didn't look too hard to pull out. The tricky part would be how to stop the bleeding with my vein open.

Then it occurred to me, silly me, I could just wave my hand over it and try to heal myself. Didn't Mrs.

Whitehall say something about my having healing power? I had never tried it before, but hey, I was learning a lot about myself these days. As soon as I pulled out the needle, I waved my good hand over my punctured hand, and sure enough the little hole closed up and the bleeding stopped. *Well how about that...*

I had an idea. There were so many things that I wanted to tell Logan, and I had to get to Summerland to do it. I was pretty sure he'd be able to lessen his sentence, if he did what I was about to suggest. He needed to try. And I thought I might be able to coax him out, *if* I said I needed his help. He seemed like a guy who wouldn't leave me hanging.

For the heck of it I tried going to Summerland without the spell this time. Because I knew the place so well, I just concentrated hard on the spot and visualized it as clearly as if I were standing in it. Not knowing if it would work or not, I just figured no harm no foul. If it didn't work, I still knew the spell.

I guess I still wasn't supposed to just pop in, because I didn't go anywhere, even though I had become familiar enough with the place that I could picture it in vivid detail. So, I whispered the spell and as soon as I open my eyes I saw the brilliant colors and heard Logan call my name.

"Genevieve!" He ran toward me with open arms. I opened my arms and he ran right into them, giving me a hard hug and actually lifting me off the ground.

"Did you miss me?" I asked when he set me down.

He laughed. "You know I did. And not just because you're the only person I've been able to talk to for several weeks."

"Awww… You miss me for me?"

"Absolutely. Plus, I've been worried. The last time I saw you, I thought…"

"Yeah, me too."

"But you're okay?"

"Yeah."

He wrapped an arm around my waist and we strolled through the beautiful soft grass.

I sucked in a deep lungful of the clean, oxygen-rich air. "Does it ever get old?"

He squinted at me. "Does what get old?"

"The beauty of this place. Do you ever get so used to it that you don't even notice it anymore?"

"Oh, no. I notice. I imagine if I went back to the regular world I'd be disappointed by how dull it is."

"It hasn't been dull lately…"

He stopped walking and faced me. "What do you mean?"

"Sit down. I have a lot to tell you."

I let him in on a lot of the recent happenings— starting with how there was a fire and we not only suspected Bossy Rando, but there was a witness, and the administration and police had been looking for her ever since.

And then I told him about the bomb, and how I was almost a permanent citizen of Summerland. He looked at me intensely and listened the entire time until we got to that part.

"I was terrified for you. I knew you were on the edge of death."

"Did you know why?"

He frowned. "No. All I knew was I might never see you again. I'd miss so much about you. Seeing your beautiful smile, talking to you, holding your hand…"

Even though I went all squishy inside, I ignored the obvious compliments and shrugged. "I imagine you'd get sick of being alone and maybe consider what your mom suggested."

"What, going back and facing my sentence?"

"Actually, I had an idea about that…"

He tipped his head and said, "What's going through that devious mind of yours?"

"Well, I had my sentence commuted, because of saving the facility. There's one more thing they really want and that's Bossy Rando on a platter. No way can I capture her by myself, but with your help I think we could track her down and hand her over to Mrs. Whitehall, and whatever board she was talking about.

"Probably the School Board or the Board of Directors, or something."

"Yeah. I'm sure there's something like that," I said. "Why don't we at least think about and discuss what would happen, *if* we were able to pull it off." That seemed like a very nonthreatening way to approach the idea of his going back. All I asked him to do was discuss it.

"Uh, let's see. They toss me back in Haven and add years to my sentence in Hell…"

"Or, you'll get your sentence commuted, like what happened to me."

He nodded, thoughtfully. While I was enjoying the warmth and pleasantness of being so close to him, he said, "It's a nice thought, but there's no guarantee they'll let me go. Even if I give them the one thing they want. Remember, I'm in for manslaughter. You're in for slapping someone with a fish."

"I'm not sure that's the only reason I was there."

His eyebrows shot up. "Is there something you're not telling me?"

"Yeah, but only because I'm just finding out about it myself. This is going to sound totally stuck up…"

He laughed. "I know you, Genevieve. You're not stuck up."

"I'm glad that's how you feel, because I don't think I'm stuck up either, but listen to this… Apparently I'm some kind of super-witch or goddess or something. My parents were afraid of me—especially when I started doing stuff without meaning to. They weren't able to suppress my powers. Even the Haven teachers couldn't. I just thought they had, so I didn't even try to use them. Pretty crazy, right?"

"That you wouldn't try to use something you didn't think you had? It seems pretty normal to me."

"No I was talking about that whole witch/goddess thing. Does that scare you?"

He grinned. "You've always been a goddess to me."

I could've melted like ice cream on earth.

"So anyway, as a goddess, what kind of superpowers do you have?"

"I'm just figuring that out. I've always been pretty good with locator spells. At least my aunt seems to think so. That has me wondering if I can locate Bossy Rando. Then I'll need your help to bring her in. I don't know how strong she is, but I do know how pissed off she'll be."

He nodded. "I totally understand that. But why me?"

"Well, she might see me coming, but she'll never expect *you*."

"So, you think that together, we might be able to grab her and subdue her somehow, then deliver her to Mrs. Whitehall. Except there's one big problem."

"Only one? What's that?"

"If I go back, will I land right back in my room at Haven with my powers suppressed? Or can you pop me out of there as soon as we arrive?"

"I'm not sure, but only because I've never tried it. I know you want me to take you to the mountains or something, but I don't want to do that. You'll be running for the rest of your life. I swear if you help me catch Bossy Rando, which will help everyone who's vulnerable to her attacks, meaning our friends, I'll help you anyway I can. If that means testifying at a new trial or just talking someone's ear off until they decide to give you a break…well, I don't know if I can guarantee the outcome, but I'll try. I'll try anything."

"Will you try because you believe in me? Or because you want Bossy Rando and you need my help."

I worried my lip. "Both?"

He smiled and said, "Deal."

I sat up straighter. "Really?"

"Really. If it's important to you to catch her, and you think we can do it together, I'm willing to go back and try it. I hope that will end my sentence, but if it doesn't, I won't hold it against you. You're right. I'm getting tired of being all alone. Even if I were hiding out in the mountains, I'd still be alone—unless you'd come to visit me there…"

"I'm going to live with my aunt in Arizona, and I have to get a job. So I doubt I'd be able to see you very much, if at all. So far I haven't discovered a way to be in two places at once. But when you're out—"

"You mean *if* I'm out…"

"I'm going to think positive. You should too."

"Oh, I should, should I?"

"Don't worry," I said softly. "I won't let anything

happen to you."

⚜

So, we came up with a plan—and oh, what a plan it was. I wanted to rub my hands together and laugh maniacally, "Muahahahaha."

But we had to be smart. I didn't want to hurt Logan in the process of transporting him off this plane of existence. I had never tried to take anything from Summerland back with me before, and I really had to know if my new boyfriend would survive the trip.

He gave me a bunch of bright blue flowers from Summerland's meadow along with a charm he kept in his pocket. We'd have to see if these items survived a relocation first.

But where to take them? Smartest move—take the items back to my hospital room. I could check on things there while at the same time testing a transport on inanimate objects, *before* trying that on a person.

I tucked Logan's protection charm—an arrowhead —into my pocket. It's funny, but I sensed it had come from Arizona. Nah, I told myself. I just had Arizona on the brain. Indians populated the whole country and most hunted with spears and arrows. It could have come from anywhere.

Holding the flowers from the meadow in my hands, I chanted the return spell three times, concentrating hard on my hospital room. I didn't know if I had to continue chanting more than once, but so far three times had worked so why mess with it?

Sounds of beeping in the background said I'd arrived. Opening my eyes, the first thing I noticed were the flowers. They hadn't wilted but they had lost their brilliance. They were the same color, but it was as if the flowers had been on a backlit screen, then suddenly became a print on matte paper.

Then I patted my pocket and smiled when I felt an arrow-shaped hard item in there. The stone had never been a brilliant color, so I doubted it would be one now.

I heard footsteps coming down the hall, so I quickly grabbed the tube I'd taken out of my vein and jumped into bed, covering everything with the blanket. I remembered the machine I'd had to turn off without sounding the alarm, and that had to be turned back on. So I concentrated on trying to do that. I heard a soft click and knew it was on again even though the numbers were facing away from me. Then I spotted the little finger thingy still dangling beside it. I grabbed it and clipped it back in place about half a second before a nurse rounded the corner and came into my room.

I breathed slowly and rhythmically with my eyes closed, hoping she would think I was sound asleep, check my machine, and go away.

Then I remembered the flowers. They were just

lying on the over-bed table where I had tossed them.

She padded around casually, as if nothing were amiss. Then I heard her enter my bathroom and it sounded like she was draining something into the toilet. Gross. Fortunately I had remembered to magically disconnect the urine bag before I went to Summerland. Showing up with that thing attached would have been real sexy, right?

Water running in the sink for a couple of minutes meant she was probably washing her hands. Soon she was on her way, and when I heard her footsteps fading down the hall again I open my eyes. The flowers were in a paper cup of water next to my bed. That was sweet of her to do that. It was good to know there were still sweet people in the world.

———

So, getting back to our plan. I needed a little help on this side or I had to hope I timed it just right. There were so many potential ways this could go terribly wrong...

I reached out with my mind and pictured Bossy Rando in all her disgusting glory. Remembering she was probably asleep, I tried picturing her that way as clearly as I could. Soon I felt the urge to go in a certain direction.

She was far away, but not too far for someone with

magical abilities. Heck, I had gone to Summerland and back. I could probably go to wherever she was. My astral body hung suspended over a city. A humongously long bridge spanned a major inlet. It might be Tampa. I could smell the ocean. Okay, let's hope she's in Tampa… How do I find her exact spot?

I wasn't sure how much could be seen by spirits from the other side, but I could try to consult Logan's mother. I think she would be happy to know Logan was willing to return and I would like to tell her that anyway.

I returned my consciousness to my body, got myself out of bed, making sure everything still looked as if I were there, except pulling the covers over my pillow so there wasn't a dent in it and no head.

I concentrated hard on reaching out to Logan's mom, Mrs. Holderness. I had to be able to speak out loud without being overheard, so I tiptoed into the bathroom and quietly closed the door.

Concentrating hard on our tether, I gave it a mental yank. "Mrs. Holderness?" She appeared almost immediately, sort of hovering in the shower.

"Did you want to see me, dear?"

"Yeah. I need to ask you something, and tell you something. First I'll give you the good news. If that's how you want to hear it…"

"Oh. It sounds like you have good news and bad news?"

"I don't know." I shrugged. "It could be good news and good news."

"Okay, then, give me the good news," she said, smiling.

"Logan is willing to come back, but only because I asked for his help with something."

She clasped her hands in front of her. "I'm glad to hear that, what does he need to help you with?"

"Well, we have a plan that I think might work to get him out of Haven. At least it got me out. It has to do with giving them what they really want. This teacher who was obviously more evil and psychopathic than anyone realized, tried to burn down the place. Then when that didn't work, she tried to blow it up. That's how I landed in the hospital."

She sighed. "I did see that, but there was nothing I could do. I felt a yank on the tether and I watched as they took you away to the hospital. I was relieved that you were still breathing, and I checked on you here in the hospital later on. I was very happy to learn you were recovering quickly."

I smiled. "Thanks. It's nice to know someone 'over there' is pulling for me." I used air quotes, although she probably knew what I meant.

"So, how can I help?"

"There are a couple of things… I'm pretty good at locating people, but to find the exact house I'm looking for I may need your help. So far I think the offending teacher is in Tampa. Can you confirm that? If Logan and I can find the exact spot, we can capture her, but first I have to find a way to subdue her. I'm kind of in the right place to find a tranquilizer dart, or something…"

She laughed. "Tranquilizer dart? I think you'd be better off at the zoo."

"You know what I mean. An injection of some kind that would knock her out. I figured Logan could distract her, especially since she thinks he's gone into hiding or is more likely dead since no one can find him. She'll be completely off guard for a moment, and that's when I sneak in."

"With the tranquilizer dart," she finished

"Exactly. Then we have to transport her all the way to Haven, which should take about two hours I think."

"And what are you going to transport her in?"

I shrugged. "I hadn't gotten that far yet, but I think I could probably hotwire a hearse and have her bound and gagged in a casket."

She leaned back and laughed. Thank goodness no one else could hear her, because it was one of her loud bursts of laughter that continued for several seconds. I loved hearing it though.

"Tell you what, I'll not only help you find her. I'll play lookout. How's that?"

"That sounds perfect. Now I have to find the drugs I need, and I think I can do that with my witchy powers."

"Oh, honey. That'll be tricky. I can manipulate elec-tricity to create a bit of a distraction and possibly unlock any doors you need unlocked. At least I can give it a try, but remember, hospitals have generators that will come on in seconds. You'll have to locate the exact place you need to be and get there quickly."

"I'm fast. I can do this. When you're ready, you can do your thing and I'll do mine."

"Be careful."

"I'll be okay with your help. Now you can probably see where the nurse is, right?"

"You mean nurses. There are two of them on this ward. Fortunately, or not, they're both at the nurses station right now. The drug cabinet might be behind them."

"How do you know that?"

Mrs. Holderness smiled. "I used to be a nurse. You didn't think I was always a spirit, did you?"

"No, of course not. Logan told me you had been on earth until he was seven. I guess you had to do some kind of job in that time."

"I was a full-time mom when Logan was little, but before I had kids I was a nurse. I had been planning to go back to work as soon as my youngest went to first grade. If you can get to the pharmacy you can get anything. First you need to know what drug to grab. You might have to deal with the security guard, if he's there at the wrong time, but that's all."

The bathroom door opened a crack. "Oh, that's all?" someone said sarcastically. "Well it sounds easy peasy, doesn't it?"

"Aunt Hilary?"

I was actually relieved she was here. Our plan wasn't a good one. We needed to think of another way to do this.

She pushed her way into the bathroom and shut the door behind her. "Honestly, Genevieve. What are you thinking?" She was whispering loudly, but I knew a scolding when I heard one. "You do realize you'd be thrown back into Haven for stealing drugs from a hospital, right?"

"But I'm working with Mrs. Holderness. She can blackout the unit long enough for me to get past the nurses and then I could take the stairs down to the pharmacy…especially if you can distract them when the lights come back on. I sense it's on the first floor down a long corridor. I can find it, I have to. We can't let Bossy Rando get away with attempting mass murder—twice, and she's probably just nuts enough to try it again."

Mrs. Holderness disappeared. "Wait!" I still needed her help. I didn't know which drugs to look for.

Aunt Hilary jammed her hand on her hip. "Hey, I did a lot of things that could have landed me in Haven before I got there, but stealing drugs wasn't one of them."

"What are you doing here anyway?"

"I wanted to pop in on you and see how you were doing. It's a damn good thing I did too."

"Look, I'm glad you're here, but not if you're going to try to stop me. With everyone's help I won't get caught."

She leaned against the door and crossed her arms. "What if I turn you in?"

I gasped, but still had to whisper our conversation. "You wouldn't."

"I should."

"But *you wouldn't!* Would you? Please…I need to get this done before the nurse comes back around."

Aunt Hilary's posture sagged. "Of course I won't turn you in, but only because you haven't done anything stupid yet. Now, get back into bed and let me come up with an actual plan. Something foolproof—because, honey, that plan's proof that you're a fool."

Ouch. I'd never been called a fool before, especially not by someone whose opinion mattered to me.

She opened the bathroom door and poked her head around to see if the coast was clear. Then she opened the door wider and pointed to the bed.

I guess I had to trust her. She knew how desperate I was to get this done, right? Logan's mom wasn't back, so I really didn't have a choice. I crawled under the covers and when Aunt Hilary finished fluffing the pillow I sank back onto it.

"Trust me, Genevieve. I promise I'll work on it, and I'll have a much better solution."

I sighed. "Okay. I trust you. When will you be back?"

"Tomorrow at the start of visiting hours. Can you promise to wait until then?"

"Yes. I promise."

She smiled and I knew she believed me. But did I believe myself? Waiting was never one of my talents. But I made a promise, and I'd keep it.

As soon as Aunt Hilary popped out, someone else popped in.

"Lake Pirate! How did you get here?"

"With a spell."

"But you're a—a…"

"A fuggle? No, I'm not. I think Bossy Rando worded her spell to affect teachers and students. I'm neither."

"Yeah. You were a spy."

He nodded.

I sat bolt upright. "You admit it?"

"There's no use keeping up the ruse now, is there? You're getting out. I was paid to watch you and report anything unusual while you were incarcerated."

"Paid…pretending to be my friend," I said with more bitterness than I realized I felt.

"I'm sorry about that. In all honesty I really did like you. It became harder and harder to remember where my loyalties were."

"Oh, boo hoo. How difficult that must have been for you."

"Look, I came here to check on you, not to ask for forgiveness."

I remembered that whole speech about love and forgiveness, but I just couldn't… Not yet.

"You seem really healthy," he was saying. "I'm happy you weren't…" He trailed off, apparently unable to put the worst into words.

"Blown to bits?"

He smiled a little. "Yeah. Look, I know I'm probably not your favorite person right now, but if you ever need a friend…"

He began walking toward me, slowly. Oh, no. He wasn't looking for a hug, was he?

He came close enough to touch, and extended his arms. "Truce?"

"I'll think about it." Then I shoved him as hard as my human strength would allow and he flew across the room, falling on his ass, but instead of crashing into the opposite wall, he simply disappeared through it.

"Yeah. I thought about it. No, we can't be friends. I can't trust you."

I guess he was smart, after all.

# CHAPTER 18

THE NEXT DAY MY WONDERFUL AUNT HILARY WAS THERE bright and early—well before visiting hours. She and my doctor walked into the room at the same time. I had just woken up and was about to sit up and stretch. Then I realized I was fully dressed and the doctor wouldn't be expecting it. Oh well, I could always say I was more comfortable in my own clothes. That's not even close to a lie.

"How are you feeling, Genevieve?" the doctor asked.

"I feel one hundred percent. Seriously, I could go home today. If you'll let me."

"You are one lucky girl. I don't know how you managed to heal so quickly, but the nurses say you're doing very well. Just let me take a quick look at your wound."

*What wound?* I didn't even know I had a wound. It must've been there a couple days ago, but I hadn't noticed anything when I got dressed, except a bandage which fell off. I suppose it must've been under that. "Oh. You won't find anything. I looked under the bandage last night. I'm wound free." I said.

Aunt Hilary just put a hand on my tummy and said, "I think you'll find she's healing nicely, and we are perfectly capable of changing her dressings at the spa."

"Indulge me." The doctor peeled back the covers and raised her eyebrows. Then she smiled, knowingly. "You don't like our fashionable gowns?"

"Not so much." I grinned back at her. She seemed like an okay doctor. I unzipped my jeans and raised my shirt. Somehow my aunt Hilary had reapplied a bandage when she touched me. The doctor lifted a corner and nodded. "You're doing amazingly well. I'm satisfied that your aunt can take it from here."

She stuck the dressing back down and whatever she saw must've been Aunt Hilary's doing. Some kind of well healing wound spell must've appeared real to the doctor, since I didn't see a thing.

"Can she come home with me today?" Aunt Hilary asked.

"I don't see why not. You can always bring her back. If something opens up or starts looking red or swollen…"

"I'll definitely keep an eye on it," she said.

"Okay. I'll send the nurse in with the discharge instructions."

Ah, yes…discharge instructions. I suppose we have to put up with those, but I really was itching to get out of there. Aunt Hilary gave me a wink, and I knew she had something up her floppy, embroidered sleeve.

As soon as the doctor left, I lowered the railing and threw my legs over the bed. Feeling fine, I jumped off and gave my aunt a hug. We both giggled.

"I'm free to go, I guess. You look like you have a good plan, and I'm dying to hear it. When can you tell me more?"

"We can talk freely after we get you out of here, but let me just say a magical solution has presented itself, and may be a much safer way to deal with another magical than waiting for a drug to kick in."

"Of course. I did think of that, but on TV you always see someone getting an injection and collapsing a second later. I figured Mrs. Holderness would know what kind of injection could do that." I didn't know how powerful Bossy was, if she could fight off the effects, or if I could even deal with her magic to magic.

Aunt Hilary grinned that knowing grin that I like so much.

"We have a secret weapon. We just have to find her, first."

Find *her?* Who was she talking about? Then I remembered… Somewhere I had a twin sister and apparently together we were unstoppable.

"Are you talking about my twin? Do you know where she is?"

"I am, but I don't know *exactly* where she is. I've narrowed it down and I'm reasonably sure you can follow her DNA since it's so close to your own. You should be able to locate her that way."

"Follow DNA?" I opened my closet and took out the cardboard box Mrs. Whitehall brought in last night. My meager belongings consisted of mostly T-shirts and jeans. How strange that my whole life fit in a box the size of a microwave.

"Here, I'll take that." Aunt Hilary grabbed the box I was about to lift, and I wondered if I really needed to be treated like an invalid.

"Are we ready to go?" A nurse said as she breezed in, carrying a clipboard.

Now I saw what my aunt was doing. She'd be looking pretty neglectful if she didn't lift heavy things for me right now.

"Here are your discharge instructions…" The nurse went over the items on her clipboard, checking off the boxes when she was sure we understood everything about wound care. Then she handed us a bag containing a few packages of sterile dressings and some tape. "Keep it clean and dry. Watch for any signs of infection, like redness at the incision site, drainage, swelling, pain…"

"We will," we both said at the same time and smiled.

The nurse nodded. "Well, the last thing is to get you a wheelchair and bring you downstairs. I'll have an aide come back with that in a minute."

I rolled my eyes. Aunt Hilary was probably reading my mind, because she said, "It's policy. You have to get in the chair and let them take you to the door. Probably some insurance regulation..."

I sighed. There were so many unnecessary things that fuggles had to do, it made me feel sympathetic for them all the more.

In about ten minutes someone showed up with a wheelchair and took us to the driveway. I knew what kicked to the curb meant, but it was more of a gentle nudge. I remembered to stand up slowly, even though I wanted to jump out of the chair and pop into Aunt Hilary's car the minute she pulled up in her dusty jeep. My belongings were already in the back.

"How did your car get so dirty?"

"I live in the Arizona desert, remember?"

"You drove all the way across the country?"

She laughed. "Of course not."

"Holy Sh... I have a whole lot more to learn, and I'm glad I have *you* as my teacher now." I was never so relieved as when we drove away, to who knows where...

"Are you sure you're up for this?"

"What choice do I have? You say, my sister is somewhere up in these hills and somehow I'm supposed to sense her through our DNA. It seems unlikely, but sure. Your itching is driving you crazy. Knowing that is driving *me* crazy. I don't really have another choice, do I?"

Aunt Hilary had been racking her brain, trying to come up with a way to figure out where my twin had gone. Adoption records were useless, because my parents didn't go through a normal agency. There was some kind of magical community that placed magicals with other magicals. It made sense, of course. What fuggle wants to adopt a kid who suddenly starts flying around the living room?

So we were coming up to a large paved road that branched off from the pebbled road my aunt lived on. It looked as if we'd be taking the scenic route up until then. This was an actual paved two lane highway. We were able to drive a little faster, but still under the speed limit. No one else was on the road, so we could go pretty much any speed we liked. She kept glancing over at me.

"What?"

"Do you feel anything?"

I paused and tuned in to my body for a moment and waited for some kind of tingle, and when nothing happened I just shrugged. "Nothing, yet."

"Okay, be sure to tell me if you're drawn in any particular direction, and I'll look at GPS to get us there."

"What if there isn't a road?" That was probably a silly question to ask her. But what if there *wasn't* a road? I somehow got the feeling that she was high up in these mountains and maybe in some kind of cave. That would be weird, right? "Are there any towns around here?"

"You mean like places with a large population like Phoenix or Scottsdale? They're about an hour away in the other direction."

"No, I mean little towns. Even ghost towns. I don't see anything around here."

Aunt Hilary looked off in the distance. "I know. It's pretty desolate out here. But there are occasional settlements along the river. There's even a place that looks like a lake, and that has some buildings near it.

"Is there a dam on that river?"

She glanced over at me and her brows lifted. "A dam? Are you having a vision of a dam?"

"Um, yeah. Not a big thing like Hoover Dam, but just a small one with a little waterfall flowing over it. I mean it's not hooked up to hydropower or anything, but it's man-made…"

She smiled. "You are amazing. You don't even have to close your eyes to see these things."

"So, there is something like that around here?"

"I think it's about an hour north, but yes, and we can get to it from this road."

"Awesome."

We drove on in companionable silence for several miles. Eventually something started to tingle. It began as just kind of an itch on my right cheek. And then I noticed it traveling to my chin and then my collarbone... "Aunt Hilary? That tingle you were talking about..."

"Yes. Do you feel something?"

"Maybe. Or maybe I just got into some poison ivy." I started scratching my cheek and collarbone.

She laughed. "Well, if it points to any particular area that's not your skin, aim me in that direction."

I tried to separate the tingling in my skin from whatever was drawing me out there and I finally latched onto something. Can you take a right up here?"

Aunt Hilary glanced at her GPS and said, "Yeah. I think I see a road coming up around the next hill. There was indeed a very bumpy dirt road that led down a steep hill.

"Is this it? Should I take this right?"

"Yeah. I think so. We're supposed to go to the right and yet I don't see anything in front of us but hills."

"Well, down below us is that dam you were talking about earlier."

"Wow. So I guess that formed in my mind for

reason. Or let's hope it did. This feels like a wild goose chase, you know."

Aunt Hilary sighed. "I know. I hope this will bring us all together, but I have no idea if it will or not. I had the feeling she was reaching out to me through the lightning strike on my back years ago. But I didn't see it as a map at that time and I just dismissed it. I wish I hadn't."

"Can you pull over and stop for a minute?"

She looked at me concerned. "Are you okay?"

"Yeah. I'm fine. I just want to see something."

She pulled off to the side and even though we were stopped on an incline, it seemed plenty safe with her emergency brake on. So I climbed out and came around to her side.

"What are you up to?"

"I want to see the mark on your back. Can you lift up your shirt and lean forward so I can compare it with the GPS?"

"Yeah, that's a good idea."

When she lifted the back of her blouse I examined both the map on the dashboard and the map on my aunt and they were identical. Little offshoot roads here and there. Not many, but in the exact same spots, and in the exact same patterns, squiggles in the same places and everything. "Hey, this is it. This is the exact match on the GPS that your back shows. The only thing is when I feel that tug toward something it's not going downhill it's straight across." The two of us studied the hills off in the distance and the place we were headed toward. The road definitely led to a river valley, surrounded by high hills and some of them showed dark spots that might've been caves.

"Good Lord and Lady, do you think she could be living in one of those caves?" Aunt Hilary asked.

A weird feeling came over me. My brain kind of spun a little. My stomach felt sick. I just leaned on the Jeep's hood and took a few deep breaths.

Aunt Hilary put her hand on my shoulder. "Are you okay?"

"Yeah, I am. But I'm not sure she is."

"Oh, dear. I hope we're not too late."

Late? What could we be late for? I had to rest for a minute then set this feeling aside and get back in the car. There was nothing around us—nothing to give us a clue about what I was sensing. It was just some kind of ominous feeling, and that could be my own imagination.

"Well, we're not getting anywhere by sitting here," I said, "so now that we think we know where we're headed, let's go."

Aunt Hilary checked the GPS and said, "Okay. It looks like this road goes down to that dam. Let's check it out and maybe we'll find someplace to get lunch."

We bought a couple of take-out sandwiches since that was the only option at the Damn Dam's General Store. Yeah, that was the name of the business. As we ate I got the feeling someone was watching us. It could have been anyone. They didn't get many tourists here.

When we were finished, I glanced across the dam. "I'm afraid I'm being drawn that way." I pointed across the river and then up.

"Up in the hills?"

"Yeah. I don't see any roads, do you?"

"Nope. How sure are you?"

"Pretty sure."

Aunt Hilary tipped her head up and shielded her eyes as she scanned the surrounding hills. "So, I guess we're going climbing?"

Ugh. Were we really going to follow this tingle? Knowing how much Aunt Hilary wanted to stop the itch on her back, I decided it wouldn't kill me to get a little exercise. Besides, if I had a sister up there, I wanted to meet her.

We wiped off our hands and threw the trash in a barrel beside the General Store. We weren't exactly dressed for climbing, but at least I was wearing my trusty old sneakers. Aunt Hilary was carrying a cross-body purse and wrapped the strap around her waist, then knotted it.

"Wow. Instant fanny pack."

She gave me the hairy eyeball. "And I assume you're okay with it since it's carrying my wallet, keys, sunscreen and an extra bottle of water."

"Yeah, yeah. I'm sorry. I'm not exactly a fashion-plate myself."

She produced the sunscreen and we both slathered some on. As soon as our hands were no longer slippery we walked across the concrete footpath which was built about five feet above the rushing water.

On the other side, we stopped to study the terrain. There weren't a lot of options. No ropes or handholds to help the average climber... Fortunately we weren't average. "We have to make it look normal, right?"

Aunt Hilary smiled. "Yup. No Spiderman webs shooting out of your fingers, I'm afraid."

"We can't even ride our brooms?" I joked.

"Nope. About the best I can do is firm up the earth and anchor the vegetation so we have something to hold onto."

"Great," I droned sarcastically.

"Unless you have a better idea."

"Not really, no." I grabbed the first few tufts of scrub brush and pulled, making sure it would hold me. Yup. It felt secure. "Okay, here goes nuthin'."

We hadn't climbed very far before we had an audience. Nobody called out to us, they just came out of the buildings and watched. It was a little creepy.

Suddenly an arrow whizzed by my head. Aunt Hilary let out a startled squeal and let go, sliding down the hill a few feet.

The crowd laughed. *Laughed!* What kind of sickos lived around here anyway?

I looked over my shoulder at my aunt, who appeared unhurt, and then at the peanut gallery, still snickering, until one of the older guys yelled, "You obviously don't know about the crazy girl living up there in the caves."

Oh, I knew all right. My DNA tingled harder with every foot of progress I made.

"Aunt Hilary? Are you okay?"

"Yeah. I'm fine."

"What do we do about this? She obviously doesn't want to be found."

"So why did she send me a damn map?"

I wasn't sure if she was talking about the map of the dam or cursing the whole experience. I'd put my money on cursing.

I backed down to where she hung on, so we could talk in a normal voice. The sound of the rushing water would obscure our conversation from the fuggles. "Want to go on?"

She hung her head and hesitated. She must have been weighing the pros and cons. Eventually she pondered aloud. "We can shield ourselves from the arrows with a protective circle of energy. But will the fuggles think it's suspicious if the arrows bounce off an invisible surface?"

"Uh, yeah. Probably."

She sighed. "I suppose we could come back after dark…"

I wasn't a fan of that idea. I wanted to get this over with. Every minute we delayed was another minute Bossy Rando had to come up with a new plan to destroy Haven—and I still had friends there.

"What are the odds that she's just a really bad shot?"

Aunt Hilary laughed. "Not good. If she's been living like a free range teenager for a few years, she can probably hit a rabbit at fifty paces."

"Do you think she knows she's magical?"

"I have no idea. We really need to find her and talk to her. We don't know how long she's been up there. She could die if she doesn't know how to conjure what she needs."

"So, do you think we could sneak up on her in the dark?" I asked.

"Do you think you can find her in the dark?"

I sighed. "Probably. Whatever DNA we share is telling me exactly where she is now."

"And she's probably sensing exactly where you are. This is more dangerous than I figured, Genevieve."

I sensed Aunt Hilary was on the verge of giving up. Part of me wanted her to, and the other part of me really wanted to meet my twin.

Another arrow whizzed by me, and soon after that another one flew toward Aunt Hilary. "Oh no you don't, asshole!" I yelled and batted the thing away before it hit its mark.

The fuggles cheered.

"Well, I'm glad we're providing such riveting entertainment," I said.

Aunt Hilary rolled her eyes. "We really need to come back later when we don't have an audience."

"Agreed."

No more arrows flew at us as we backed down the hillside and crossed the footbridge. She must not have wanted to waste her ammunition—or she was only trying to scare us. Or both.

## CHAPTER 19

That evening, after taking a short nap in the car, we stretched and popped the kinks out of our bodies.

"I have an idea," I said.

My tired aunt brightened. "I'm all ears."

"If she does come after her arrows, we can be lying in wait for her."

"But what about her sensing us?"

"I'm not sure if it's possible, but do you think I could separate my energy from my body and send it in a different direction, then maybe sneak up behind her as she's going the wrong way?"

Aunt Hilary thought about it. "That sounds really difficult, and risky. I'm not sure it's something we should attempt. We'd need a well-worded spell for that. It's not natural, and The Goddess may not even allow it."

I crossed my arms and tried to come up with a

rhyming spell I could use. Poetry wasn't my forte. Maybe I could leave that up to Aunt Hilary, but she didn't even bother rhyming. "Do you think it needs to rhyme? They taught us to rhyme at Haven."

Aunt Hilary smiled. "I know they did. That's to get the The Goddess's attention. Since we're kind of like minor goddesses ourselves it's easier for us to get *The Goddess of All* to listen. So about rhyming? I don't think we have to."

"Whew. I'm terrible at rhymes. So okay. What should I say? Please move my energy away from my body to attract my sister away from me?"

"I don't know, that doesn't seem quite right. How about…Please shield my energy from other beings. May I appear invisible, until I'm ready to reveal myself."

"Oh, yeah. I never thought about an invisibility spell and containing my energy to sneak up on her without being seen. That makes more sense."

"She seems like a smart one. We're going to have to be smarter."

I nodded.

"It's dark now and I don't think anyone is around. Let's start out with shielded energy and invisibility…or should we wait until we're ready to climb?"

"I thought we weren't bothering to climb this time. We're just going to wait for her to come for her arrows."

"If she hasn't already."

I was dying to get out there. Something told me she was on the move. "Let's try the whole invisibility and energy shielding spell now just to be sure she can't sense us coming. We can hold hands so we don't lose each other."

"Good idea."

We jumped out of the car, meeting in front of it. Holding hands, together we chanted "Goddess of all, hear us. Our intention is pure and requires your help..."

Aunt Hilary continued on her own. "Please shield our energy and image from all sentient beings, until we ask you to return us to our natural state."

Together we chanted, "If it be your will, so mote it be."

"I guess that'll do it." I squeezed the hand I felt in mine, even though I couldn't see my aunt or even sense her. I moved forward.

Still holding my hand, she walked with me. "Can you hear me?" I whispered.

"Yes."

We crept quietly down to the footbridge and crossed it. I spotted an arrow and pulled on my aunt's hand, indicating that she should come with me. I didn't know if we could be overheard, since we forgot to ask The Goddess for the opt-out of audio option. We just asked her to shield our energy and our images. Since The Goddess is notoriously literal, she hadn't bothered to shield our voices. Just as well…as long as we didn't scream.

I spotted movement above us. Glancing up, I saw a figure in the dark advancing expertly down the hill. I guess shielding my energy from her also shielded hers from me, because there were no tingles—but there she was.

As she came closer I was able to make out her features in the moonlight. I can't tell you how shocking it is to see your own face, but dirty and gaunt. Her hair was longer than mine and stringy. And the clothing? Well, it had obviously seen better days. The pants were filthy, ragged and looked like she had outgrown them a while ago.

As she came closer I managed to come up behind her, still holding Aunt Hilary's hand. I knew I was going to have to let go of my aunt at some point because even though my sister looked skinny, I imagined she was strong. She had to be to shoot those arrows and climb that hill. Eventually I was so close, I could smell her. *Peuwww.* I don't think she had bathed in a while.

I let go of Hilary's hand, grabbed both of my twin's arms and said, "Gotcha!" and quickly added, "Goddess reveal us!" The whole time I was struggling to hold her. As soon as Aunt Hilary came into view I saw that she was hugging my sister's legs, so she couldn't run. We wrestled her to the ground, and both of us held her there while she struggled and grunted.

"It's okay, we're not going to hurt you." Aunt Hilary's voice was more soothing than mine, so I let her do the talking.

"Please, stop struggling. If you calm down we can let go and talk."

I felt her arms sag and her muscles relax. Eventually Aunt Hilary let go of her legs and I let go of one arm, keeping my hand around her wrist. She was so thin, my thumb and index finger touched. My heart went out to her. How many days had she gone hungry?

I decided to introduce myself. "I'm your sister Genevieve. What's your name?"

She stared at me, but said nothing. Aunt Hilary introduced herself but my twin kept staring at me. I think she was as surprised to see her doppelgänger as I was.

"Can you speak?" Aunt Hilary asked.

"I… I remember how."

*Remembered* how to speak? That means she's been up here for a while. When had Aunt Hilary experienced that lightning strike? Four years ago?

"How long have you been here?" I asked.

"I don't know. A long time."

"How did you get here?" Aunt Hilary asked.

"My mother took me here."

She must've been talking about her adoptive

mother. I couldn't imagine my mother taking her and dropping her off in the middle of the desert. My parents weren't cruel, just neglectful and distracted."

Aunt Hilary was rubbing her legs soothingly. "Where is your mother now?"

She hung her head. "She's with the great spirit."

That sounded like a Native American expression. I wonder if she grew up with the indigenous people from this area? I guess we could get the whole story later. The important thing was to get her cooperation, now. Aunt Hilary seemed like the best person to do that, so I stayed quiet and kept a firm but gentle grip on her wrist. Then I thought, it's probably been a long time since she's had a hug.

"May I give you a hug?"

She leaned back and stared at me. "Why?"

I smiled, or tried to despite my anxiety. "I didn't know I had a sister until recently. I've been excited to meet you. I hope we'll be good friends."

"Oh. I didn't know I had a sister, either."

Aunt Hilary sat back and smiled. I guess we were bonding. I could only hope…

"My name is Tawania," my sister said.

We were having this surreal conversation in Aunt Hilary's kitchen. We had magically transported her here, not knowing if she'd change her mind during the long car ride. She was understandably hesitant to come with us, but seeing her obvious twin helped, I think.

As Aunt Hilary set three cups of herbal tea on the table and sat down she asked. "How did you wind up living in the mountains?"

Tawania took a sip and groaned. "That's good."

I didn't know if she was avoiding the question or just enjoying her warm beverage. Either way, we stayed silent and waited for her to offer more information.

"I was raised by a powerful shaman."

"Like Native American shamans?" I asked.

"No. They weren't Native Americans. My father was a witch, like you, but I think he just liked the word, 'shaman' better.

Aunt Hilary nodded. "There are plenty of new-agers who call themselves shamans. It's probably just semantics."

"Yes. When my father died, my mother didn't feel safe anymore. I don't know why. She moved us to the town on the river and worked at the General Store. She kept talking about how someday we'd live off the grid. When she didn't have to work, she took me up into the mountains and taught me how to hunt."

"She must have done a terrific job, because I thought for sure you were going to kill us."

She smiled, slyly. "If I wanted to kill you, you'd be dead. I just wanted you to go away and leave me alone."

"Did you know who we were?" Aunt Hilary asked.

"No. My body was tingling, but I thought it was telling me I was in danger. Now I know my twin and I can sense each other that way."

"Did you reach out to me four years ago, by any chance?" Aunt Hilary turned around and lifted her blouse, exposing the map. "With a bolt of lightning?"

Her eyes widened. "No. I would never do that. Besides, I didn't know about you. Perhaps my father sent the lightning when he knew he was dying."

Aunt Hilary nodded. "That makes sense. He would want someone to look after you. Maybe he knew about your birth family."

"Maybe." She took another long sip of her tea and smacked her lips.

"Would you like to take a shower?" I asked. "Not that you're stinky or anything. I just figured you might like a hot shower instead of a cold river."

"I would like that," she said.

Aunt Hilary rose, "Let me show you where it is. Meanwhile maybe Genevieve can find some clean clothes for you to wear afterward."

"Sure. No problem," I said. In my room all I'd have to do is pick out one of my t-shirts and a pair of jeans, then shrink them down four sizes. While I was at it, I magically removed the nice queen bed and conjured a bunk bed instead. She'd have no problem climbing to the top bunk, and maybe we could conjure a skylight over her head, so she could sleep under the stars. I didn't know if she'd be staying, but I hoped she would.

When Aunt Hilary and I converged in the kitchen, she leaned down and whispered, "I'm so glad we found her. I think she needs us more than she's letting on."

"I wouldn't say that to her though. She seems proud."

"Agreed."

"Aunt Hilary, I need to go for a walk. This has been a lot to take in."

She nodded. "Don't be too long. I think she feels calmer, around you."

"I won't. Maybe half an hour?"

"Yeah, that should be okay. I can deal for half an hour. I'll just pretend she's you." She winked.

I stuck my hand on my hip and gave her a smirk. "Very funny."

Outside I immediately walked around to the back of the cabin, remembering where the invisible room was so I didn't accidentally bump into it. That would be embarrassing, having a big thump from the back wall giving away my plan.

As soon as I reached a discrete spot in the woods, I whispered the spell to visit Summerland.

I felt and smelled the place before I opened my eyes. The air smelled flowery and fresh. Like when my mom used that 'April Fresh' fabric softener. There was always a soft breeze here too. In my head, I kept trying to liken it to a real place on earth, but there's nothing exactly like it. Dull down the colors and it could be some beautiful spot in the wilderness...not that I had been to many places like that. One summer we visited a few National Parks for educational purposes. That's the closest memory I had to this.

Logan came striding toward me. He had a lopsided grin on his face. When he reached me he gave me a big hug and kissed me. "I was hoping you'd come back soon. I missed you."

"I missed you too, but to be honest I've been a little busy."

He took my hand and we started to stroll through the tall grass of the meadow. Even the grass felt softer against my legs than normal grass would. Just for the heck of it I kicked off my shoes to really feel the grass under my feet. It was as silky as I imagined.

"So, what kept you so busy?"

"We found my sister. Or, maybe I should say she found us."

"I thought you didn't have a sister. You said you were an only child." He leaned away from me, scrutinizing me, as if he'd caught me in some kind of devious lie.

"I didn't know about her until very recently. It turns out I have an identical twin, named Tawania. I guess her name was Joy when we were infants, but she was given up for adoption and her name was changed. That's a whole story too, but one thing at a time.

"I don't remember if I told you about my aunt's weird scar on her back. She got it during a lightning strike about four years ago. It turns out that my twin was raised by a shaman/witch and he may have reached out with what he had to draw a map to my sister on my aunt's body. Lightning."

Logan sat down cross-legged in the grass and pulled me down facing him. He held both my hands. "No shit? Really?"

"Really."

"So, what does that mean? Is she going to live with you and your aunt?"

"Hopefully. She's…a little wild. She was living alone in the mountains, hunting for her food."

His jaw dropped. And then he grinned. "Wow. I thought that might be cool to try, but she actually did it."

"Yeah, but I don't think you would look good losing 40 or 50 pounds, wearing clothing you outgrew years ago and covered in dirt."

"That's how you found her?"

"Yeah. Pretty much. I was able to sense her because we're twins, and the only way to get to her was to climb these steep foothills, so we tried and then wound up dodging arrows."

He laughed. "I can just see it. Obviously you're okay,

because you're sitting here with me, but how is your aunt? Is she okay?"

"Oh yeah, she's fine. In fact, she thinks I'm out for a walk. I told her I would be back in a few minutes. I just wanted to check on you and tell you we have this possible secret weapon against Bossy Rando."

"Secret weapon? Your twin?"

I bit my lip, not knowing if I could speak for Tawania or not. She didn't have any stake in this and could easily say no. But I had a feeling she might actually enjoy the hunt and capture of a 'bad guy'. "Possibly."

"So how would we go about this? Does your aunt know about the plan?"

"Yes and no. I told her what had happened with Bossy and she understands the importance of getting her either into a magical jail or committing her somewhere magicals can be treated for mental health issues. I'd say she needs both."

"Yeah. I'd say so too. So, do you think I could visit your place in Arizona? I should be completely safe getting there. Right?"

"I haven't tried to take you anywhere yet. I got the flowers back to the hospital without killing them and your charm is okay. So I'm guessing it'll probably work, but is *probably* enough? I really, *really* don't want to kill you."

He chuckled. "I know you don't, Genevieve. Or

should I call you Fish Face, and then you might not be too afraid of killing me?"

I laughed. "Let's walk and talk a little more. I think we could spend some time coming up with a solid plan, and then I'll have something to present to my aunt and sister."

Logan leapt to his feet and extended his hand to help me up. We walked hand-in-hand. I took a good look around, knowing that once he left here, there would be no reason to come back. He glanced over at me a couple of times.

"What?"

I shrugged. "Do you think you'll miss it here?"

He looked thoughtful as he gazed around the area. "Yeah. But if I can clear my name and spend more time with you, it'll be worth it."

"You're willing to come back to Haven and clear your name?"

"I'm willing to try. If they won't consider letting off their number *two* most wanted magical criminal for capturing their number *one* most wanted, then I might take off. I just can't spend my life in prison."

I nodded. "I get it. But I'm going to operate under the assumption that your contribution to her capture will be enough to show you've changed. That's what they needed from me, so I imagine that's what they'll need from you too." *If not, I'll come up with another plan.*

He draped his arm around my shoulder. It was as if

he couldn't get enough human contact. Not that I minded...at all.

"So, how are we going to run this sting on Bossy Rando?" he asked.

"I think you're still the best one to surprise her. You're taller than she is, and she knows you broke out of Haven. That automatically gives you some intimidating bad boy cred."

He laughed. "I guess it does, doesn't it? I never thought of myself as a bad boy, but I kinda like it." He growled at me, and we both laughed.

"Okay, so you're the one who's going to confront her first. Maybe you'll have time for a quick incapacitation spell. If not, I can get my twin on board, and with one of us on either side of her, we can hold her and you can prevent her from running. Seeing double trouble will shock her even more. Then my aunt can covertly approach her from the back."

"With what? Another spell?"

"Yeah and a Taser. She might have protection from others' magic in place."

"Do you think a Taser will do it? It might incapacitate her for a few seconds, but how are we going to get her all the way back to Haven?"

"I actually spoke to your mom about that. She said she would be the lookout and I think I can arrange transportation for us."

His brows rose at the mention of his mom. "She's going to help us?"

"Yeah. She kinda likes you and wants to see you get out of here. Even as pretty as it is, it's nowhere to spend the rest of your life."

"You're right. Being alone and talking to myself is getting old."

"Great! Then we're agreed. I'll pop back to my aunt's place now and tell my sister what's been going on. Hopefully she'll trust me enough to let me drag her into this. According to my aunt, we're more powerful when we're together."

"If not, don't pressure her. It sounds like she's been through a lot. Maybe we can do this without her."

I cuddled up next to him. "That's one of the things I like about you."

"What?"

"You think about other people and what they might be feeling and needing."

"Yeah. And sometimes I'm wrong."

I looked up at him, trying not to act as shy as I felt. "You're not wrong about me."

He didn't respond, but on the other hand, what could he say, exactly? Clearing my throat I refocused myself to the important mission at hand. "So are you ready, Lawless Logan?"

He took my hand and smirked. "I'm as ready as I'll

ever be, Fish Face. You're sure the flowers made it okay?"

"Yeah. Oh! Your good luck charm. You should probably have that." I dug in my pocket until I found the arrowhead and handed it to him. Oddly enough it seemed brighter, possibly because we were in Summerland or maybe it just got polished in my pocket. Either way, he was happy to see it and tucked it in his pocket with his free hand.

"Remember, everything will seem much less colorful and bright. Even the air smells less fresh. Not that my aunt's house smells bad. It doesn't. It's just that you might notice the lack of this fabulous fresh air."

"Okay. Let's go before I change my mind."

We held hands as I recited the spell and pictured my aunt's little cabin. I was hoping we wouldn't surprise them or anyone else. So I pictured the two of us in my room. It had been empty when I left.

On the third recitation, I held on tight and concentrated really hard on the guest room in my aunt's cottage. I had replaced the Queen bed with bunk beds, and I tried to picture it exactly the way it was when I last saw it, bunk beds and all.

I heard a scream.

"It's okay. We're not going to hurt you!" Logan said.

I opened my eyes and saw my twin sister soaking wet wearing only a towel, scanning the room frantically, probably looking for a weapon to throw at

Logan. I got to her just as she picked up the lamp and wrestled it out of her hands.

"He's okay. He's with me. You don't have to worry. He's one of the good guys."

"I thought I was a bad boy."

I gave him the stink eye, then refocused on my sister. "No one here to trying to hurt you. He's here to help us."

She gradually relaxed but maintained a ready stance, glancing back and forth between the window and the door.

Aunt Hilary burst in. "What's wrong?"

"Aunt Hilary, this is Logan—the boy I was telling you about."

She scrutinized him and hesitated. "From Summerland?"

"That would be me," Logan said with his charming smile.

Finally, she approached with her hand out. "Nice to meet you, Logan."

"Same here. I've heard great things about you."

"Nothing I have to live up to, I hope."

She smiled and he grinned. Tawania seemed to relax as well. *Thank the Goddess!*

I took a moment to revel in my own accomplishment. I had done it. I had transported a person from Summerland to an entirely different place than the one he had come from.

And now I hoped he would stay. For that matter, I hoped my sister would stay. There was a whole lot riding on people deciding to cooperate. And, selfishly, I hoped everyone would stay. I finally had people I loved who could love me back.

# CHAPTER 20

I DIDN'T REALLY HAVE TO WORRY. AFTER EXPLAINING TO Tawania the lengths Bossy Rando had gone to, trying to poison the inmates, set fire to the facility, or just plain blow it all up, she was completely on board. I remembered that Logan's mother offered to help, so I called on her too. Happily, she was able to appear to all of us and speak through her own mouth, even though her voice sounded a little tinny and far away.

"What do you need, dear?"

"We were just brainstorming how we could capture that dangerous teacher...well, after we find her. I haven't really located her house yet, but I'll probably be able to find the exact location once I really concentrate and astral project there."

"What does she look like?" Mrs. Holderness asked.

"Oh, yes. It might be good for everyone to know that. She's kind of on the thin side, her skin color is sallow, kind of pale yellowish, and I think she's a smoker. She has stains on her fingers and her teeth."

"Don't forget about her wild red hair," Logan said.

"Yes, short red hair, frizzy, and it curls around her ears. She never wears jewelry in it though."

"Jewelry?" Logan asked.

"You know, barrettes, headbands or combs—nothing like that."

"Oh, sure. Now I know what you mean."

"Is she apt to be alone?" his mom asked.

I shrugged and looked to Logan.

He shrugged back. "I'd have to be really desperate to live with someone like Bossy Rando," he said.

"You never know," Mrs. Holderness said. "There's a lid for every pot."

I laughed. "I haven't heard that one, but I get it. So, she might not be alone. How can we check that out first?"

"I can," Mrs. Holderness said.

"Of course. You're a spirit, so you can go anywhere."

"Aren't you glad you invited me?"

"I didn't even have to tug on your tether."

"I did," Logan said. "I knew this was going to be dangerous, and I figured she would warn us if we were walking into a trap."

*Trap?* As far as I knew no one was luring us anywhere. Although I guess people don't always know when they're being lured. She could be holed up somewhere with a million wards and snares surrounding her. Come to think of it, that's what I'd do if I was wanted for attempted magical murder.

"I sense we have to move fairly quickly. As soon as we know where she is and that she's alone, what will you do?" Mrs. Holderness asked.

"We'll have to wait until she's vulnerable and then move fast. The element of surprise might shock her into just enough hesitation for us to capture her," Aunt Hilary said. "If not, we could all be in trouble. We have to catch her without her wand handy. Wands can harness and direct energy."

I'll bet Aunt Hilary was picturing getting another scar, only this time on her stomach.

Logan cracked a smile. "We could get her while she's on the toilet," he said.

We all burst out laughing.

"He has something there," Aunt Hilary said. "Not on the toilet, but in the shower. If she doesn't see us coming, we can grab her then wrap her in the shower curtain and use that to keep her from getting away. Do you think that might work?"

"That sounds like a good possibility," I said. "But if we use a Tazer to subdue her, we could electrocute her in the shower."

"I can help," Tawania offered. "I can use a poison tipped arrow. I used to have to do that to bring down large dangerous animals."

"Good thinking," Aunt Hilary said. "What do you need for that?"

She reached her hand out and her quiver of arrows appeared. "I'm all set."

*Huh. I guess she does know how to use some of her magical abilities.*

"Since it's morning in Florida now, it beats waiting until she's sound asleep, even though that would be good too," Logan said.

"Yes, time is of the essence," Mrs. Holderness said. "She may be coming up with a new plan as we speak."

"I have to find her right away, then," I said. "We can't let her get away."

Aunt Hilary held out her hands, "Everyone stand in a circle and grasp each other's hands—tight. Genevieve I want you opposite me holding onto Logan and Tawania on your side. I'll hold onto them on my side…"

I nodded, knowing what she was getting at. Two who knew how to use their super-witch powers would be safer to transport the other two, who might get scared as we fly through three time zones. If either of them let go, one of us would be holding onto them.

We formed our little circle and Aunt Hilary looked at me. "Do your thing, Genevieve."

I closed my eyes and followed the energy that I identified as Bossy Rando's. It was weak at first, but we were far away. I could find her more quickly alone.

I open my eyes and said, "I need to go alone first.

When I find her, I'll come right back and then bring all of you with me."

"I don't want you going anywhere without me," Logan said. "Someone needs to be with you to protect you."

Although, that made me feel all warm and fuzzy, and it was wonderful that Logan wanted to be the one to protect me, I had to explain further... "I'll be right here in body. I'm just going to astral project to her location, and then I'll be right back. I mean in body *and* mind, instead of just my body."

"As long as she can't hurt you." Logan squeezed my hand before he let go.

I smiled at him and took a step back. Closing my eyes, I concentrated on where I thought she'd be and planned to latch onto her energy from there.

I did get a Tampa vibe and mentally cruised the Florida Gulf Coast. Soon my astral body was dragged to a dicey spot where I wouldn't have expected her to reside. Although I could see the privacy it afforded, and who knows what kind of crazy stuff she'd want to shield from the fuggles, the place was butt ugly. Maybe that was her way of making the place so uninviting that no nosy fuggles would want to drop in.

Her house was more of a run-down cabin. Some woods backed up on an industrial park, and those businesses were her only neighbors. Her place was about a hundred yards into the woods and only reachable by a footpath. Her car was probably one of the few in the parking lot. There might be more cars there later on, but it was early morning. This could be a good time to find her in the shower. Just in case we were too late to catch her there, I wanted to peek without tipping her off. Since I wasn't actually there in body, I could descend through her roof, but would she pick up on and recognize my astral energy?

The only way I knew how to check without the possibility of getting caught was with Mrs. Holderness's help. I tugged on the tether and her voice came through whispering in my ear, "Do you need me, Genevieve?"

Thank goodness I was reminded to whisper in case Bossy Rando had the ability to hear spirits or astral projections. "Yeah. Can you be the scout until we're here in body?"

"I'd be happy to."

"I need you to take a look inside and see if the woman we described is in there and see if anyone else is with her."

"You got it."

She disappeared and returned in literally two seconds.

"The woman you described is in there, and she's alone. That's good, right?"

"Perfect, I'll get the others. Can you wait here for us?"

"Of course. I'll keep watch and let you know if she wakes up or comes outside. Now where are you going to land?"

"I don't know. I'd like to take everyone to her living room, but we'll have bodies reforming and I don't know if the others have the power to go through walls. Some of us could make quite a crash landing. Where was she when you saw her?"

"She was in her bedroom still asleep. Why don't you land on the roof as lightly as you can, so you don't disturb her? If for some reason she hears something and looks out a window, you won't be discovered. I'll let you know when she's in the shower and you can all quietly float to the ground and tip toe in the door."

"As long as my aunt and I can disarm any wards that sounds like a good plan. I don't know how long I'll be, but I'll get back here as soon as I can with the others."

"Good luck."

And with that I returned my energy to my body and open my eyes. The other three were chatting and stopped as soon as I raised my head.

"Did you find her?" Logan asked.

"Yes, and with your mom's help we know she's alone and in bed."

"Perfect. I hope we can catch her in the shower."

I glanced at Tawania, whose hair was still wet. Now we just have to hope Bossy's someone who cares about her hygiene.

I looked at Aunt Hilary's wall clock, knowing it was later out there. "It's almost five o'clock here, six in the next time zone, seven in Tampa. She's not an early riser, I guess."

"She may be waking up soon, though." Aunt Hilary said, "We should get going."

We formed our little circle. Aunt Hilary holding onto Logan and Tawania's hands. His and Tawania's other hands holding mine. I felt an enormous power building. Aunt Hilary nodded to me and I closed my eyes.

"Hold on tight!" I had transported one person, but not three. Hoping everyone had power enough to make this work, I concentrated extra hard and went for it.

Halfway there I realized I'd forgotten to tell them to bend their knees to minimize the noise when we landed on Bossy's roof. To make sure we didn't blow our element of surprise, I pictured all four of us landing in a tree that bent over her roof.

"Ooph."

"Ouch," Aunt Hilary muttered as she straddled a large branch and glared at me.

"Hey, was this the landing you were going for?" Logan whispered.

"Sorry. I meant to land on her roof, except I forgot to tell everybody to step really lightly. We don't want to tip her off."

Tawania must've climbed trees before because she

was already halfway to the ground, with her quiver of arrows on her back.

"Wait for me," I whispered loudly. Logan uttered a spell under his breath and jumped, landing on the ground safely. Aunt Hilary floated down.

"Show off," I whispered.

She grinned at me.

"So now what?" Tawania asked.

"Mrs. Holderness?"

"I'm here. You want me to check and see if she's in the shower yet?"

"Yes please, meanwhile all of us should stay out of sight of the windows and the Industrial park across the way. People will be arriving for work soon, I imagine."

We tiptoed over to the side of the house that was blocked from the parking lot, crouched under the windows and then waited. And waited, and waited...

"I kind of thought your mother would be back by now," I whispered to Logan.

"I thought so too. I wonder... Never mind." I noticed worry lines etched across his forehead.

"Relax, she's probably just waiting until the coast is clear."

"I hope so."

Mrs. Holderness appeared and all of us were able to see her. At least we were all looking in the same direction...

"She just stepped into the shower. Can you go in without making any noise?"

"I can transport us right outside the bathroom door, I think."

Or we could just walk in the front door, extra quietly," Logan said.

"She probably has it warded. I wouldn't try it." Aunt Hilary said.

"Oh, yeah. I guess I would do the same thing, if I were an evil maniacal witch," he whispered.

"Let's reform our circle," Aunt Hilary said. "Genevieve and I can transport us inside."

The four of us held hands and in the blink of an eye we were all standing in Bossy Rando's living room. I didn't take us there. Aunt Hilary must have.

We followed the sounds of water, and found what had to be the bathroom. Aunt Hilary counted on her fingers, so she didn't have to speak, she held up one, then two, then three, then she threw open the door. Tawania had her bow drawn and let the poisoned arrow fly.

*Damn!* The shower had a glass door and it bounced off. But the shock factor was all we needed. We rushed in as Aunt Hilary removed the glass with a wave of her hand and grabbed Bossy's wrist. At first, Bossy laughed. Then she struggled and screamed obscenities at us.

Logan grabbed her around the knees and lifted her

off her feet. I quickly grabbed her other hand and the three of us got her facedown on the floor. Tawania picked up her poison-tipped arrow and poked her in the back with it. We then trussed her up like a turkey with magical twine.

She laughed. "You think I can't break this thing?"

"Try it," Aunt Hilary said.

She mumbled a few words under her breath and pulled. It held. She pulled harder and harder. Nothing worked. I was never so relieved!

Mrs. Holderness whispered in my ear, "You're ride is waiting."

"Let's take her out the back door and transport her to Haven."

The four of us carried her still wiggling but hopelessly bound naked body outside where a hearse and driver sat idling.

"Perfect." Logan laughed, now that we didn't have to whisper. The rest of us giggled.

"You didn't say you were going to kill me," Bossy Rando said.

"We won't, unless you make us." I quipped.

Tawania's eyes sparkled. "Can I run her through with a spear? I can't understand why my poison didn't work."

"No, no spears. We're going to try and take her alive to face the justice she deserves."

Bossy started to scream, but Logan made a zipping

motion and her noise ceased. Finally we reached the hearse and she looked defeated. I guess she decided that staying alive was more important than being a pain in the ass all the way to Haven. Or…maybe the poison from the arrow was finally kicking in.

We opened the back of the hearse, rolled out the coffin, opened it and threw her in. Aunt Hilary slammed the cover shut and placed her hands on the seam saying, "Hold tight, magical locks. Let her not escape from this box."

"Oh, and give her enough air for us to get her there," Logan added. He shrugged.

He was about as good at rhyming spells as I was, but I'm glad he thought to add that. We did agree we'd try to bring her in alive.

He shoved the coffin back into the hearse, slammed the door, and all of us piled in. Aunt Hilary and I sat on the black bench seat next to a very confused looking driver.

"Where am I taking you?"

"Haven."

His eyebrows shot up. "Did you say—"

"We'll give you directions." I conjured a GPS unit, typed in the address and handed it to him.

He looked at it and whistled. "That far away?"

"Yeah, all her old friends want to pay their respects. That's where they are."

The gentleman shook his head slowly, as if his

whole morning had been a blur. It probably was. *Someone* transported him here. Okay, I admit it. The whole hearse thing was my idea and I was kind of proud of myself.

As he pulled out of the parking lot, Logan tapped me on the shoulder.

"Nice work, Genevieve."

"Thanks, Logan."

Then he proceeded to rub my tense shoulders. It felt so good, I groaned aloud. "You could do that professionally, you know."

Aunt Hilary turned around. "I might know of a certain spa looking for a good masseur. Of course you'd have to train for that first."

I could only hope that meant she was inviting him to come to Arizona after he had finished clearing his name.

## CHAPTER 21

WHEN WE REACHED HAVEN AND PULLED THE COFFIN OUT of the back, Bossy Rando finally called out with a question.

"Hey, which one of you little basket cases turned me in for leaving the library door unlocked and unwarded?"

My eyes widened in shock, and I looked at Logan who was wearing the same expression.

"You left the door open, on purpose?" Logan asked.

"Of course I did," she yelled from the coffin. "Did you think I'd *forget* to lock it? I was going to see which one of you little fart-heads would try the door and smuggle out some sort of contraband. Then I could tip off the guards who'd search everyone's rooms and whichever one of you did it would get caught."

"And add months or years to the kid's sentence," Logan said, through gritted teeth.

I shook my head. I guess I'd turned in the right person for the right crime after all. How weird is that?

"So where the hell did you go?" Bossy Rando asked Logan.

"Wouldn't you like to know?"

We carried her coffin into the facility and deposited her right on Mrs. Whitehall's desk.

The administrator jumped up and backed away with her mouth open. "What is this?" she demanded.

Aunt Hilary jammed her hands on her hips and said, "This is your criminal. Caught and wrapped up in a nice magical bow," she said.

"Are you telling me you killed Bessie Randall and brought her coffin here?"

Maniacal laughter came from inside the coffin.

"Ah, no," I said. "She's very much alive in there. I thought you might want to bring her to justice, since she was the one who left the library door open on purpose, made us all sick, tried to burn down the place, and last but not least—blow us up!"

She glanced between Tawania and myself. Then she narrowed her eyes at Tawania. "And you are?"

"Who do you think I am?" she asked as she slid over right next to me.

Mrs. Whitehall glanced between the two of us and finally let out a defeated sigh. "Oh good Goddess... There are two of you."

I couldn't help but chuckle. Then she pointed at

Logan. "And you, young man... Where did you go and how did you get there?"

Logan tipped his head and smiled. "I'll make you a deal," he said. "I'll tell you where I went and how I got there, if you'll commute the rest of my sentence. You want to see change? I was part of this group who delivered your criminal teacher on a silver platter—or actually in a satin-lined wooden box—with enough air to breathe to keep her alive."

"Get me out of here!" Bossy Rando demanded.

Mrs. Whitehall just shook her head. She plopped down in her office chair and looked at the four of us. "I'll have to speak to the board about this."

"How long is that going to take?" I asked.

She sighed. "The next meeting isn't for a week."

"Can't you call a special session?" Aunt Hilary asked.

Mrs. Whitehall rubbed her temples as if a migraine was coming on. "Yes, I suppose I should. I can't leave Ms. Randall in this box for a week."

"Great," Aunt Hilary said. "If you need us as witnesses we will all be at my cabin."

"Mr. Holderness will stay here," Mrs. Whitehall stated, not as a request. It was an order.

I glanced over at Logan.

He shrugged. "I can stay here a few days. As long as I get a fair retrial, and just so you know, Mrs. Whitehall, the whole reason I'm here is because I was defending myself. The guy I was fighting was huge and trying to beat the snot out of me, like he did his daughter. When he was on the ground and tried to get up, I just kicked his chest to keep him down. I didn't smash his head into the pavement repeatedly as the prosecuting attorney said I did. Check the autopsy." He folded his arms and jutted out his chin.

I interjected my two cents. "Since Logan delivered your problem teacher right to you, I think you should pardon him completely, just as you did me. By coming back here, he has demonstrated his willingness to do the right thing. You can see that, right?"

Mrs. Whitehall closed her eyes and remained quiet for a few seconds, as if she were praying for some kind of guidance.

"I can discuss that with the board. I'm sure I can make them see reason. Then she focused on Logan. "And you, young man will tell me what happened. That's our deal, correct?"

"That's what I said, and I won't go back on our agreement."

"I'm happy to hear that," she said.

From inside the coffin Bossy Rando called out, "Hey, I want to know where he went and which spell he used to break out too."

"Shut up, you!" Mrs. Whitehall yelled at the coffin. I took a step back. I had never seen her lose her temper, I didn't think it was possible. But I guess she's only human-ish.

She focused on Aunt Hilary. "Ms. Howe, is that still your last name?"

Aunt Hilary nodded. "Yes."

"I'm expecting you to keep a close eye on this one." She pointed to me, of course. "And you will return with her when I call. Can I have your word on that?"

"Absolutely," Aunt Hilary said.

I couldn't have been more relieved. She was going to let us go and then I remembered my promise to Logan...

"Mrs. Whitehall, I would like to speak for Logan at his retrial."

Mrs. Whitehall shook her head. "That won't be necessary."

"Why not?"

She focused her gaze at Logan. "I can speak for him. I do believe that both of you have accomplished what we set out to do. And that is to see you change enough to make good decisions, stand up for what's right, and prove you can be trusted to use your magic that way."

"And you believe that I've achieved that?" Logan asked.

She nodded. "I'm confident you learned your lesson. We'll just have to discuss where you're going to go and who's going to look after you."

"I can go back to my dad's house in upstate New York. Or... I hear there's an opening for a job in Arizona," he looked between me and Aunt Hilary.

"Ms. Howe, is this something you would be in favor of?"

"I'm the one who suggested he take a job at the spa," Aunt Hilary said.

Mrs. Whitehall crossed her arms. "Well, I will have to call his father and ask him to get here as soon as possible. We need to hear what he would like to see happen." Addressing Logan she added, "You're not yet eighteen, so he's still responsible for you."

Logan sighed. "That's true. Then he looked at Aunt Hilary. "Do you think they'll hold that job for me? I turn eighteen in a month and can start training then."

She smiled. "Whenever you're ready."

Mrs. Whitehall looked at each of us in turn, and then focused on Logan. "You can return to your room. I'll make the arrangements for the board meeting and your father's attendance."

"Can I say goodbye to my friends first?" he asked.

She nodded.

He hugged Tawania who stood stiff, but didn't push him away. "I hope to see you again, Doppelganger," he said. Then he hugged Aunt Hilary and whispered in her ear. "Thank you, for everything." Then he came over to me and smirked. "I'm going to miss you most of all, Fish Face."

I couldn't help laughing. Then he grabbed me and hugged me hard. I hugged him back just as hard.

"Okay you two, break it up," Aunt Hilary said. But

she was smiling, so I knew she wasn't upset. Logan backed out the door, giving us one last sad wave. As he disappeared down the hall, I prayed to the Goddess we would see him again.

"Ms. Howe…"

Both Aunt Hilary and I answered "Yes?" at the same time and then giggled.

"I was speaking to your aunt, Genevieve. In fact, maybe it would be better if we spoke alone."

I looked to my aunt for her preference and she shrugged. "Is it okay if they stay? If it has anything to do with my being here twenty years ago, they're aware."

Mrs. Whitehall nodded. "As you wish. I was going to tell you I am proud of who you've become. You were pretty mixed-up there for a while, but I'd like to think you rose to the occasion and overcame the challenges you had at the time. You'll make an excellent role model for these young women. I'm going to recommend you for Elder status."

Aunt Hilary gasped. "An Elder? You think I'm fit to become an elder? I thought… Well, aren't I a little young for that?"

"Age has nothing to do with it. A certain amount of maturity may come with age, but there are no guarantees older witches are better suited to guide us. I believe you have achieved the kind of maturity needed to guide the next generation."

Mrs. Whitehall turned into teaching mode, holding her hands behind her back, pacing slowly. "It turns out that growing into elderhood is like becoming a self-actualizer. Wise elders are self-actualized people.

"According to Abraham Maslow, self-actualization is everyone's overall aim. He says, that the more we learn about our natural tendencies, the easier it will be to learn how to be a good person, how to be happy, how to be fruitful, how to respect ourselves, how to love, and how to fulfill our highest potential. Have you heard of Maslow's hierarchy of needs?"

"Yes, of course," Aunt Hilary said.

"I haven't," Tawania said.

I didn't even realize she'd been paying attention, but she seemed to be acutely interested.

"Picture the hierarchy of needs like a pyramid. You need to build upon the foundation before the next layer can be added. Then when that group of needs are achieved, the next layer can be attempted."

I wasn't picturing a pyramid. I was picturing a German chocolate layer cake. Yum.

Mrs. Whitehall continued on. "The base of the pyramid is physiological needs. Things like food and water. Warmth and rest."

Tawania nodded. I'll bet for her there were times when even those basic needs were tough to achieve.

"What's the next layer?" she asked.

"Safety and security."

"And next?" Tawania asked as if checking off the list. Apparently she felt her arrows and spears took care of the safety problem.

"Next is belonging and love. Intimate friendships."

She hung her head. "Oh," she said softly. "I guess that's where my layers stop."

I draped an arm around her shoulder. "Don't be so sure."

Aunt Hilary slipped her arm around Tawania's waist and gave her a side-squeeze. "You've got us now."

Tears sprang to my sister's eyes. Aunt Hilary enveloped her in one of her long, warm hugs. I rolled my eyes and said, "Aw, heck…" and wrapped myself around both of them, surrounding my twin in a loving group hug.

Mrs. Whitehall didn't even know the circumstances but her eyes glistened like she was thinking about shedding a tear or two.

When we finally parted and stepped away, Tawania reached for my hand and smiled. I happily grasped it and we held hands for the rest of the conversation.

Aunt Hilary sighed. "If all goes well, I imagine these two will help me with the next level. 'Self-esteem and a sense of accomplishment.'"

Mrs. Whitehall smiled. "I certainly hope so, but whatever happens with them I hope you'll never lose sight of the many things you've accomplished already."

Mrs. Whitehall turned to me and Tawania. "The last

and final step—the top of the pyramid—is called self-actualization. It's when a person achieves their true potential, including their creative best."

"I imagine that's a long way off for us," I said.

"Most young people have a ways to go before getting to that level, but that's as it should be. Right now you're just finding your way."

Considering I wasn't sure what I wanted to be when I grew up I couldn't argue with that logic.

"There's one more thing I want to leave you all to think about. Maslow suggested practices that can help lead us toward self-actualization. Be your own person. Don't conform just to fit in."

I took a good look at my beloved aunt. Her bohemian clothing was out of style, but she didn't care. She wore what she liked. Her hair was done in whatever fashion was practical at the moment. Down and flowing when she wanted to look nice or in braids, a ponytail, or up in a messy bun to keep it out of her way when working or gardening. She took care of others with her knowledge of massage, herbs, and natural medicine and continued learning, even studying Eastern practices like acupressure Reiki and reflexology.

"Do you have any last minute advice for me before I get these two home?" she asked.

"Sure. Since you asked..." Mrs. Whitehall smiled. "Experience life fully. Listen to others with an open mind. Know yourself by listening to your body, your reactions and intuitions. Be honest and take responsibility for your feelings and actions. Dare to follow your own path. Basically, keep doing what you're doing... And try to have more peak experiences. You'll know what those are, because you will feel at one with the universe."

"Oh, is that all?" Aunt Hilary said and snapped her fingers. "Piece of cake." And we all laughed.

Eventually Aunt Hilary heard from the Elder's council. I wondered if Mrs. Whitehall was part of it, but I forgot to ask. Oh, well. It didn't really matter. Regardless of what the council decided, Tawania and I would have our very own 'Elder' to guide and teach us about our powers, as well as when and how to use them.

Aunt Hilary had said she really didn't care if she achieved elder status or not. She was happy doing what she was doing and might not want the responsibilities that came with the title. Meanwhile Tawania and I were on our own for a while. We had all kinds of home-schooling homework to do. But it was nice to have a study-buddy.

"What do you think Logan's doing right now?" Tawania asked.

I glanced at the clock on the wall. "Let's see... It's

ten o'clock here, so eleven o'clock Central time, and noon Eastern. He's about to eat lunch."

"What did you eat for lunch there?" she asked. "I'll bet it wasn't raw fish or rabbit."

"Raw?"

"Sometimes. Depended on how hungry I was."

My stomach churned whenever she talked about her former diet. But the processed food we got at the detention center wasn't much better. "No, we had sandwiches with processed meat and cheese. Might as well put a pile of salt between two pieces of cardboard."

Her laughter bubbled up from her diaphragm and spilled over, making my heart glad we'd found her.

"Can I meet our parents sometime?" she asked out of the blue.

Shock momentarily silenced me. "Why would you want to?"

She shrugged. "I don't know. I'm just curious."

"Well, they're in Africa for a year. I guess someday we can go there and visit them, but I wouldn't without Aunt Hilary knowing about it."

"Yes. Of course," she said.

But it felt like she wasn't sharing everything. "Are you wondering why they gave you up?"

She looked sad, but didn't seem like she was going to cry or anything.

"Yeah. And why only one of us? Why not both?"

I supplied the other unasked question for her. "And since they kept one of us, why was it me and not you?"

She nodded.

"Well, Aunt Hilary said some stuff that made sense…kind of. I guess together we were more powerful than they could handle."

"But there were two of them and they're adults."

"Yeah, but sometimes even adults are easily overwhelmed. They're not mean or bad people. They just have different priorities than raising children. I guess it's a wonder they kept one of us."

"Aren't they teaching children in Africa?"

"Yes, and adults too. I guess it's different when you can spend a couple hours with them and then send them home for someone else to worry about the rest of the time."

Her posture sort of slumped, but I think she understood.

"Don't worry," I said to her. "Everyone is happier this way. Plus we'll visit them sometime. We'll have to give them plenty of advanced notice, so they can get used to the idea."

"What would happen if we just popped in? The two of us?"

I tipped my head and thought about it. I could see my mother's eyes bug out of her head, and she might forget to breathe for a minute—which would lead to her having to lie down—which would lead my father to taking care of her and ignoring us. I shook my head. "Nothing good could come out of a surprise like that."

"Okay. But do they even know I'm alive?"

"Yeah. I'm sure they do. Aunt Hilary wouldn't hide anything like that from them…for long."

"What does that mean?"

"Nothing. Just that it's been a busy few days. Between finding you, capturing a magical criminal, having two kids dropped in her lap, and at the same time keeping us educated and out of trouble, plus having to go before the elders…I imagine she hasn't had a moment to think about it."

"True. Should we offer to help her?"

"How?"

"Before my mother got sick, I helped her at the General Store."

"What did you do?"

"I got cans and stuff out of the back storage room and refilled shelves. They wouldn't let me near the cash register though. And I couldn't be there when my mom wasn't working. I was just a kid, plus I'm pretty sure they just didn't want to pay me."

"Well, I don't think we can help Aunt Hilary with massages or dispensing natural medicine. We'd probably get arrested."

She laughed. "Yeah, and that wouldn't help her at all." Then she became pensive. "But I still feel like I should do something to earn my keep."

"Why? We're kids. Our job is to do our schoolwork and stuff."

Tawania shrugged. "I'm not used to that. When my mother couldn't work anymore, I helped her by hunting and fishing and preparing our food."

"Well I don't want you to go hunting or fishing. Someone at the spa might see you and have a fit because you killed something." I glanced around. "I guess we could help clean up the place."

She smiled. "Yes. That's something we could do."

I went back to my book, and while I read about X+Y=Z, I snapped my fingers and the room sparkled with cleanliness.

She giggled. "How did you do that?"

"Magic. You can do it too. Did you know that?"

"I knew I was good at some things. If I pointed my arrow toward a bird and told it that I needed to feed my mother, my arrow would go straight to its heart. If I wanted to catch fish and there were no fish nearby, I chanted like my father taught me. Fish would swim right up to me. I didn't even need to use a fishing pole or bait a hook.

"I'm learning more about magic every day, just watching you. But your Aunt—I mean *our* Aunt doesn't want us using magical means to get what we want."

Tawania was still getting used to being part of our little family. "She just doesn't want you to do any magic where we can be seen. But we're all alone today. No one is even apt to come here since she had to take a couple days off to go to…well, wherever the elders hang out."

"I'm here," a tinny feminine voice said.

"Mrs. Holderness? Is that you?"

"I'd say 'in the flesh,' but, well…you know."

I smiled. She was making a joke.

"I just wanted to let you know that Logan is getting out of Haven. He'll be home with his father and brothers tomorrow."

I jumped up from the table and whooped. "That's great! And nobody will be looking for him? He got his retrial?"

"Nobody will be looking for him. They took a look at the whole case again and decided due to the nature of the fight and because it escalated to a situation where he had to defend himself or presume he'd die— even with his magical abilities, he was innocent and his record was expunged."

"Expunged? What is that? Wrung out, like a sponge?"

She giggled. "Pretty much. It means erasing something unpleasant completely."

I jumped around and pulled Tawania up out of her seat so she could bounce around like a loon with me.

The lock clicked in the door and Aunt Hilary walked in. She took in the scene of Tawania and me holding hands and grinning.

"What did I miss?" she asked.

"Mrs. Holderness just told us that Logan's being expunged!" Tawania said.

Aunt Hilary's eyes widened. "He's what?"

"His *record* is being expunged," I explained. "His retrial found him innocent."

"I didn't think he even had a retrial," Aunt Hilary said. "I spoke to his father a few minutes ago."

"Oh! What did he say?"

"Just that the whole unfortunate incident was looked at again and the verdict was overturned. A whole new trial would have taken so long he'd have aged out of Haven before it happened."

"I guess that's even better then. He didn't have to sit on the stand or anything."

"How do you sit and stand at the same time," Tawania asked.

I chuckled. "It's another thing you don't need to know yet. Maybe you never will. If we pay attention to our powers and don't let our minds wander, we should be okay."

I winked at Aunt Hilary and she smiled back.

"So what did they say? Are you going to be an elder? Do you have to go someplace else to do your job?"

"Like sit on a cloud or something?" Tawania added.

I could have asked more questions, but I'd just end up babbling and I was anxious to know what was going to happen to her…and to *us*.

"Relax, girls. I'm not taking the job."

"You're not? Why not? Didn't the interview go well?"

"It went fine. In fact they wanted me to come back and go through some kind of test to prove I have what it takes. But I was more concerned about what it would take out of me."

"Oh. So you're not even going to try to go through the testing part?" Tawania asked.

"Not yet. I told them I'm doing important work right here, and maybe if I got sick of you two…" She couldn't keep a straight face and eventually cracked up laughing.

"Nice. So, *we're* the important work now, huh?"

"You bet you are." She hugged each of us in turn, then said, "Hey, let's take a walk. It's too nice to be inside."

"Give me five seconds to get my sneakers." I was more than ready for a study break.

"Let me see if I can do it in one," Tawania said. She closed her eyes, then pointed to her feet and said, "Sneakers."

Sure enough, she had sneakers on her feet. They were on the wrong feet, but it wasn't a bad start.

# CHAPTER 22

As we were walking, I thought I should bring up something that had been weighing on me for a couple days. I hoped it wouldn't create a problem. I didn't need a new one. Not that anyone needs problems.

"Aunt Hilary…"

"Mmm?" she answered. I could tell she was communing with the beautiful puffy white clouds, maybe finding pictures in them. At least that's what I would be doing—if I weren't concentrating.

"I wish I'd taken the opportunity to say goodbye to Just Jen and Alien."

Tawania's brows rose. "Alien?"

"It's a nickname. Long story. I'll tell you all about it later."

Aunt Hilary stopped walking. "Do you want to go back and say goodbye?"

"I don't know. Well, I do but I don't…"

She smiled with one side of her mouth. "Okaaayyy… When you decide what you want to do, let me know."

We resumed walking and I mulled it over a little more.

She glanced over at me a couple times. Finally she asked, "What are you afraid of?"

How did she know I was afraid? It was a stupid fear —one I would be embarrassed to admit. Finally I sighed, and said, "I'm afraid they won't let me out. That they'll say they made a mistake and I'm not really reformed."

She started to laugh and then quickly covered her mouth. "Sorry. I didn't mean to make light of your feelings. For what it's worth, your pardon is real. I signed the papers accepting you into my care."

Okay, that was helpful. Wish I had known that before. "In that case, yes. I would like to go see them on visiting day, just to say goodbye."

"I think that's a nice idea. Closure is usually a good thing."

"Usually?"

"Well, almost always. How's that?"

I shrugged. "I don't know much about closure. I didn't get to say goodbye to anyone at my old high school—not that I want to. I don't. My parents came to say 'Goodbye, we're going to Africa'… See you in a year, maybe."

Aunt Hilary cleared her throat. "About that…"

"Oh, no! They're coming back, aren't they?"

She looked a little shocked, but quickly schooled her features. "No earlier than planned." We strolled up to the edge of the ridge. Looking out over the landscape the clouds rolling by made soft shadows move across the ground. "What I need to tell you both is that I called to tell them about Tawania."

Tawania who had been looking at her feet snapped to attention. "Me? You told them about me?"

"Yes, and they're anxious to meet you. I was just realizing we could probably take care of both situations at once."

"How do you mean?" I asked.

"Well, I can transport Tawania to Africa and leave her for an hour or two with her birth parents and then take you to Haven to say goodbye to your friends."

I pondered that for about ten seconds. "Why would you stay with me and just drop off Tawania?"

"I think I should be with you, Genevieve. Then each of you has a responsible adult nearby."

*Whew.* "Okay. I just don't want to be left alone there with no way to get back if they've discovered a way to ground minor goddesses, or super witches…or whatever we are. We really need to come up with a name."

This time she didn't try to cover her laugh. "Just continue to act in a mature way and nobody will think they made a mistake."

Oh, sure. *I'll try* to do that. "I wasn't trying to wreak havoc before though. The whole 'fish to the face' incident was accidental."

"You've been able to keep stray thoughts from conjuring real things most of the time though, haven't you?"

"Yeah…"

"Well, there you go. The exercises they gave you were meant to discipline and refocus your thoughts. Also to see the positive potential in any situation. I can see the change in you. Can you recognize it in yourself?"

"Yeah, now that you mention it. I guess my time there wasn't totally wasted."

"Of course not. They wouldn't let me take you, if they weren't confident in your ability to learn and grow. You might make a mistake or two along the way, but you'll correct it quickly."

"I will?" I couldn't hide the smirk.

"Oh, you naughty witch."

Suddenly I heard a deep 'ahem' throat-clearing behind us.

I whirled around and came face-to-face with a familiar grin. "Logan!"

We gave each other a tight, but quick hug and then he stepped back and pointed over his shoulder. "My dad's coming down the road. I just couldn't wait and ran ahead."

Okay. I guess that's why I didn't get a kiss or longer hug. But I wasn't complaining, I'd take whatever I could get since I wondered if Logan was just here to say goodbye and get closure.

"What are you doing here? Other than visiting me, of course…"

"Of course," he said. "I was also wondering if I need to set up an interview or something. I'll be turning eighteen soon and my dad agreed that getting a job for now and saving some money for college later might be a good idea. So, I'm thinking about taking a gap year."

Tawania tipped her head like I do sometimes. "Gap?"

"Yeah, it's when somebody has a gap in their education. They just work for a year or travel or something. Before they go to college."

She nodded. "Okay, that makes more sense than what I was picturing."

"Like working at The Gap?" Logan said and smiled.

"No. I just saw you straddling a huge gap in the landscape."

"Do you have visions?" I asked her.

"Yeah. Lots of times, but I don't always know what they mean. They're kind of metaphorical."

Oh, wow. She knew the word 'metaphorical'. Maybe it won't take her that long to catch up.

Logan must have thought she was teasing, because he raised one eyebrow and looked to my aunt. "Anyway, I'm just wondering if there's something I can do around here without special training—just for a while. Something that might pay enough for me to rent a place and still save money. I'm not too proud to get dirty."

I was tempted to say he could always go to Summerland and sleep for free, but I was pretty sure we were both done with that.

"Do you know anything about maintenance?" Aunt Hilary asked.

"I helped my dad fix things around the house. Speaking of…"

Logan's father, or at least a man who looked like him but about thirty years older came strolling towards us. Sweat puddled on his brow and rolled down his cheeks. When he reached us, he said. "It's certainly hot here. Are you sure you want to work in this heat, son?"

Logan put his arm around my waist. "I'm sure. Dad, this is Genevieve."

He smiled at me and we shook hands.

"So this is the place?" he asked.

Aunt Hilary spoke up. "Not all of it. The spa is kind of hidden behind that ridge over there," she pointed.

I slapped myself upside the head. "Oh, I'm sorry. I should introduce you to everyone. This is my Aunt Hilary." They reached for each other's hands and something seemed to pass between them as they touched.

They each looked surprised, but quickly recovered. They shook hands and let go quickly as if stung.

Mr. Holderness glanced all around. "It's pretty, when you get past the heat. Lots more trees than I expected. And lots of hills. I kind of thought the Arizona desert would be sandy and flat."

Tawania spoke up. "Arizona has a lot more to offer than desert."

"Sheesh. I'm sorry again. This is my sister, Tawania."

Mr. Holderness glanced between the two of us. "You look very much alike."

"That's because were identical twins." She and I smiled at each other.

"Well, I wouldn't have guessed identical, but you're definitely sisters."

I knew we had to do something to either fatten Tawania up or skinny me down, if we wanted to pull off 'twinning' pranks. Frankly, I wanted to stay about the same, so I'd just slip some extra calories into her every once in a while.

"So, about that job," Mr. Holderness said. "Is that a real thing?"

Aunt Hilary smiled. "Oh, it's real. It may not be exactly glamorous, but if your son is willing to work hard and do physical, sometimes dirty, labor, he should be great."

"What you think, son? Does that sound appealing?"

He looked at me and said, "Very appealing."

I couldn't help feeling surprised and pleased at the same time. I honestly didn't know if what Logan and I had was only due to the circumstances of the moment —or if when everything went back to normal we'd ever see each other again. It looks like we might see each other quite a lot. That was very okay with me.

"Let's go back to my cabin," Aunt Hilary said. "I can get everyone a nice cold glass of iced tea and we can get to know each other better."

Mr. Holderness smiled. "That sounds great, but I have to get back. My youngest son is on his own."

I guess young boys are a little harder to leave unwatched than sixteen-year-old girls. Maybe Tawania would like to meet the youngest Holderness… No. She has to learn how to be a modern teenager first. Later we can figure out how much she knows about boys. That's a conversation I'm not looking forward to. Maybe I can get Aunt Hilary to give her the low-down.

"So when is your birthday?" Aunt Hilary asked Logan.

"On the 27th. Do you think I could pop by and bring some leftover cake with me?"

"I'll have a whole new cake for you, if you want," I offered.

He leaned down and kissed me on the nose. "Thanks, Fish Face. You can never have too much cake."

Then he and his dad waved and disappeared.

I settled into the visiting area with my aunt. Soon Just Jen and Alien burst through the door and ran toward me. Just Jen reached me first and we gave each other a long tight hug. As soon as she stepped back Alien threw herself into my arms and hugged me too.

"Oh my Goddess, where have you been?" Just Jen asked. "We were worried, especially when Mrs. Black-Hole said you weren't coming back."

"She didn't tell you why?" I asked.

Alien crossed her arms. "No. She just said something about you having completed your program, and we figured that meant you were reprogrammed. But we didn't know how or why. Maybe you were a cyborg."

"Spill it," Alien said. "What did you do? In other words, what's the secret to getting out of here?"

"Have a seat on the couch, and I'll tell you everything."

The two of them sat on the comfy couch and I pulled a chair over, so I could see both of their faces. They were so different, and yet in here everyone was in the same boat and differences made little difference.

"So, I knew if I could get Bossy Rando to stop trying to destroy the place, I could save not only myself but all of you too."

Just Jen reached over and squeezed my knee.

"Believe me, we all appreciate that. We knew you took a big blast. Some people thought you were dead and it seemed like the administrators were covering their collective asses. That's why we're so happy to see you."

I sucked in a breath. "You thought I was dead? And they didn't tell you differently?"

Alien laughed. "We knew you weren't dead. They said you were in a coma, but we didn't know if you weren't *still* in a coma. You sure looked bad when they carried you out to the ambulance."

I glanced over at Aunt Hilary, who was sitting far enough away that she may or may not have heard our conversation. She seemed to be studying her nails.

"My Aunt Hilary is a healer. She helped me through the worst of it, and now I'm going to be living with her."

Just Jen smiled and said, "I guess that worked out well. I know you weren't looking forward to going back to your school in Pennsylvania."

"You got that right. There's no one I really miss at my old school. No one I felt close to. I actually feel closer to the kids here. That's sad, right?"

They giggled and Alien said, "I don't want to answer questions when I get back home. Maybe I can spell them all to forget the thing ever happened."

"We understand." Just Jen said. "I'd do that too, if I knew how."

Yeah, they'd understand like no one else would. I

wouldn't want to go back to the place where it all happened and have to answer question after question about how a two foot fish got up my sleeve—especially since fuggles wouldn't believe the truth anyway. Or if they did, they'd want to use me for their own selfish purposes.

"So, you weren't dead and you weren't in a coma *and you didn't tell us?"* Just Jen said, accusingly.

I leaned back in the chair and shook my head at myself. Why would I assume the Haven teachers had told them everything? They're not usually known for transparency.

"It's okay, I'm here now and I can explain whatever you want to know. I really thought they would've told you more."

"Are you coming back to visit sometimes?" Just Jen asked.

"And how do we join you out there? That's what we really want to know," Alien added.

"I don't know what to tell you. I just asked to come back and say goodbye to you two. Is Lake Pirate still here?" I asked, out of curiosity.

"No, he left the day after you were blown up."

So I guess he really was there just to spy on me. I'm betting the administration knew how powerful I was and wanted an extra eye on me. I didn't want to freak out my friends with that little tid-bit. Time to change the subject. "Well, there's more I can tell you of interest."

"Tell us!" They both said, as if hungry for gossip of any kind.

"There's nothing interesting happening here," Alien added.

"I found Lawless Logan before he turned himself in."

Jenika's mouth dropped open. "Where was he?"

"You wouldn't believe me if I told you, but I can tell you he wasn't here. He wasn't hiding anywhere in Haven."

"I didn't think he could be," Just Jen said. "He was gone too long and they looked everywhere."

"Who's Lawless Logan?" Alien asked.

"Oh, that's right. He disappeared the day before you came. So you never met him. Well, you missed a great guy. He's doing well, though. He helped me capture Bossy Rando, and now they pronounced him 'reformed' too." I used air quotes around the word reformed.

The girls just rolled their eyes.

"Okay so we've got that news. Anything else?" Alien asked.

"As a matter of fact, yes. I recently learned I have a twin sister."

Both of their eyes widened. "You're kidding. You didn't know?"

"Nope."

"How the heck... What happened?" Just Jen asked.

"It's a long story, but yes. I have an identical twin, and I didn't know anything about her until a few days ago. My aunt and I found her living in a cave. She's still a little on the uncivilized side, but we're gradually introducing her back into society from the wild."

"Into captivity, you mean. That sounds...awful," Alien said.

"Why?" Just Jen asked.

"Well, if she was used to being wild it must be kind of difficult to have to do things others tell you to—just like here. To have no freedom when you're used to total freedom to do whatever you want? I kinda know how she must feel. I used to get away with everything."

I laughed. "I don't think any of us quite know how she feels. She was hunting for her food and sometimes eating it raw. Drinking out of the river and trying to stay clean without shampoo or soap..."

"Ick," Alien said. "So when you found her, was she disgusting?"

"Not really." I didn't want to embarrass my sister, even though she wasn't here. "But she was really skinny and still is. I think she's happy to be somewhere with a hot shower and three reliable meals she doesn't have to kill."

"So did she grow up like that? Raised by wolves or something?" Just Jen asked.

"No, apparently she was raised by a shaman and his wife. But they died. She had to take care of herself at an early age—like twelve or so. I'm still learning all the details myself. But she'll have quite a story when she finally makes the transition. Right now, it's like she's just growing up."

Jenika breathed, "Wow. Speaking of growing up, do you finally know what you want to do next?"

"I think I want to become a massage therapist. Or maybe an aesthetician."

"Doing facials and stuff?" Alien asked.

"Yeah. That sounds kind of nice, doesn't it?"

Alien laughed. "You know you have to pop zits if you're an aesthetician, right?"

"Ewww. But I could do it magically. If they have cucumbers on their eyes, they'd never know…"

They looked at each other and laughed. "Yeah, I guess. If it works for you…"

"I'll have to look into all the spa stuff and see what's involved. I'll be living at the spa in Arizona where my aunt works."

"Oh, that must be tough." Alien smirked.

"Arizona? That's so far away! I thought Pittsburgh and Detroit were too far apart to see each other much, but oh my Goddess, you're going to be on the other side of the country when I get out?" Just Jen looked disappointed but she wasn't about to show tears or anything.

"You can come and visit me. Can't you?"

"Maybe. I'm only fifteen right now, so when I get out of here I'll be sixteen. Maybe that's old enough. I just have to get permission so they don't think I'm a runaway."

"How hard will that be?" Alien asked.

Just Jen shook her head. "Not hard at all. It's just me and my step-dad and he barely pays attention to me when I'm there."

"So, you'll be closer to Haven West now, right?" Alien said. "Do you think you'll ever go there for a visit?"

Mrs. Whitehall strode in and said to her inmates, "I'm sorry to interrupt, but your dinner time is starting soon, and I need to speak to Genevieve and her aunt before they leave."

"Awww…" my friends said in unison. We rose and gave each other long hugs goodbye.

As soon as they left the visiting area Aunt Hilary and I stood shoulder to shoulder alone with Mrs. Whitehall.

"There's just one thing I need you to understand before you go, Genevieve…"

"Okay, what is it?"

"You're not to visit Haven again. I'm glad you had a couple friends here, but it's time to go into the real world and make healthy relationships. They still have a ways to go, so you shouldn't interfere with their process. And I'd highly discourage you getting together with any of our alumni after this."

Aunt Hilary looked over at me, as if expecting me to argue.

I was standing with my hands behind my back anyway, so I simply crossed my fingers and said, "Okay."

**SNEAK PEEK: LIVE AND LET
WITCH**

Look for Jenika's story coming soon!

Live and Let Witch
*by E. B. Lorow*

"WHAT DO YOU WANT?"

"I want what every kid here wants. I want my freedom and I want my powers back!"

"Well, that's not going to happen. What else do you want?"

I let out a deep sigh. "I guess I'll have a chocolate pudding."

The cafeteria woman retreated to the back of the kitchen and returned with a tiny plastic container of the requested pudding. *'Please sir, I want some more...'* The famous line from Oliver Twist ran through my mind as I took the tiny dessert.

"Here you go Jenniker."

My name is Jenika. Jen-EE-ka. For some damn reason, people insist on mispronouncing it to sound like Jennifer with a K and a Boston accent. As a result I wound up accidentally giving myself a nickname. "It's just Jen."

"Okay, Just Jen."

*Oh, yeah. That never gets old.*

"Some prize," I muttered as I dropped the pudding cup on my tray. I probably wouldn't be recommended for 'student of the month' again for a while, not that my stepfather would proudly display a bumper sticker on his car or anything. *My juvenile delinquent was named inmate of the month at the Haven School for Wayward Witches!*

Yes, they have the nerve to call us students here. We're inmates. Incarcerated in a juvenile detention center for magicals. That's what they call witches. It's as if someone said, "Let's get rid of all the negative connotations, so they don't know they're in witch kid jail. And while we're at it, let's have a real good laugh and call it Haven."

I dropped my tray with a clang on one of the tables. A long metal picnic-size table bolted to the floor with two cold benches attached on either side. Everything here is either nailed down, too heavy, or too awkward to lift. Goddess forbid some understandable frustration results in impulsive violence and injury since we're unable to use our powers—even to protect ourselves.

I hadn't quite sat down when fellow inmate Francine, also known as Alien, ran up to me and grabbed my hand.

"Come with me," she hissed.

"What?"

"Come on! I have to show you something."

Normally I'd be a little scared if any of these kids zeroed in on me and tried to drag me off, but I could probably take the willowy blonde in a one-on-one fight. She was some kind of pampered princess from Connecticut, and I was from the mean streets of Detroit. 'Nuff said.

I groaned when I thought about what might happen to my lunch if I left it untouched. "Can I eat first?"

"No. The surprise might disappear, and trust me, you don't want to miss this!"

"Shit," I muttered, grabbing my roll, which was the only thing I could eat without a spork—the combo plastic spoon and fork with tines too short to stab any vital organs.

I let her drag me out of the cafeteria and down the white cinder-block corridor to the front entrance of the building. "Look!" she said when we reached the glass paneled door.

I peered through the wire reinforced double paned glass. *What the...*Across from the curved gravel driveway rested a huge stone vat, maybe ten feet around, with a naked boy made of green copper, peeing a stream of water. The water ran over a scalloped edge pan and down the rocks, pooling into the bottom receptacle. "Is that a fountain?"

"Yes. And it wasn't there yesterday, was it?"

"Not that I remember."

"Do you know what that means?"

"Not really, no."

"Somebody in here still has their magic! We know the staff would never put that there. Right?"

"Yeah, I doubt it. Goddess forbid we drown ourselves."

"More like drowning our sorrows!" She almost jumped up and down. Then she glanced around and when she was sure we were alone, she whispered, "It's filled with vodka!"

I was momentarily speechless with so many questions vying to come out of my mouth at the same time. "How the heck did that happen? And how do you know it's vodka?"

"I tasted it." She glanced behind her at the corridor and waited a moment to be sure no one was coming. Opening the door, which was usually locked, she whispered "Come on!"

Crunching across the gravel driveway and quietly as we could, we made our way to the fountain. I was sure we were going to get in trouble, but for what?

Investigating a strange fountain? And what could they do? Take away my pudding? Big whoop.

Francine was already leaning over the rock wall, slurping up the contents. For a moment I wondered if I was being punked—set-up to be the butt of some joke. But with no one around to witness the humiliation, it wouldn't be a very well thought-out prank.

I leaned over and took a sniff. Anyone who thinks drinking vodka won't give them away because it doesn't have a smell is delusional. I could smell vodka on half my old neighborhood every weekend. The other half smelled like pot.

But just to be sure… I leaned over and touched my tongue to the liquid. Nothing terrible happened. I don't know what I expected. It's not like my tongue had the power to make a fountain of vodka burst into flames or anything. And like I said, we don't have our powers in here. The first thing they do to us when we arrive is suppress the powers we had.

The liquid tasted like escape from strict rules with a side of naughtiness. Just like Francine, I began taking bigger and bigger mouthfuls and swallowing the straight alcohol, even though the taste was gross.

"Nice view," someone said from behind us.

We both whipped around to see a boy about our age, bending to one side, as if admiring our ass-etts.

"Who are you?" Francine demanded.

"My name is Patrick. Do you like my gift?" He pointed to the fountain.

"You put this here?" I asked, relieved that it wasn't some kind of 'test' created by our teachers. If so, we would have failed miserably.

"Uh huh. It looks like I'll be joining the general population tomorrow, and I thought I'd make a few friends before I got here."

"What makes you think you can buy our friendship?" Francine asked, almost angrily.

I put my hand on her arm and muttered, "Down, Alien. He's just looking for allies. Can't say I blame him."

I called her Alien, because she made the mistake of telling some inmates that she alienated people. I just used her old nickname to remind her of that fact.

I rose and faced him. "So, you put this here now, knowing they're going to suppress your powers tomorrow?"

"Yeah. I was told a little bit about this place. My uncle was here for a while. I guess they only give your powers back when you demonstrate you can handle them. But how do they know you can use them responsibly, if you have no powers?"

I laughed. "That's what our classes are for. We only get our powers back one at a time, and only for a few minutes. If you don't accomplish whatever assignment you're given, using spells correctly, you won't get another chance for weeks. It's a good thing you got this out of your system now."

"Great," he said, sarcastically. "Well, after you've drunk your fill, or filled up and got drunk…" he smirked, "tell your fellow inmates about my gift. You might as well have a little fun before I get here. After that, we'll find more creative ways to have fun." He raised his eyebrows a couple times,

I threw up in my mouth a little bit.

"I wouldn't count on that," Francine gurgled.

Then he disappeared. Which was weird, because this place was warded up the wazoo against intruders.

"How do you think he got in?" I asked Francine.

"I don't know. Maybe because he's already been sentenced, technically he belongs here?"

"I guess that makes as much sense as anything else. So, should we pass the word, like he said to?" I asked.

"In a minute." She whirled back around and practically stuck her whole face in the fountain, gulping down enough Vodka to get a grown man hammered. She was tall and might weigh 110 pounds, soaking wet —which she was now. I was shorter, but weighed about the same.

"Careful. You're going to feel that tomorrow," I warned.

She pulled her mouth out of the liquid just long enough to say, "Yeah, or I could die tomorrow, meanwhile I'll be feeling no pain today."

I didn't quite know what to do. We'd be in trouble the minute one of our teachers smelled us. I might still be able to get away with it, if I changed my shirt and brushed my teeth quickly.

"Okay, I'm going in. I'll try to send out a couple of the boys, since he wants friends."

Francine gave me a thumbs-up, without even lifting her head.

⚔ ⚔

Just as I was hurrying down the corridor to my basic cell, which they call a room simply because it has walls and a door, a teacher caught my eye.

"Oh, Jenika! Jenika Jones? Come here, please."

*Oh crap.* I didn't know if she could smell me from that distance, or if she had something else to talk to me about. Either way, it was too late to pretend I didn't hear her. I stopped where I was, leaving about twenty feet between us. "I was about to go to my room for a minute. Do you need to talk to me right now?"

She smiled. Not something most teachers do a lot around here. "It's important."

I sighed. I didn't have much choice but to obey. I walked over to her slowly, keeping as much distance as I could between us as I tried to figure out which way the breeze was blowing from the air conditioning units so I could stand downwind.

"It's all right, Jenika. I'm not going to hurt you."

"I, um… I didn't think you would."

"Why don't we go to my office? We can talk more privately there."

She still had that smile on her face. Was it creepy or nice? Who could tell in here? Some teachers were a little bit of both.

I followed her to a door with a shiny new name-plate screwed into it. It said Ms. Broome. That's weird. A witch named Broome. Well, that's not as weird as some names I'd heard. Any football team can supply an impressive amount of jerseys explaining why those guys had to become so tough.

She opened her door, magically, I'm sure. No key was involved and yet she wouldn't leave it unlocked. Other teachers had keys concealed somewhere or just used magic.

"Come in, and sit down." She gestured to one of the two turquoise upholstered chrome chairs on the other side of her chrome and glass desk. Her empty desk didn't look like she had a lot of work going on at the moment.

"I've been assigned to you, and I was hoping we could get to know each other."

"Assigned? One on one? I didn't know we had teachers assigned to us for anything. Don't we have guidance counselors and social workers already?"

"Some of the social workers and guidance counselors could use an extra hand. I volunteered to take on a few kids."

"You're new here, aren't you?"

"Yes, I am. I just got here last week."

I smirked. "I knew it the minute you said you volunteered. You won't volunteer much after this."

She leaned back and grinned, crossing her arms. "Oh, no? Why do you say that? Are you going to give me a hard time?"

I sat up straight. "Oh, no. No, that's not what I meant. Believe me, I'm trying to be as trouble-free as I can. I mean, I'm not a troublemaker. I mean, I don't want any problems and I won't cause any, either."

She must have understood because the smile slowly faded and she leaned forward, clasping her hands on top of her desk. "I understand that you're one of the easier students here. However, easy isn't always a good thing. There are concerns."

"Concerns? How could you possibly have concerns, if I'm behaving appropriately?" *Ninety-nine percent of the time.* "I have nobody interfering from the outside. No visitors to screen. No packages to search. I get no letters to be redacted. I keep my room clean and free of contraband… What are you talking about?"

She let out a low breath and said, "Exactly that. You have no outside contacts. We tried to get in touch with your stepfather, but he never responded. I understand your mother was killed a few years ago…"

"Yes. She was in the wrong place at the wrong time."

"That's all you have to say about it?"

"It's not like anyone murdered her on purpose, it was just a drive-by."

"*Just* a drive-by?"

I knew I had kind of stepped in it. She was staring at me without the expected pity—or any other expression on her face. But I'm an empath, and I can read people's faces better than anyone I know—even without my powers. Right now I believe she's trying *not to* show her emotion and if she did, it would be pure pity.

"Okay. So, it wasn't *just* a drive-by. It was a really horrific incident. It changed my life forever. I'm not making light of it, I've just learned to live with it."

She waited a few beats and then nodded. "I understand that, and I commend you on making a difficult adjustment, but there's been more, hasn't there?"

I sighed deeply. "Yes. What else would you like to know about?"

She leaned back in her chair and opened her hands. Even though I didn't have my magical abilities to confirm I was reading her right, I knew body language. She was open to my side of the story.

"Why don't you tell me whatever it is you can think of that might still be affecting you."

I was confused again. "I don't know what you mean. I really don't. What's affecting me here? I'd say not a whole heck of a lot. This place is pretty tame compared to my old high school."

A tiny ghost of a smile appeared again. "That could be what's affecting you here. Not necessarily in a bad way. Relief is an effect. You seem fairly comfortable here. Maybe too comfortable. Are you more comfortable here than you were in your old high school?"

I had to think about that for a minute. Here I was ensconced with magicals like myself, but none of us had our powers. Here we were just commonplace thieves, vandals or other more nefarious problem children.

I was here because I electrocuted someone. That's terrible. But it wasn't intentional. The guy came up behind me and covered my eyes. Before he had the chance to say, "Guess who?" I whirled around and defended myself from a perceived attacker. I didn't even know I had the power to shoot 220 volts out of my fingers. It was a knee-jerk reaction, and I was already on edge. I truly wish I had just thrust my knee into his groin.

I shrugged. "It's really about the same."

"Except for the school shooting, I imagine."

I sighed again. "Yeah. There was that."

A long pregnant pause followed. Finally she said, "I understand if you're reluctant to go through it all again. I know a little bit about you, but I'd like to hear the story from you."

I groaned. "Do I have to?"

She shook her head. "No. You don't have to tell me anything, but it would help both of us. I'll be checking in with you periodically. I can ask you about the same things over and over again, hoping you'll open up to me in time, if you would rather do it that way."

It was all I could do not to groan again. I really *really* didn't want to go through the whole story again. I had talked to police officers, detectives, guidance counselors… Maybe I could think of some way to abbreviate the trauma and give it to her in one quick summary. Stupidly I said the first thing that came to mind. "I think I have PTSD."

Her smile lit up her whole face. I thought by diagnosing myself we could move on. Her body language said we were just getting started. *Damn.*

"I have to get to class. Can we talk later?"

"Yes, but we need to address your past as soon as possible. You're scheduled to leave here in a couple months. I want you to have the best chance at succeeding out there."

"Uh huh. I really have to go now."

She rose, strolled to the door, and opened it for me. As I walked past her, she said, "I don't think changing your clothes and brushing your teeth will help. I can smell vodka all over you."

I clamped my lips shut as I exited her office, waved goodbye, and ran to my room.

# A WORD FROM ELISABETH LOROW

This is where a reader would expect to find a list of my previous work. However, it's confusing to know what to do here. This is my debut young adult novel. I have over 30 published titles under another name. I've won awards and had novels in the top ten bestseller lists on Amazon. I've even had one of my books made into a video game!

I can't tell you my other pen name or list my previous books, because your parents would kill me if you started reading my adult romantic comedies too soon. So you're going to have to trust me. I'm not a total newbie, I'm just new to you!

One way to motivate an author is to write a review. Most of us really do want to know what readers think.

Plus reviews sell books, sales feed authors, and well fed authors write more books!

Thank you for reading Don't Mess with This Witch. I really hope you enjoyed it.